The Year of Chaos

Third Book in the Sunflower Beach Series

Dolores T Puterbaugh

Dolores T Puterbaugh

Copyright © 2026 by Dolores T Puterbaugh

All rights reserved.

No portion of this book may be reproduced in any form without written permission from the publisher or author, except as permitted by U.S. copyright law.

Cover art is detail from original painting and copyright Dolores T Puterbaugh

The Crow logo is original art and copyright Dolores T Puterbaugh

ISBN Softcover 979-8-9916758-4-0

ISBN E-book 979-8-9916758-5-7

Contents

Dedication and Comments	1
Chapter 1	3
Chapter 2	9
Chapter 3	16
Chapter 4	19
Chapter 5	28
Chapter 6	35
Chapter 7	41
Chapter 8	48
Chapter 9	55
Chapter 10	61
Chapter 11	69
Chapter 12	75
Chapter 13	80

Chapter 14	85
Chapter 15	93
Chapter 16	99
Chapter 17	105
Chapter 18	112
Chapter 19	120
Chapter 20	129
Chapter 21	142
Chapter 22	153
Chapter 23	161
Chapter 24	169
Chapter 25	176
Chapter 26	186
Chapter 27	191
Chapter 28	200
Chapter 29	209
Chapter 30	218
Chapter 31	228
Chapter 32	232
Chapter 33	239
Chapter 34	243
Chapter 35	247
Chapter 36	252
Chapter 37	259

Chapter 38   267

Chapter 39   273

Book Club Conversations   278

Dedication and Comments

D edications and Thanks

Most of all, thanks to Gerry, my husband and best friend, for unflagging encouragement and patience.

Thanks to Dora Campbell, for advice on the often puzzling process of writing and publishing.

Thanks to Savannah Grace, for input on developing the artistic theme for the Sunflower Beach series.

Thank you to Trista Smith, my patient and gifted editor.

Thank you to Eva Polakovicova, designer, who creates beautiful book covers out of my art.

Disclaimer

When I was a child, I created an imaginary monster to scare my siblings – tales of a slimy beast that lived beneath the house and could emerge, wet and terrifying, from the sump in the darkest, dampest corner of the basement. Naturally, I scared myself more than anyone else and, as helping with laundry was one of my chores, I ended up spending a few years racing up the stairs, heart pounding, several times each day, hoping to lurch out the basement door into the warm kitchen before The Sump Pump monster could get its terrible webbed grip on me. Going downstairs was even worse, and it didn't take long before even the flap of the door of the laundry chute in the bathroom could trigger a surge of adrenaline as I rushed out before that terrible, scaly arm could reach me.

That being said…the people and situations in this book are entirely the fruits of my regrettably over-active imagination. Except, of course, for the animals: some of the animals memorialize much-loved and much-missed animal companions.

Chapter 1

One of the little lambs was smacking another little lamb with the shepherd's crook. A shepherd and one of the Magi were swapping costumes. The front and back ends of the camel were lounging around, giggling and stoned. A man and a woman who were not married to one another were shouting at one another as if they were, over the burning question of how best to hang the cardboard star over the makeshift stable. Their respective spouses were urging them to give up the argument, just walk away, but the Star of Bethlehem was too important to surrender to an idiot. The Star of Bethlehem swung back and forth wildly over the mayhem.

Gloria Quinn stood in the middle of it, hands on her hips, nodding to herself. *Everything seems to be going according to plan.* The preparation for the annual nativity pageant for the Christmas Eve children's Mass was going splendidly.

Her eyes slid around the scene again, pausing. Yes, that was one of her grandchildren whacking another child and shouting, "Baa! Baa! I'm a baaaad sheep." She rolled her eyes. *His mother is being ineffective, as always, trying to get him to hand over the crook.* Her eyes moved on, taking in everything, the way they had for all those years of teaching kindergarten. She briefly considered asking the camel halves to leave, then thought better of it. No one else had volunteered who was big enough to handle the camel costume. She continued scanning the scene. The Magi was out of her costume and now the shepherd, who had peeled off her costume, was slipping into it. Gloria shook her head. At least that was settled, although she was disappointed that Marta would not be one of the Magi. Her twin brother Sean hadn't objected. She wondered, for a moment, if this were Alexa's fault. *Honestly, encourage someone to come out of their shell and the next thing you know, they're sowing chaos.*

"Mom, enjoying the show?"

Gloria turned, smiling. Her oldest son, Cody, was grinning at her. He nodded over his shoulder. "Looks like Veronica has her hands full with Bobby. You want to head over, or should I?"

Gloria kissed his cheek. "I'll take care of it. The twins are over there." She pointed. "Marta opted out of being a Magi." She pressed her lips together in disapproval. "Some nonsense about not wanting to be a possession."

"Ah." Cody nodded. "Yes, I bet she didn't want to be in the procession. Too much attention."

"It's an honor to be one of the Magi," Gloria said firmly. "She's old enough to know that."

"She's old enough to know what she wants," Cody said mildly. "I'll go see what's up."

"Your Aunt Alexa, I suspect," Gloria said with a slight huff, and headed off to put an end to the sheep-swatting.

"*My* Aunt Alexa," she heard Cody remark, "means you're annoyed."

Gloria marched over to the lambs and their hapless young mothers. She took the shepherd's crook, gave Bobby the bad lamb a gentle tap on the backside and patted the head of the victim with her free hand. Her voice cut across a church hall full of chaos. The two moms began calming down and even smiling.

Gloria looked toward Cody. He had turned and headed over to where his children—one a Magi and the other now a shepherd—were waving to him with excitement. He hugged them and then hugged Aunt Alexa—his mother's best friend since all their children were small. Gloria's trained schoolteacher ears caught part of their conversation despite the din.

"Mom's a bit annoyed," Cody said, grinning. Alex shrugged and rubbed her jaw, caught his look and grinned.

"I'm working on it," she said. "Seriously." He nodded. *That's odd*, Gloria thought. *Working on being annoying?* She made a mental note to see if Alexa was a bit confused about what it meant to come out of her shell.

"So ... a Magi and a shepherd, huh?" Cody said to his children, and they began talking in their usual half sentences, filling him in on the details. Having settled the sheep, Gloria then strode toward the wildly orbiting Star of Bethlehem.

At the end of rehearsal, Gloria stood again in the middle of the church hall, having a last look around before heading home. She nodded approvingly. *Everything will go fine.* Yes, rehearsal had been a bit chaotic, but it was to be expected. Christmas Eve, everyone would be eager to please—if not her or their parents, at least Santa. *Except for that camel*, she thought regretfully. She wondered, briefly, if she could talk her husband and one of her sons into being the camel. *Well, no use bringing it up in advance*, she told herself. *Wait and see if the teenagers show up stoned for Christmas Eve.*

Back at home, the kitchen had exploded. There were dishes in the drainer. *Honestly, can the man not simply put things away? Finish a job?* She shook her head. *How he has managed to run his optometry practice all these years is beyond me.* She thought, not for the first time, that his office manager, Doreen, was some sort of saint. Gloria was sure she would have thrown something at him long ago if she had to put up with his constant disorganization there, too. She moved to the spice shelves, scanned them. Yes, as she suspected. He must have doctored up the frozen enchiladas. The cumin was between the cardamom and the cinnamon; it clearly belonged on the other side of the coriander. She straightened the spices, went to the refrigerator, put the salsa back where it belonged—on the left door, with the other savory condiments, instead of with the jellies on the right side.

"Gloria? Inspecting the kitchen?" Bob called from the other room. He appeared in the doorway, came over, kissed her cheek. "Welcome home, honey. How's the pageant going? All well?"

Gloria kissed him, a perfunctory peck on the cheek. "Oh, it's the usual mess, but it will be fine. Alexa is not as helpful as I'd like." She sighed. "I swear, she's a bad influence on the twins."

Bob chuckled. "Alex? A bad influence on anyone?"

Gloria scowled. "You have no idea. One minute she's a little mouse and the next minute, she's got Marta rebelling."

"Rebelling."

"Yes, rebelling. She won't be a Magi like Sean will. She doesn't want to be in the procession. She wants to be a shepherd."

"That sounds like a perfect role for our Marta. She's not one for attention hogging."

"She needs to get over that."

"Can't we be grateful she's not like her mother?" Bob asked mildly, ambling back toward the living room. Gloria clamped her lips tight and her eyebrows flared up.

Gloria made herself a plate of leftovers and headed in to join Bob in the living room. They spoke of the upcoming Christmas holidays, his time off from work, his fishing plans with Joe. They wondered if Jenna would put in an appearance for the twins this year, and whether Bobby would behave himself during the Christmas pageant. Bob wagered a slice of pie at their favorite diner that Bobby couldn't pull it off; Gloria was sure she was able to intimidate him into keeping it together for fifteen minutes, especially with a church full of people.

Bob remained skeptical. "You overestimate your powers."

"I taught kindergarten for years. I can manage a naughty sheep." Gloria sighed. "A 'baaaad' sheep, he keeps saying."

"Ha!"

"Maybe you're right," Gloria sighed. "Maybe I've met my match in little Bobby Quinn."

"You met your match with old Bobby Quinn years ago," Bob teased, and Gloria rewarded him with a smile and a kiss on the forehead as she went toward the kitchen with her empty plate.

After carefully washing, drying, and putting away her dishes, she clicked off the kitchen light. The night-light under one cabinet glowed softly. Gloria leaned on the edge of the sink, looking up at the night sky. Stars were showing through tree branches. She was sure she saw a little owl on one branch, leaning sideways, as screech owls did, trying to disguise themselves as broken off branches. A glint—yes, those big eyes blinked. Gloria's mind drifted from the owl to her best friend. Alexa. Gloria shook her head and pressed her lips together. The woman was a mess.

Inviting her to help with the pageant again, after all these years, was supposed to be helpful. And perhaps it is—to Alexa, Gloria thought resentfully. She was anything but helpful to Gloria. She seemed to be leading a revolt. *Honestly, talk someone into a holiday manicure and taking time for herself, and the next thing you know I've got rebelling Magi and half-naked shepherds in the middle of a Christmas pageant rehearsal.* Perhaps it's some sort of menopausal thing, Gloria considered. She vaguely remembered some mood changes herself, or at least that was what her children had asserted, quite often. Her coworkers, as she recalled, had made vague remarks about the temperature in her classroom and there had been a few upset kindergarten parents, but hadn't kindergarten parents always been ridiculously demanding? Half of them seemed afflicted with some sort of paranoia that the school was against their little brats. Thirty years of kindergarten; Gloria Quinn had seen it all.

She headed off to start the evening ablutions. There were grandchildren to babysit tomorrow, and there was Christmas baking to be done.

Chapter 2

"Gloria, we really appreciate you watching the kids again. You know how it is this time of year." Veronica's eyes slid over to where Bobby and Gina were manually inspecting the antique blown-glass ornaments on the Christmas tree. "Just need to get a few things wrapped up."

"Of course," Gloria replied, nodding. *Good Lord*, she thought, *the woman is a mess.* Veronica's eye makeup, as usual, looked as though she'd slept in it. *I suppose it might be the current fad; who knows? Perhaps it is an artistic statement.* She pressed her lips together and nodded again. "What time do you think you'll be here to collect them? Should I plan on a nap time?"

"Oh, no." Veronica was emphatic. "Please, no naps. I should be here before four thirty; we want to be home before Kevin gets home." She knelt down. "Bobby! Gina! I'm out of here. Be good for Grandma." She hugged each one, and then took Bobby by one shoulder. "Bobby! No poop on the cookies. Seriously."

Gina giggled and Bobby said, "Okay." Then, after a gentle "harrumph," from Gloria, he added, "Mommy. Okay, Mommy."

Veronica smiled, stood up, gave Gloria and hug and, with more "byes" all around, headed off. The children looked up at Gloria expectantly.

"Okay," she said, half sternly. "Marta and Sean will be here soon. Then we're going to bake and decorate cookies. Gingerbread cookies," she emphasized. Gingerbread cookies were a nice, golden brown—much less tempting to use yellow sugar and chocolate chips for urine and poop. Gloria had also strategically only brought out cookie cutters that were not humans or animals. Trees, drums, and stars were unlikely to attract Bobby's fixation with bathroom humor. She had attempted, once, to elevate the conversation by using "feces," but its rhyming with "pee-pee" made things worse. She shook her head, remembering.

She had the table spread with a plastic tablecloth, the decorations in small dishes, ready to go. She would help Bobby and Gina roll and cut their cookies; Marta and Sean, who were nine, were able to do their own rolling and cutting, with a little watchful eye to be sure the dough was somewhat consistent in thickness. Gloria sipped a mug of coffee and watched Bobby and Gina. They had moved from ornament inspection to carefully rearranging the figures in the crèche. Bobby had both sheep in his hands and she decided to interrupt before he reenacted his pageant rehearsal hijinks.

"Bobby! Gina!" Gloria put her coffee down firmly. "Please come with me." Better to have them help with the daily movement of the Magi figures, who were spending Advent winding their way through the house until they reached the crèche on Epiphany. At present, due to Sean's decision yesterday, they were in the usually unused shower stall of the guest bathroom. She assumed Bobby would no doubt find this hilarious, and he obliged by laughing and pointing.

After some deliberation, the decision was made to have the Magi go from the damp valley of the shower stall to a lookout point on the bookshelf in Rachel's bedroom, where various environmental flyers and seashells had to be moved slightly to make room for all three Magi and a kneeling camel.

Gloria was just gently shooing the children out of Rachel's room when she heard the door from the garage open and Cody, Marta and Sean calling out greetings. Bobby and Gina took off running, with Gloria close behind. The twins hugged her and then Marta hugged both of her cousins. Gina hugged back; Bobby wriggled around, rolling his eyes in mock disgust.

Gloria reached out to hug Cody, noticing the dark circles. She held him an extra moment. Her oldest son was tall, but not much taller than she. She held his shoulders, tilting her head. "You're too tired," she announced. He gave a grinning shrug. She turned, shaking her head. "You work too hard. It's too much, the practice and kids with no help."

Cody followed her toward the cookie-decorating setup in the dining room. "I have plenty of help. You're the best, Mom. Couldn't do this without you."

Gloria watched her grandchildren. Cody's twins, energetic and sweet-natured; out-of-control Bobby; and barely less chaotic little Gina. Marta already had Gina by the hand, talking about how fun it would be to decorate cookies once Grandma got them started, and Sean was trying to distract Bobby from eating the decorations in advance. She knew the difference was that Cody was attentive and consistent, and Veronica was attentive and very concerned with being child-centered. Gloria shook her head. Sometimes she felt that if she watched Veronica squat down one more time to be at Bobby's level and talk to him about his feelings when the only feeling he needed was a quick little smack to the rear … well, they were grandchildren, not her children, and Kevin had picked an art major. She sighed. *They are still married and she loves her children, so perhaps he knows better than me. Whatever happens, I will never play matchmaker again.*

Cody interrupted her thoughts. "Mom. I'm off early tonight, four thirty, unless there's an emergency."

"Which there always is on a Friday."

Cody shrugged. "Fair enough. But I should be here by five to pick up the kids. Thanks again for watching them."

"Marta and Sean," Gloria said pointedly, "are never a problem."

"Bobby is a handful," Cody replied mildly. "I think you might want to intervene about now—"

Gloria lurched toward the table. It was too late: A shiny, damp cinnamon hot, now pink and white, was just dropping out of Bobby's fingers into the dish of red candies. *Not again – just like Halloween.* Gloria's shoulders stiffened. "Bobby Quinn," she began, her voice cycling upward. Cody grinned and, with a quick "Have fun! Be good for Grandma," made his exit.

Overall, cookie decorating was a success, Gloria thought. At least, bathroom references were absent. She had scrupulously picked the sucked-on red hots off the cookies before they were baked, replacing them with intact red hots, and told herself that a 375-degree oven for twelve to fifteen minutes would certainly kill even Bobby's no-doubt ironclad germs. Marta had, predictably, carefully used individual nonpareils to make garland on her trees, an idea Gina attempted to borrow but became frustrated with—she was, after all, only three—and then just dumped too many nonpareils onto her cookie and smashed them in with the side of her fist for good measure. Sean had been scrupulous about having the candy decorations on his tree be in colors that "went together," by which he meant the blue and orange of his father's alma mater, or red and green Christmas colors. Now all four were piled up on the couch, watching their allotted thirty minutes of a Christmas show for the day. It was a weekday indulgence for Marta and Sean, and starvation rations for Bobby and Gina.

Gloria packaged up the few decorations that were salvageable, and had the entire room put back to normal in short order. She tilted her head; quiet giggling, the sounds of the show about half over. Good. The rotation of cookie sheets through the oven continued, of course, but the children were no longer involved. She glanced at the clock. Two hours to go before Veronica thought she'd arrive. Two hours in Bobby and Gina time was two days in Marta and Sean time, in terms of aggravation. Gloria's eyebrows lowered. *I wonder how long board games, stories, and a snack could entertain them. Probably forty-five minutes total*, she guessed.

The garage door flew open and Rachel came rushing in, Aidan right behind her. *Saved*, Gloria thought. Aloud she said, "Back already! Hi, dear." She hugged her daughter and then gave a quick hug to Aidan. Rachel was chattering about the traffic, their errands, and the fabulous hot cocoa.

"It was delicious," Aidan agreed. "Very rich."

"So are these," Rachel said around a mouthful of carefully decorated tree. She held up the half that was left. "This is Marta's work, isn't it?" She turned in the general direction of the family room and shouted, "Hey, guys. Nice work on the cookies!" Marta and Sean came rushing in, followed by Gina. Bobby was last. After a quick hug for Rachel and bashful smiles for Aidan, they rushed back to their Christmas show.

Gloria's "Please don't shout through the walls" went ignored. She offered Aidan a cookie. He selected a small one, patted his nonexistent belly and said, "You Americans certainly pile it on this time of year."

"You'll have to fill us in on your customs," Gloria remarked. "I'd love to be able to serve you something you'd enjoy."

"I've enjoyed everything you've ever served me," Aidan said with surprise. "I'm sorry if I ever gave the impression otherwise."

"Oh, you haven't. I just wanted to be … sensitive." Gloria pursed her lips after the word. It was a troublesome word, as far as she was concerned. Just loaded with all sorts of weird connotations. No matter what the context, if someone started throwing "sensitive" around, you knew some sort of fiasco was around the corner.

Veronica and her child-focused parenting was just being "sensitive." People who barely knew Matt had tiptoed around her with innuendos about his "sensitivity," as if she couldn't tell he was gay before middle school. She shook her head, remembering thinking Alexa was an idiot when she had mused once about how nice it would be if her Sandy and their Matt ever married. Was the woman blind? Jenna had been "sensitive," in that way that turned out to be voraciously sensitive to herself and oblivious to others' feelings. Based on how unpredictable she could be, she figured Alexa probably considered herself "sensitive," too.

"Mom? What's wrong?" Rachel looked concerned.

"Hmm? Wrong? Nothing."

"You shook your head. That usually means something is wrong."

"Oh. Hmm. I was thinking. About the Christmas pageant." Her eyes slid toward the family room. "Rehearsal was … interesting. Yes, interesting."

"Trouble?"

"Yes, but nothing I can't handle," Gloria asserted, lifting her coffee cup and thinking, suddenly, of the shaggy-haired teenagers who would be inside the camel costume.

Chapter 3

It wasn't that he complained, actually. It was just that huffing and puffing, the dawdling. Gloria rolled her eyes toward the dark sky. A simple stroll around the neighborhood to admire the holiday lights wasn't exactly a marathon. They were about the same height, and the slow pace was uncomfortable for Gloria. She imagined her kneecaps were going to fly off from trying to take such short steps.

"Sorry about being a turtle," Bob said. "I guess I'm just more tired after a day's work than I used to be."

"Not to worry," Gloria said crisply. "Once the holidays are done, we're getting back in shape. Both of us," she added, in case he thought otherwise. Babysitting grandchildren daily, managing the house and yard, and various other activities kept Gloria on her feet most of the day. *More*, she thought, *than my optometrist husband. I don't like the sound of his breathing.*

"Back in shape as in ... what, exactly?"

"Nothing arduous. Daily walks. Less starches. A lot less." Gloria glanced sidelong at Bob. "We do need to get your sugar under control. Remember what the doctor said."

"Yes, I know." Bob paused, stood still. "Look at this house! They've got the stable set up with real hay again this year. Such a great job."

Gloria nodded. She appreciated this particular house. The baby Jesus was not out yet; Mary and Joseph were staring piously at the empty manger. The family always brought Jesus out sometime Christmas Eve night. The baby Jesus was about the size of a five-year-old, compared to His mother. The Magi appeared in their side yard on Christmas Day, and advanced toward the stable, arriving January 6. By then, the warning letter from the Homeowners' Association would have been out for a few days, advising them that all holiday decorations were due down no later than January 2. Which was, as half the association members would complain at the next meeting, before the end of their holiday season. It was a perennial argument.

"Maybe I'll run for the HOA after the twins are a bit older," Gloria mused.

"Look out, everyone," Bob said mildly.

"What's that supposed to mean?"

Bob squeezed her hand. "You know exactly what it means. You'll run the neighborhood like you ran kindergarten: orderly, neat, well-mannered, and everyone happy about it. Well, almost everyone. You had your challenges."

"Challenge. One challenge."

"And you managed to keep him in the circle by becoming best friends with his mother. And I wouldn't want to go without Joe in our lives, either."

Gloria nodded. *Jonah Bonhall. The one and only ... what a loathsome child.* She'd tried; God in heaven knew she'd tried her best to get him to fit in, to accept other children. She'd tried to look the other way when he took an active dislike to her Matt, the same age, but that was asking a lot. "Well, Jonah is a singular person," Gloria sniffed. "And we hardly ever see him. They might be at church Christmas Eve, but that's barely a nod and a hello for pictures after Mass."

"His wife seems pleasant enough."

"Hmm." Gloria thought about Beth. "She's certainly pleasant. A bit vanilla." Beth was bright, brighter than her husband, but so insipid, as if she were perpetually about to apologize for breathing. She was worse than Alexa. She'd heard that boys marry their mothers, but you couldn't tell that by either Kevin or Cody. And Matt's Tim was certainly nothing like her, either. In Jonah's case, he may have succeeded.

Bob stood still again. He took a few deep breaths. "Honey, I'd just as soon we head home. I'm sorry. Maybe we can cover the other side of the neighborhood tomorrow. I'm just not feeling up for it."

"No worries," Gloria replied, and linked her arm through his. But she had a flash of concern, which she dismissed. Everything was fine, and she would push him into getting back into shape after the New Year.

Chapter 4

Christmas Eve day at last. Gloria let herself sit to admire the tree, musing on the past week. Another successful Christmas cookie decorating session, this time with Rachel, Sandy and Alexa in addition to all four grandchildren. Rachel and Sandy had spent time with the twins, giving Gloria a much-needed break to prepare for Christmas. Now there was the pageant, and after that, the holiday season should go smoothly.

"What time do we have to be there?" Bob interrupted her musing.

Gloria looked up. "We should be there just before three. Mass is at four." She paused. "I don't expect any problems."

Bob squinted at her. "I know that look. So, what is it … Bobby? Or the camel again?"

She nodded. "Both, I think. I'm pretty sure I can corral Bobby into behaving. Maybe you can distract Veronica so she doesn't baby talk him into having a meltdown. The camel, on the other hand." She stared out the window briefly and then turned to him. "Well, if they are unable to perform, I have a plan B."

"Plan B ... as in Bob. Me. And who else?"

"Oh, probably Cody. Or Matt."

"How about Matt and Tim?"

"That could work. They'd probably be great at it." Gloria pressed her lips together. "I wonder if Father Anthony would object."

"I don't think Father Anthony knows, or cares," Bob remarked mildly. Gloria looked skeptical. She pushed herself out of the chair, giving her back a bit of a loosening twist.

"I'm going to get ready early," she said.

Gloria wanted to be dressed well for church. Of course, it was important to always dress appropriately for church, but Christmas Eve was special. She also wanted to set an example for the parents. She pulled out a satiny red tunic with a smattering of sequins: perfect. Long sleeves, longer hem in the back. Black dress slacks, her red flats. Gloria was nearly six feet tall and didn't need to wear high heels. Besides, at her age, her feet didn't appreciate the unnatural angle and pressure. Dressing, she wondered how the parents would behave. She frowned. One of the smaller angels' mothers was the one who insisted on taking pictures up by the altar last year. She had been wearing what was supposed to be a dress but looked more like a butt-length white tube top with sleeves. What a debacle. She had spent more time pulling her skirt down, and the bodice up, than taking pictures—not that all the tugging helped.

She wondered if she could talk Alexa into taking that one under her wing. No, probably not; Alexa would just say something silly about the Sistine Chapel and the image and likeness of God, as if Michelangelo's artwork had anything to do with Brooklyn Smith's thong-clad behind showing during the Christmas pageant. *No, Alexa will be no help at all.*

Gloria glanced at her hair: short, crisp, no-nonsense. *As if I have time for all that fussing*, she thought. *Honestly, how do people get anything done?* She put on bright red lipstick and long, dangly Christmas earrings meant to look like a few Christmas lights. They had been a gift from a student years ago and they suited the spirit of the day. Gloria gave herself a stern nod of approval before heading to the kitchen.

Gloria and Bob arrived well before the mad crush of a Christmas Eve Mass. She scanned the parking lot area and sighed; the two boys who would be the camel in the procession were hanging out on the rock wall near the entry to the sacristy. She could hear the laughter before she stepped out of the car, which Bob had parked in such a way as to be able to leave the parking lot quickly. She rolled her eyes. Why Bob imagined he needed to park like the getaway driver for a bank robbery, she could not understand. She would complain about being parked at an angle, on the grass, under a tree, half on the pavement, and Bob would say mildly, "Well, honey, you know what it's like," and flap his hand toward the rest of the parking lot. To hear Bob tell it, the entire parking lot turned into a kind of apocalyptic Mad Max nightmare within a minute of the final blessing.

Gloria strode toward the teenagers and stopped in front of them, hands on her hips. "Good evening, gentlemen."

They both looked up at her. Chris, the blond one, pushed his long hair off his face with one hand and held out a cardboard box. "Hi, Mrs. Quinn. Want a brownie?" His partner in crime, dark-haired Luke, burst out laughing, except he tried to hold it in and then snorted instead, which resulted in bits of brownie coming out his nose.

"Gentlemen," Gloria said sternly, "I hope you won't disappoint the little ones. Or your parents." She drew her eyebrows together sharply, lips pressed shut.

Chris sat up straighter, said, "No, ma'am," and put the brownie box down on the wall. Gloria trained her gaze straight onto Luke, who chimed in, "Yes, ma'am. I mean, no, ma'am, we won't. Disappoint them." Gloria nodded and strode toward the church, Bob right behind her.

When Bob had caught up, he said, "Stoned again this year, eh?"

"Apparently. But don't say anything to Alexa. You know how naïve she is."

Bob opened his mouth to protest, and then clamped it shut, shaking his head. He stayed alongside his wife as she strode purposefully toward the gathering area adjacent to the narthex. The high-pitched cacophony of many children and their mothers, with the occasional lower tones of fathers, resonated throughout the entire church.

As always, the pre-liturgy organization was wanting. Alexa and Joe weren't there yet, and she suspected Alexa wouldn't be much help, anyway. Veronica and Kevin were there, with Bobby and Gina, and Cody with his twins, Marta and Sean. Bobby was being ... Bobby. Veronica was crouched down, talking to him yet again about his feelings and other people's feelings. Bobby was busy manipulating the headband with sheep's ears he was wearing. Sandy, Rachel, Matt, and Tim would be arriving soon, she presumed.

One of the young mothers, Fiona, rushed up, face red. "What about pictures? When can we take pictures?" She pointed toward the church. "Father always says, no pictures during the liturgy. But I was thinking I could just sit up front—"

"Where the reserved seats are for handicapped persons?" Gloria asked.

"Oh." Fiona sighed.

Gloria smiled benevolently. "It's taken care of. Veronica"—she pointed toward her daughter-in-law—"is a professional photographer. She will be handling all the photography, before, during, and after. We have permission for one photographer to be discreet during the pageant part only, not during the rest of Mass. Veronica will be sending photos to all the participating families."

"Oh." Fiona nodded, chewing on her lower lip. Her eyes slid over to where Veronica was now wrestling with Bobby over his fuzzy sheep sweater and ears. "Will she be available, do you think ..."

The woman had a point. "I'm the grandmother of that one," Gloria said, frowning. "Trust me. He'll behave when the time comes and his mother will be available."

"I didn't mean to criticize your daughter."

"Daughter-in-law," Gloria said. "And don't worry about it." She headed off to manage Bobby and his hopelessly inept mother. When she had handled that disaster, she looked around. The camel had shown up and Joe Bonhall was trying to help the boys into their costume. It didn't usually require help, but apparently they were a bit less coordinated than usual. Gloria sighed. Everyone else seemed to be handling things well. She felt a hand on her shoulder and turned. "Cody."

Cody grinned and kissed her forehead. "Mom. I don't know how you do it." He gestured at the teeming crowd of costumed children and anxious parents. "Everyone looks great."

Gloria shrugged. "Well, you know. All those years of kindergarten classes." She glanced around and sighed. "Oh, no. It's Brooklyn. Okay, I have to give her a job or she'll be at the front of the church like last year. And the year before." Gloria rushed off to handle Brooklyn Smith.

Brooklyn Smith was the mom of two of the smaller angels and had not yet learned to dress like a parent. *Or even a law-abiding adult*, Gloria thought. This year it was a bright red strapless dress—once again a sort of tube, this one with sequins. It ended only a few inches below her behind. In what Gloria supposed was a nod to decency, she wore a black lace bolero that was more ventilation than crochet. Once again, Brooklyn spent half her time pulling the tube up and then wriggling the bottom part down. Gloria stepped up beside her, smiling with gritted teeth. "Brooklyn! How ... festive."

Brooklyn smiled up at Gloria and unthinkingly gave a tug to the top right edge of her dress. "Thanks, Gloria! Merry Christmas!" She smoothed the front of her dress and then gestured at Gloria's tunic. "We match!"

"Yes, I suppose we do." It occurred to Gloria that perhaps Brooklyn had some sort of mental problem. "Merry Christmas," she said aloud. "Brooklyn, I wondered if you would be willing to take on a special task this year. I'm sorry I didn't ask earlier, but it suddenly occurred to me that the families would really benefit from a second set of eyes for the photography." She thought about how, last year, Brooklyn had rushed up to the front of the church, squatted down, and proceeded to take lots of pictures when she wasn't tugging at some part of her dress. The bottom edge of her behind had been streamed to the entire online viewing audience, and her posterior preserved for posterity on the parish website.

"Oh, sure." Brooklyn glanced toward the sanctuary. "Up front? Where?"

Gloria shook her head. "We have special permission from Father for one photographer up front, so we're going with the parent who is a professional for that. However, I'd really like someone to be back here"—she walked Brooklyn just inside the doors to the sanctuary—"to catch each and every child on the way in, before they've had a chance to have their costumes slip out of place." Gloria placed one finger on her chin, pausing. "Do you think it would be possible to get a photo of each of them? If I try to control how quickly they come through the door in procession?"

"Absolutely." Brooklyn nodded. "But what about the ones up front? The ones who don't process?"

"Very thoughtful of you," Gloria replied. "But they won't be moving around much, so they're less likely to be messy by the time they get up front. The procession members, on the other hand ..." She paused as an angel who had been talking to her parents in the pews rushed past, tripped on her robe and caught a wing on the door as she stumbled. She didn't fall, but when she straightened up, her wings and halo were askew.

"I see your point," Brooklyn said. "Yes, I'll stay right here and catch them on the way by."

"Thanks," Gloria said. "I'm so glad I can count on you." She walked off to straighten up the Magi. Sean needed help with his costume; she looked around for his father. Cody was off on the side, talking with Alexa's daughter Sandy. She frowned. Sandy was probably trying to talk him into recycling something. Probably wrapping paper, she thought grimly. That would figure. She waved vigorously but Cody didn't notice. She sighed and looked down at Sean. "Okay, it seems your father is busy."

Sean nodded serenely. "Yeah, he's talking to Aunt Sandy. Grandma, could you just help me with this one part? Please." He pointed to the front of the robe, where it draped on the floor. She nodded, pulled a few safety pins out of her pocket and made two discreet folds to the shoulders in front. Now the robe draped nicely and was ankle-length in front—less likely to cause kingly stumbling up the aisle.

Somehow, everything fell into place. The parents went off to their seats. The children became quieter. Gloria nodded approvingly. *Get the parents out of there and everyone could calm down.* Just like the first day of school; the parents were always worse than the five-year-olds. At least the five-year-olds stopped crying as soon as their parents left. Everyone for the procession was lined up properly. The Holy Family and angels, as well as the shepherds and sheep who would be placed nearby, were walked up to the area reserved for them near the front of the church. Alexa, Joe, and their daughter Sandy would sit with those children, as well as Gloria's daughter Rachel, and Veronica. Veronica would, of course, have her hands full with Bobby until it was time to do the photography. Kevin, Cody, Matt, and Tim would be in the pew just behind all the children.

The pageant went off fairly well. The camel, of course, was high on marijuana-laced brownies, walking a bit unevenly and doing its best to control laughter. The result was a snorting sound that gave the impression of a gassy camel. This made the two boys who were Magi turn red with constrained giggling. Jolie, who was the tallest and oldest Magi, controlled herself very well. Gloria had hoped to have Marta be a Magi, but Marta had insisted on being a non-speaking, non-processing shepherd. Jolie had stepped in and Gloria had to admit; she made a very good Magi. She was tall, dignified in her bearing, her dark, curly hair flowing from under the turban, her head held high. Jolie would definitely be tapped for a Magi next Christmas.

Brooklyn stayed at the back of the church as the entire procession passed but then decided to ad lib things; she followed the procession up the aisle, snapping away and occasionally pulling on her dress. Gloria followed her up, calling her with a stage whisper, which only led to Brooklyn turning, grinning, waving, and then going back to photographing the procession. Gloria was halfway up the aisle; she sighed and just went up to step into the pew beside Matt, who put an arm around her shoulder and whispered, "Great job, Mom."

Gloria shook her head, glancing at Brooklyn and back at Matt, who whispered, "Mom. Let it go. It's all okay." Gloria pressed her lips together, frowned, and then nodded. It wasn't worth arguing about, anyway.

Chapter 5

Ryan Michaels had made his debut at Starfish Elementary School on the first day of kindergarten, rolling off the school bus in the midst of a fist fight and landing at the principal's feet on top of another student. Mr. Smith sighed and grabbed Ryan by one elbow, nearly lifting him off his feet, and then helped up the other student. The other student was Danny Scott. Danny was a notorious bully, a third grader. Big for his age, Danny was almost ninety pounds; he played football. Ryan was nearly a foot shorter and just shy of thirty-five pounds. Ryan's hair was ruffled and the neck of his apparently new shirt was stretched. Danny had a split lip, a bloody nose, and the pink puffy look that promised a black eye was to come. Danny had started it and not been prepared for Ryan Michaels, who didn't look upset at all.

Something similar had happened two days later at recess, when Georgie, a much bigger boy, began pushing Ryan around. Ryan told him to stop it—there were witnesses, including several teachers—and walked away, but the agitator, this time a boy in second grade, was a bit of a slow learner.

Ryan's mother was called in. She looked too young to have a child in kindergarten and was the adult version of her son: on the short side and small framed. She sat demurely with Gloria, who was Ryan's teacher, Mr. Smith, and Mrs. Graham, the school nurse who had done her best to patch up both Danny and Georgie.

"Mrs. Michaels," Mr. Smith had said, starting out with his best school principal voice, "your son has been in two fights, and it's only the third day of school."

"Actually, my son has been attacked by two much bigger, older students," Mrs. Michaels said. Her voice was calm and her big eyes looked right at Mr. Smith.

"Be that as it may," he continued. Gloria watched him. He was waffling. This always happened.

"That is true," Gloria said. "Ryan has been very well-behaved otherwise, and—"

"He hasn't been badly behaved at all," his mother said calmly. "Unless you're telling me he started these fights?"

"No," all three school personnel said in unison. Gloria added, "However—"

"However what?" Little Mrs. Michaels frowned a bit and tilted her head. "Isn't he allowed to defend himself? I mean, especially since apparently the school failed to do so. Twice."

Gloria had watched Mr. Smith. He rubbed his temples and made the perplexed face of a man who was watching his well-controlled meeting go sideways. *This is not going according to his plan*, Gloria thought. *Mrs. Michaels looks as if she should be in high school.* The young mother was supposed to be embarrassed and apologetic, not …

well, she was not argumentative. She was as soft-spoken as her son, and landing every hit.

It must have occurred to Mr. Smith, too. He sat up straighter. "Mrs. Michaels, it appears as if Ryan were ... unusually well-prepared to defend himself. Almost." He paused. "Almost as if someone had taught him to fight."

"Huh," Mrs. Michaels had said. "Children do fight and wrestle around. You do have children, don't you?"

Mr. Smith nodded and attested that his children did not fight. He did not add that his daughters were, of course, two rather ladylike girls and kept under strict supervision by his wife. The conversation with Mrs. Michaels was not going well.

Gloria suddenly pictured the last bit of the "fight" between Georgie, the bully, and tiny Ryan Michaels. She thought of the small clenched fists, the wiry little arms, the clearly aimed punches, one straight from the bony shoulder that peeked through the stretched-out neck of his T-shirt, the next hooking upward into Georgie's chin. She looked at Mrs. Michael's small, thin hands and wondered.

Gloria had watched the whole thing and wondered what sort of a year it would be, with a tiny boxer in the class. But there was, of course, nothing to worry about; Ryan Michaels was delightful. Half the girls had crushes on him, the boys liked him, and he was never anything but polite and cooperative with the adults. On occasion, another student—usually someone older and always someone bigger—would begin something. Ryan would always say, casually, "Leave me alone." And then, if he was ignored, Gloria would watch the subtle change in posture: the angle of the torso, the front shoulder slightly raised in front of his tucked little chin, the tension in the thin arms. Usually that was enough to lead the erstwhile troublemaker to back off, and only someone watching carefully would have seen anything unusual. Then Ryan would turn back cheerfully to what he'd been playing with his friends. Gloria always wondered if Mrs. Michaels—or someone—had taught little Ryan how to throw a punch, but she had never asked.

And now, here Ryan was, at Gloria's front door, his hair ruffled, wearing his police officer's uniform. He was saying things that made no sense whatsoever; for a few moments time seemed to stretch and contract rhythmically while little Ryan Michaels, who had never started a fight and never lost one, told Gloria there'd been a serious accident and if she'd like, he'd drive her to the hospital. The kindergartner told her Bob was alive. That made no sense, either; of course he was alive. In a kind of a daze, she'd grabbed her bag and her cell phone and found herself sitting in a police car with her former student.

Ryan explained the situation. There'd been a one-car accident—Bob's car—and he was seriously injured. He had been rushed to the hospital and Ryan figured he'd let Mrs. Quinn know.

"Ryan, you can call me Gloria," Gloria said robotically and then, with a nod, "Can you do that?"

"Gloria," Ryan repeated tentatively. He glanced sideways at her and then coasted his glance across the screen on his dash and then to the road. "Bob is in pretty bad shape. Do you need any help contacting anyone? Your kids? Any other family?"

Gloria shook her head slowly. "No, I'll get in touch with them all." She waved her cell phone. "They're all in here." She turned to watch the world race past them. *Ryan is in a hurry,* she thought. *Strange how the police can weave like maniacs through traffic so seamlessly.*

The next couple of hours passed in a blur that Gloria could not quite put into order. She had called all her children, as well as Alexa. The boys immediately set up a tag team to cover keeping her company; Rachel had packed up things for her father and for Gloria and brought them to the hospital; Alexa had gone off to babysit the twins so Cody could work and then come to be with Gloria at the hospital. Joe had stayed with Gloria until Matt and Tim had arrived. The first doctor was very young and wanted to keep even Gloria out of the room at first. Gloria did remember being firm about that, and that worked as well on the young resident as it did on most people.

The information kept coming; it was hard to keep things straight. Did he have a ruptured spleen? A punctured lung? Broken pelvis? Fractured femur? Was he unconscious? What surgeries were needed? The first night was a vortex of ever-shifting news.

Cody was with her when the clearest assessment arrived at seven a.m. By then, she had been at the hospital overnight, with a parade of her children coming to be with her. A different doctor came into the waiting area on the intensive care unit to speak with her. Except for Cody, no one else was present.

"Mrs. ... Quinn."

Gloria looked up. "Yes."

The doctor looked at Cody.

"This is my eldest son. You can speak in front of him. Freely." Gloria's voice was quiet.

The doctor nodded. "I'm Dr. Moore. The hospitalist on duty. Your husband, Robert, was seriously injured." Gloria drew her eyebrows together. The doctor swallowed and glanced at Cody. "He has multiple contusions, broken bones in his pelvis and legs, he has significant swelling, inside and out ... and we are monitoring his heart." Dr. Moore glanced at the notes. "Bob has a history of heart disease? Is that right?"

"No. Not that I knew of. He has diabetes, we knew that." Gloria's hands twisted in a knot in her lap. "Was this a heart attack?"

"It appears so. Yes, we have the diabetes here, he had a card in his wallet. The bloodwork indicates ... yes, there seem to be some important markers. His A1C is quite high. Yes, very much so. Glucose levels aren't well controlled, are they? Isn't he on medication?"

"And a diet," Gloria replied grimly. "But he's not the best patient."

Dr. Moore nodded. Gloria looked up at him. *I wonder how he stays so expressionless. At least the young resident had looked concerned; Dr. Moore looks nonchalant. He could have been rattling off a weather report.*

"Well, he's going to be a patient. For a while. And then a patient in rehab, and then at home." Dr. Moore paused. "It's going to be a lot. A lot of work for him to recover, a lot for his caregiver."

"Which will be me. And my children."

"You have ... four? Five? A daughter and a few sons, right?"

"Three sons. Well, four"—she counted Tim—"and yes, one daughter." *Of course he noticed Rachel*, she thought. *Now that she's dating a teacher, suddenly Rachel's attracting doctors.* Gloria wondered at herself thinking such things while Bob was lying attached to all sorts of tubes and monitors.

Dr. Moore continued. "He's going to need monitoring here, and several surgeries. The surgeon will be doing rounds at nine a.m. So, you'll want to be here for that." Dr. Moore frowned a moment, and then looked straight at Gloria. For the first time, a glint of kindness showed. "Mrs. Quinn, it would be helpful to have at least another set of ears with you. Maybe two. With so much distress for all of you"—he glanced with a nod at Cody— "more people listening and able to ask questions and take notes always helps. That's what I would do."

"Thank you," Gloria said. She stared at the doors to the ICU behind Dr. Moore. "Any chance I can get in there to see him? To be with him?"

"Of course." The doctor stepped aside. "But I'd recommend getting a bite to eat, maybe some fresh air. The surgeon takes her time when she's making rounds, and comes after the early morning surgeries. Nine o'clock rounds could mean eleven when she gets to your case... your husband. The cafeteria here isn't bad," he added, "if you're wanting to stay close."

Gloria nodded. "I'd like to see my husband, and then we'll go take a break." She stood up slowly, Cody right beside her, hand at her elbow. They headed toward the door. Cody paused. "Thanks, Dr. Moore."

The hospitalist smiled. "You're welcome. It's nice to see a whole family together like this. Thanks for being here."

Cody nodded as he followed his mother through the double doors to the unit.

Chapter 6

It was the rustling in the kitchen, the sound of someone trying, unsuccessfully, to be quiet that woke Gloria. She opened her eyes and felt confused, and then she became painfully aware of her back and neck. She sighed. Another half-night's sleep in the living room, too restless to go to bed right after coming home from late visitors' hours at the hospital, too tired to rouse and get into bed when sleep finally came near.

"Rachel? Is that you?"

Rachel stepped into the living room and clicked off the television. "Good morning, Mom." She kissed her mother's cheek. "Get any rest at all?"

Gloria leaned forward, hands on her knees. "Yes. I think so. Yes." She blinked. "You're getting ready for work?"

Rachel nodded. "It's back to work day for faculty; the kids come back tomorrow. Supposedly that gives us all time to put away the holiday decorations and put up the January stuff."

Gloria said, "We used to get two days. That was nice." She heaved herself up, her breath huffing with the effort.

"I made oatmeal," Rachel said. "And there's coffee. Can I get you set up before I head out?"

"Thanks," Gloria said, "but I can do that. You get ready for the day." She watched Rachel getting her lunch packed while she sipped a mug of coffee. On faculty-only days, Rachel dressed casually. Today she wore jeans and her "Save the Turtles" sweatshirt, her hair pulled back in a ponytail. Gloria wondered when Rachel would come close to dressing her age. "You look like a high school student," she commented.

"Thanks," Rachel said mildly. She grinned at her mom. "Don't worry. I'll look like a pro tomorrow when the kids and parents can see me."

Gloria nodded approvingly. "It's important," she began. "If you want people to take you seriously—"

"Then take yourself seriously," Rachel finished. "I know, Mom." She paused. "When are you heading back? To the hospital?"

Gloria pressed her lips together. "Soon. I need to change. Grandpa Quinn, Matt, Tim and Alexa are meeting me. There's a pre-discharge meeting and I need to have a few sets of ears."

"Good luck. Call me if you need anything. Anything," Rachel repeated. She glanced at her phone and slipped it into her back pocket. "Okay. Gotta go. Bye, Mom." And with a kiss on the cheek and a wave, she was gone.

Gloria glanced around the kitchen. The dishes were done. She opened the refrigerator; it was stocked with the usual fare, although, she noted, it was almost all organic. *Organic*, she thought. *A euphemism for beaten-up produce and overpriced dry goods. Oh, well—the kids were stepping up.*

She showered and dressed, managing a cursory attempt at pulling herself together. She had to pull the shower chair out of the stall; in a burst of enthusiastic helping, the boys had installed grip bars next to the toilet and in the shower and placed a shower chair in for Bob's use on his return. She appreciated the help, really; she just wished they would take a bit of direction. Although, she considered, she didn't know what she would have directed differently. She hadn't thought of the bars or the shower chair at all. Gloria shook her head and left for the hospital.

She parked the car and checked herself in the rearview mirror. Her hair was at least in place; she wondered where she put her lipstick. She looked like a ghost. She pressed her lips tightly and lowered her eyebrows in disapproval. *A woman ought not go wandering around in public looking ghastly*, she thought. *What would people think?* She marched into the hospital. She went past the reception desk with a wave at the volunteer trying to control the coming and going of visitors before hours began and went up to Bob's floor to see him and check with the nurses that the meeting was still scheduled. *You never know with these physicians. You would think that only physicians had emergencies! Imagine! Why the devil are all of us here in the hospital, except that we, too, all had unexpected emergencies?* Then she headed down to meet Alexa.

Alexa was standing in the area near the elevators, jaw clenched and hands twisting. *Goodness*, Gloria thought, *you'd think it was her husband dying upstairs.* Still—she was here, ever loyal. Gloria enveloped her in a hug.

"I'm so glad you're here," Gloria said. "Let's go into the cafeteria. The boys will be here soon."

"Which of the boys?"

"Matt and Tim," Gloria answered as they stepped into the line. "I wanted a lot of ears." She paused. "Bob's father is here, too."

Alexa expressed surprise that Bob's father had made it, and agreed that it was a good idea to have lots of ears. They navigated the line; Gloria was surprised at her own appetite. Suddenly everything seemed appetizing. Alexa, she noticed, was being picky. Gloria pressed her lips in disapproval. "Maybe you should eat something more substantial," she commented.

Alexa shrugged. "This is fine for me. This, and a big coffee," she added.

They settled down with Grandpa Quinn. He hugged and kissed both of them, fussing over "our Little Alexa." Gloria shook her head slightly. *Look at Alexa, turning pink and simpering like a teenager over being fussed over.* She turned her attention to Grandpa Quinn, handing over his plate of potatoes. She excused herself to go to the restroom, and on her return, they all settled into breakfast.

There was a strange pause of near-silence in the cafeteria: The hum of conversations, the clanking of dishes, all was silent. *Perhaps it's my imagination*, Gloria thought, *but it's almost as if—*

It was. Gloria squeezed her eyes shut hard and her lips harder, and then turned to see her former daughter-in-law, Jenna, all nearly six feet of her, even taller in high-heeled thigh-high boots. Her fur jacket wrapped around and over her sizable bustline, amplifying the effect. She was scanning the cafeteria. She caught sight of them, squealed, "Gloria! Oh. My. God," and came rushing over, leaning over their table. Alexa slid her hand over her coffee cup; Jenna's furry bosom was dangling dangerously close to the food and beverages. "Oh, Gloria. I just heard! From the children!"

"How nice that you saw the children," Gloria managed to say through clenched teeth.

"Oh, I didn't see them. We spoke last night," Jenna said. "I'm so upset!" Grandpa Kevin stood up, chivalrous as ever, and then sat again.

"Jenna. Beautiful, as always," he stated, in his courtly way. Jenna turned her attention on him briefly, blinking her eyes slowly, and then seemed to recall he was her ex-husband's grandfather. She turned back to Gloria.

Gloria was annoyed. *Jenna is intruding. It's hard enough to orchestrate all this without chaos. Of course she doesn't pay any attention to a word I say.* She pursed her lips. "Jenna. Bob is quite seriously injured. We have a care meeting this morning. I need my family with me; we're preparing now." She looked past Jenna's shoulder. Matt and Tim had arrived. Matt headed toward them and Tim went to the food line.

Jenna seemed oblivious. "Of course, I wanted to be here just as soon as I heard! How absolutely dreadful." She waved her hands. "Naturally I was just so upset."

Once Matt was seated, Gloria took a deep breath. *Apparently, I have to be blunt. Fine.* "Jenna, we have a meeting coming up and we need to prepare. A *family* meeting."

Matt rubbed her shoulder. "Mom, we're all here for you. Whatever it takes."

"Family! Aren't I family?" Jenna's voice spiraled up. She pointed at Alexa. "She's not family."

"Alexa is my best friend; that's family for me," Gloria replied icily. *Honestly, the woman was thick-headed. How had she ever graduated with a teaching degree?*

"And him?" Jenna pointed imperiously at Tim, who had just sat down with coffee and a muffin. Tim looked up at her, his face serene, blond bangs hanging over one eye.

Gloria straightened up and her voice became stronger. "Tim is my son."

"And aren't I your daughter?" Jenna straightened up, tossing her long hair and somehow managing to loosen her fur jacket, revealing a red lace camisole. "What about me?"

Gloria glowered at her. "Jenna, please leave us to prepare. We have important things to do here."

Jenna made a vaguely exclamatory sound; Matt would say later he thought it was an obscenity and Tim would shrug—he wasn't quite sure, but probably so. She flounced through the cafeteria, nearly knocked someone over, and further humiliated herself, Gloria noticed with satisfaction, by thinking a rebuke at her crashing through a line was an approach and briefly trying to engage with the young male staff member.

The Quinn family breathed. Near them, a small girl, part of a large family group, pierced the stunned quiet. "Her's mad," the child announced. "Her's mad because no one likes her best."

Matt grinned and turned to Alexa. "Doesn't that little one remind you of Sandy?"

Alexa smiled. "Absolutely."

Chapter 7

There was nothing like a project to take one's mind off troubles. Gloria took a sip of coffee and stared at her back fence, shifting her weight in the chair. Overhead, a blue jay was calling its family to the sunflower seeds she'd tossed into the grass; meanwhile, a squirrel was having a feast.

"You're a thief," Gloria commented. "Not that you care. *Rodents.*" She went back to considering what project would be a helpful distraction. Certainly, there were plenty of things in need of attention. She realized that Bob actually had been doing a better job than she'd noticed in keeping up with the yard; just a few weeks since the accident and it was looking rather wild. She debated pulling out the lawnmower and decided she'd just mention it to the boys. Certainly, one of them would have time. Maybe Cody?

Rachel had offered to "take care of the yard" just last evening but she'd put her off. She didn't trust Rachel to actually do it Gloria's way; she had already done a "little something," as she put it, but it turned out that meant she'd put out more birdseed and carefully left the greenery under the back shrubs longer because the bunnies were nesting there. She'd also mentioned that they needed just to make "a change or two" to qualify as a national wildlife property or some such thing. They could get a certificate and a sign for the yard; wouldn't that encourage the neighbors to think more about nature? Gloria shook her head. No, better to just have Cody take care of it, and she'd have fun with the twins.

Alexa popped into mind. *Alexa. Certainly, there's a project waiting to happen.* She'd been trying to help Alexa get out of her shell during the fall, before the accident, but Alexa, being Alexa, had gone traipsing off track, and ended up with crazy purple hair and a bit of an attitude problem. Perhaps she could do more work on Alexa. *That would be gratifying. The woman needs direction, that's all. A bit of a push.* She pulled out her phone and dialed Alexa's number, forgetting, for a moment, that it was a work day and Alexa would be at the college. She left voicemail and decided this would buy her time to figure out what to invite Alexa to do. What would be helpful to her scattered friend?

Gloria leaned forward, pondering. She finished her coffee and went indoors, leaving the glass open. The winter breeze, mild and soft, wafted through the screen and rustled the pile of papers on the dining room table. Gloria looked disapprovingly at it. How it piled up so quickly, she could not imagine. It seemed that just a few days ago she'd stood right here, sorting things into piles: shredding, bills to pay, letters to write, and the ever-expanding pile of paperwork related to Bob's accident, therapies, and treatment planning. Her shoulders slumped; she didn't have time for this. She needed to prepare for Bob's discharge from rehab, scheduled in four days. He would come home, using a walker, with a wheelchair for longer outings and when he was fatigued. He would be on a strict diet, monitoring his glucose levels and having home care for a few weeks to get things settled.

Gloria wandered through the house. The area rugs were gone, rolled up in the foyer closet, to reduce the likelihood of Bob tripping. The boys had taken care of the bathrooms weeks ago, with grab bars and a shower chair. There were different groceries in the refrigerator and pantry; the sugary snacks Bob loved were gone. Rachel and Sandy had taken care of that last weekend. Gloria wondered, briefly, if she would lose weight and thought, *well, that would be nice.* She patted her stomach. A little less would make her doctor happy, although why Dr. Meredith was obsessed with her weight was beyond her. Everyone knows, Gloria had said huffily at her last physical, that a few extra pounds are helpful as a woman gets older. Dr. Meredith, raising one eyebrow, had agreed, yes, that can be the case, a few, and they had both left the topic at that.

She sank into Bob's armchair, leaned back, closed her eyes. She imagined she could smell him—his favorite soap, the old-fashioned hair oil he insisted on using. She wondered what he was doing, right now. Maybe he was lonely, or in pain. Gloria sighed; perhaps it was not too early to go and see how he was doing. She opened her eyes, glanced at the clock. It was only eight a.m.; he was probably flirting with a nurse who was trying to take his blood pressure, telling her those ridiculous old-man jokes and thinking that her smile was genuine. *Ha, he's an old fool,* she thought. *How nice that he can't tell patronizing smiles from sincere ones.* She leaned back into his chair, turned her head to take in the smell of hair crème.

"Mom? Are you okay?"

Gloria's eyes flew open. "Hmm? What? Kevin?"

Kevin was leaning toward her, hands on the arms of the chair. "Mom. You were really out. I've been trying to wake you up."

She sat up, rubbing her neck. "Well, I'm awake." She blinked. "Why aren't you at work?"

"It's lunchtime. I thought I'd pop over and see if you needed anything. Or a little company."

"Lunchtime?" Gloria squinted at the clock. Yes, it was after noon. Of course it was lunchtime; Kevin would never just be absent from the optometry practice now that Bob wasn't able to be there at all. "Ah. Lunchtime. I must have lost track of time."

Kevin stood up straight. "How about some lunch before you head over to see Dad?" he asked. "Want to go grab a bite? Or should I make us some sandwiches?"

"Oh, let's just have something here," Gloria said. "I've been eating so much hospital food, a nice lunch at home is just what I need."

Kevin was already in the kitchen, rustling around. "Mom," he said, head in the refrigerator, "exactly who did the grocery shopping?" He held a package up over his shoulder. "Vegan chicken? Mom, there is no such thing. It's either chicken or vegan. Was this Rachel or Sandy? Or both?"

"Both," Gloria sighed. "Dig deeper. There's real ham and some cheeses in there somewhere."

Sandwiches were assembled, with slices of pickle and what was left of an old bag of pretzel sticks. Kevin was cutting the sandwiches into triangles. "Any bets on how much Sandy will rub off on Cody?"

Gloria squinted at him. "What?"

Kevin grinned. "Cody. Your son. Sandy. Your best friend's kid. Hello, Mom." He waved a hand. "I mean, I know things have been busy with Dad, but ..."

Gloria pressed her lips together. "Cody is fine."

Kevin shrugged. "And so is Sandy. And I mean that in an appropriate way," he added.

"What exactly are you implying?"

"I'm implying that ... well, no. Not implying, exactly. Okay. It seems to me that Cody has been going on a lot of beach cleanups lately and I don't think it's because he likes spending time with his little sister. Just saying."

"The twins enjoy the outings," Gloria sniffed. She bit into a sandwich. "Delicious. Thank you."

"The twins do," Kevin agreed. "Well, if you haven't noticed anything, I'm probably just imagining. You know, happily married people like to see everyone else married happily, too."

"Mm-hmm," Gloria said flatly. She looked over his shoulder at the refrigerator, and a picture of the last beach cleanup Rachel had printed: Sean and Marta in front, Rachel and her boyfriend Aidan, Sandy and Cody. Everyone was grinning at the camera except Cody. He was looking at Sandy. Kevin turned to follow her gaze and returned his attention to his sandwich, but not before catching his mother's eye, raising his brows and saying, "Yeah. That." He took a satisfying bite out of his ham-and-cheese sandwich.

Gloria munched on her sandwich and wondered how happy Kevin actually was. She studied his face; he looked tired, but of course, he had been picking up extra hours due to Bob's accident. She assumed Veronica was of little help, and besides, she had her hands full with the children. Gina was already three. She wondered how long it would be before they announced Veronica was pregnant. She'd had that mildly smug look lately, which had always preceded a baby-on-the-way announcement.

"... and Veronica's been volunteering at the preschool a couple mornings a week." Kevin's voice interrupted her thoughts. Gloria blinked a couple of times, trying to look attentive.

"How nice," she said. "I had encouraged her to do something with her time," she added. *Finally*, she thought, *all these years of hints that something besides the occasional photography gig for a friend or family member would be a good use of her time and energy.* Gloria nodded with satisfaction.

"She's enjoying it," Kevin agreed. "She's helping out with their website and social media presence. It's vital these days. If you're not online you might as well not exist."

"That's ridiculous," Gloria said firmly.

"Just having a website isn't enough."

"Hmph."

"I mean as a business entity, Mom. People look stuff up online. They don't use phone books."

"I know," she said irritably. "I knew what you meant. It just sounds very dismissive."

Kevin shrugged. "I'm sorry. No offense meant. But it's the twenty-first century, and online presence is a must. Even for church-based preschools."

Gloria pressed her lips together. *Veronica can't just volunteer; she has to press her art school self on the situation. Why not just make laminated handouts and read stories like regular moms?* "I'm sure she enjoys it," she offered.

"Absolutely." Kevin stood up, clearing his dishes and reaching for his mother's. "And she's driving me crazy with ideas for the practice now." He glanced over his shoulder as he rinsed off plates. "Not that I'm making a single change without consulting with Dad. Obviously. But it's nice for Veronica to have something to talk about besides whatever Bobby did today."

"Bobby does keep her busy," Gloria agreed. "As does Gina."

"Oh, Gina's a sweetheart," Kevin said serenely, drying his hands. "She is a lot like Rachel, which is great because, really, two Bobbys would be pretty terrible."

"Mm-hmm." *Maybe a little consistency would make Bobby a nicer child to be around.* She said nothing, just stood to kiss Kevin goodbye and wished him a good day. After he'd left, she stood still, looking around. The house was so silent. She shook her head and began to prepare to go see Bob. Opening her closet, she thought of Rachel. Perhaps she needed to take Rachel shopping, help her pick out some appropriate work clothes, something that made her look like the responsible guidance counselor she was.

She made a mental checklist as she passed a few shopping centers on the way to the rehab center, noting the places most likely to have guidance counselor clothes. That might be a nice project, once they had Bob settled safely at home. What Rachel needed were a few pairs of dress slacks, a few blouses, and one or two cardigans to mix things up. A jacket, too, of course; something in a sensible neutral color to pull it all together. One of those ten-piece wardrobes would do, something she could combine lots of ways. Gloria nodded thoughtfully as she pulled into the rehab center parking lot.

Chapter 8

It occurred to Gloria as a passing thought, that tomorrow she would regale Brenda, her childhood best friend, with all the details. She would emphasize all the ways in which aftercare planning meetings are, as it turned out, much like parent-teacher conferences. But at this moment, to her dismay, Gloria herself was on the receiving end of what seemed like a cascade of criticism. Gloria resented being talked to as if she were some sort of failure. Brenda would be, of course, extremely empathetic.

But that would be tomorrow. At this moment, around the little conference table, Gloria asked why Bob wasn't part of the meeting. They all looked at each other quickly, looked down, and then Alicia and Nate had looked to Carmen, who offered, glowering at her coworkers, "We—the entire team—thought it might be better to start with the four of us."

Gloria nodded, and then it became clear why Bob was not invited to this part of the meeting. The barrage kept coming:

"Bob isn't as cooperative as he could be with treatment."

"Bob keeps sending the food back to the kitchen and asking for something decent to eat."

"Bob complains that we're trying to starve him to death and then asks when euthanasia without patient permission became legal."

"Bob is only interested in physical therapy that he thinks will help him go back to work or go fishing."

It went on and on. Gloria sat and simmered. Honestly, what did they expect? It wasn't as if she had given birth to him; she was his wife, not his mother. *My children*, she thought indignantly, *would behave far better. Well, except for Rachel with the food*, she reflected, and then had to refocus quickly. Carmen, the social worker, was repeating her name.

"Gloria? Any questions for the team?"

Gloria sat, lips pressed together, brows drawn down, and looked around at the treatment team. The occupational therapist, Alicia, looked ridiculously young and had ended every statement on an up note, as if she were asking instead of telling. The physical therapist, Nate, was leaning back, arms crossed, smiling amiably; he always looked as if he'd been interrupted in the midst of a lively basketball game, from the askew T-shirt to the baggy shorts. Carmen, with her sensible cardigan, shirt, and khaki slacks, was the only person who appeared professional. Gloria nodded and asked, "Is there anything my husband is doing right?"

The team looked at each other sheepishly, she noted with satisfaction. *Good. That should teach them. Always lead with strengths, it softens them up. It worked almost every time with parents. Your little Maribeth is such an angel. The other children just love her. She's so willing to share ... The parents would swell with pride, and that made it easier to slip in the needed corrective feedback. If only Maribeth would be sure to not hide the food she doesn't like. It's becoming a problem;*

we've had mice and it always tracks back to some moldy sandwich in Maribeth's cubby. Could you talk to her about that?

"Well, the staff say he's always cheerful. They all appreciate his sense of humor," Carmen offered.

Alicia smiled and said, "And he's always ready to practice the things that have to do with fishing?"

It's not a question, Gloria thought wearily. She turned to Nate.

Nate grinned broadly. "Dr. Bob's great. He works on what he wants to work on, but it's a hard sell to get him to see how the other things we ask feed into what he wants." He leaned forward, elbows on the table. "For example, he's in a big hurry to get back to driving. And he doesn't see how, say, doing the little 'around the house' things that Alicia's been working on are all helping him with the balance and coordination, and the confidence, to get back behind the wheel."

"Ah, that's helpful," Gloria said. "Yes, I can see that."

"You can help with that—keep reminding him how it all fits together. I mean, he's an eye doc, right?"

Gloria nodded. Never mind correcting these people about terminology; it was a waste of time.

Nate continued. "So, no doubt he talks about sun exposure and nutrition and blood pressure and all with his patients, things they wouldn't see as related to eye health."

"Thanks." Gloria nodded. "That's good. I can help with that."

So that was it; Bob was being too narrow. Good Lord, she'd have to cut back his time with Joe Bonhall, possibly the most single-minded human being on the planet. He probably had Bob's head filled with ideas of that ridiculous sabbatical fishing expedition dressed up as historical research. *I can put a stop to that nonsense.*

Carmen sighed with apparent relief and stood up quickly. "I'll let the nursing staff know we're ready for Bob to join us. Then there will just be some paperwork, and home you both will go."

"Thank you. Two of my boys are there waiting; they're going to help get Bob set up."

"Very good," Carmen said and left the room, the door swinging shut firmly behind her. Alicia stared out the window and Nate just sat back, grinning, arms folded, and nodded at Gloria.

"Bob's not done with me," he remarked. "I've signed on to do the home visits."

"I'm sure the consistency will do him good," Gloria replied.

"I hope so." Nate glanced toward the still-closed door and leaned forward conspiratorially. "Truth be told, I'm kind of excited about this big fishing trip. I'd really like to see him do the work to be ready to go."

Gloria pulled her lips all the way into her mouth and sighed. She felt, vaguely, as if an army of enthusiastic do-gooders were lining up against her.

They arrived home. Gloria was extremely tense, feeling that Bob was some sort of fragile infant without a car seat. They had wheeled him out and helped him into the car. Some adjustments were made to the seat height to make it an easier maneuver, and Nate had taken the time to give some coaching on how to navigate the move from chair to supported stand to sitting. "You're going to need a lot of support at first, partly because of the awkwardness," he explained to Bob, glancing up at Gloria. "Don't let being embarrassed about it get in the way. No one worth paying attention to is going to judge you, and this stage should only last a couple of weeks, if you do the work."

Bob smiled. "I know, I know. Ask my wife ... I'm a good student."

"Hmph," Gloria snorted. "We shall see."

Nate stepped back from the car. Carmen handed Bob the folder with instructions, phone numbers, and the first two weeks' schedule of appointments, all of which would involve people coming to their home. "No fishing trips for now," she teased, and then stopped smiling quickly at Gloria's scowl.

Gloria glanced at Bob at every red light. He was staring out the window, up at the sky. "It's so beautiful out here," he said wistfully. "I've been inside for such a long time, and this is such a beautiful time of year."

"It is," Gloria agreed. "We can take you out to the patio later if you'd like."

"I'd like that," Bob said. He shifted a bit, grunting.

"Pain?"

"Just a little twinge," he said, sitting up. "I have a lot of little twinges and they tell me it's just part of the process, the injuries are still healing." He made a small huffing sound. "Ha, wait until you hear me with the Marquis de Nate. The bastard." Bob grinned.

"He seems pleasant," Gloria replied, "and very responsible."

"Absolutely," Bob agreed. "And the SOB is convinced he can get me into shape to do everything I want to do, if he doesn't kill me in the process." Bob smiled sheepishly. "I've never been the no-pain, no-gain type, but Nate has other ideas."

Gloria wondered whether she loved Nate or wanted to strangle him. *Metaphorically speaking, of course*, she added to herself, rolling her eyes up to heaven. He'd be at the house at least a handful of times, so the jury could stay out on which it would be.

They had just turned into the driveway when Matt and Tim stepped out of the open garage door, waving and grinning broadly. The boys had built a temporary ramp inside the garage to the door into the house. Gloria stood by and gave instructions about moving

Bob from the car to the chair, but Matt and Tim, as if they did this all the time, seemed to have Bob halfway into the house before Gloria was done with step three. Matt turned and said, "Mom—never mind Dad's stuff. I'll come out for it in a few minutes."

She nodded, following. They wheeled Bob through the kitchen into the living room. He sat in the wheelchair, looking around, blinking. His eyes were wet.

Gloria frowned, bending over, hands on his shoulders. "Bob? Are you okay? Anything hurt?"

He shook his head, wiped one eye. "No, no. Everything's fine." He smiled at them, weakly, and shrugged. "Just a little ... well. I'm so glad to be back home. To see all of you. To be here. And ... " He looked around. "You know, last time I was here, it was Christmas time. The tree was up, the Christmas cards. And now it's practically Lent." He glanced at Gloria. "You're probably five minutes away from putting out all those rabbit and egg decorations."

"Oh, no," Gloria assured him. "I'll be waiting until closer to Easter."

"Not if Marta starts asking about it," Matt teased her. Tim laughed and put an arm around Gloria.

"Mom," he said firmly. "We all need to eat. It's way past lunchtime."

"And I would like." Bob paused and Gloria steeled herself. "I would like," he repeated, "a big salad. But with enough protein for a change. These rehab people were trying to starve me to death."

"Well, you're in luck," Matt said lightly, heading toward the kitchen. "Because Tim and I brought over a big slab of salmon, which we will now grill. It'll be a little while, then; how about some veggies in the meantime?"

"Veggies," Bob repeated. He sighed and looked at Gloria beseechingly. "Honey. I just got here. How about a little celebratory deliciousness?"

Gloria did not have time to answer before Tim announced, "We have arranged for that: fresh strawberries, vanilla frozen yogurt. All good." He glanced at Gloria. "Mom, you're in charge of portion control. I don't want to go there."

"Got it," Gloria said with satisfaction. "Now, Bob: Stay in the chair and go out on the deck? Or sit in your chair in here?"

"I'll take the deck." Bob sounded firm. "It will be nice to smell grilling and see the sunshine."

"Well then, let's go." Tim maneuvered the wheelchair toward the deck. Gloria waited behind for a moment, looking around. Somehow, she and the children had managed to put Christmas away; the last of it had been just a week or two ago. She wondered if she ought to have left something out for Bob and then thought, no, certainly not. She recalled that one, precious planning day after Christmas vacation each year, when all the teachers tore down holiday decorations so no remnants would be there to distract students on their return. *Bob*, Gloria decided, *needs to face the reality that this is a new season in more ways than one.* She gave a firm nod to the fireplace and strode toward the deck, following the sound of male laughter.

Chapter 9

Alexa came in through the door from the garage to the kitchen, announcing, "I'm here! Good morning!" She put her purse on the countertop near the pass-through to the dining area and then gave Gloria a big hug.

"It's good to see you," Gloria sighed. Her eyes flickered over Alexa. *The purple hair is growing out, thank goodness.* She wondered if the woman owned a hairbrush. Still, here she was, ready to help. "It's been"—her eyes darted toward the living room—"a lot."

Alexa nodded sympathetically. "I know. It seems like a lot. How are things going?"

Gloria shrugged, turning toward the coffee maker. "Everyone's very happy with how Bob is doing."

"But you? What about you?"

Gloria half turned to hand a mug of coffee to Alexa. "I'm tired, to tell the truth. It just seems ... endless."

"Thanks." Alexa lifted the mug a bit in acknowledgment. "Yes, it sounds like there's a lot going on."

Gloria turned, leaning against the counter, her hands wrapped around a steaming mug. "It's the chaos. Everyone coming and going! The boys, the professionals, the phone calls." She shook her head. "No one explains how chaotic it will be. These people can't be on time; the schedule is constantly in flux." She pressed her lips together firmly. "I can't organize my week. Someone's coming at ten—no, it will be eleven fifteen. Oh, and tomorrow it's two, or maybe three thirty."

Alexa sighed. "It must be frustrating. How are you managing?"

Gloria put her mug down, carefully aligning the handle to be parallel to the edge of the counter. She reached over to the sink to grasp the sponge and wipe the counter around the coffee maker, soaking up any droplets that might have bounced from the mugs when she'd poured them. She followed this up with a careful toweling and then hung the dish towel carefully on its hook near the sink. She picked her mug up and took a sip. She looked straight at Alexa's gently concerned face and said, "Oh, I'm fine. Really."

"Hmm." Alexa shrugged. She glanced at the living room. Bob was reading. She called over, "Hey there, Bob, how are you?"

He looked up, beaming. "Everything's going great! I'm feeling better every day." He held up the book. "Getting ready to go fishing with Joe," he explained, pointing to the title. Alexa squinted and he obligingly explained, "It's about fresh-water fishing in the mid-Atlantic states."

"Ah," Alexa said. "I'll let Joe know you're doing your homework."

"See," Gloria hissed through clenched teeth. "That's what I mean. Chaos." Alexa looked confused. Gloria scoffed. *The woman is clueless. What is Bob, who was barely alive, doing imagining he would be going fishing anywhere anytime soon?*

Alexa nodded slowly. "It's beautiful outside; why don't we get some fresh air?"

When they were ensconced in the deck chairs, Alexa turned back to Gloria. "So ... out of earshot. How are you, really?"

"I am just exhausted. Like I said, it's just chaos—chaos everywhere." She pointed at the canoe on the lawn. "Exhibit A. The canoe, so the physical therapist can help Bob with his functioning. Matt and Tim got it all set up with the bricks to hold it in place."

"That seems useful."

"Useful? It's feeding his delusion. It's like agreeing that someone's ... oh, I don't know ... Napoleon! He's not going fishing anytime soon."

"But what do the professionals say?"

Gloria shook her head disapprovingly. "They seem to think that the injuries are healing very well; that if Bob follows instructions and does the work, he'll be almost as good as new. The main concern is his heart and his blood sugar. Good as new, and in some ways, even better—so they say." She snorted. "They apparently have managed to *treat* Bob without actually *meeting* Bob."

"Oh, Gloria, that's not fair. Bob seems to be trying."

"And he argued with them about food at the rehab center."

Alexa nodded. "Well." She paused. "Did he have a point?"

"Meaning?"

"Meaning hospital food! Bland? Boring? Limited menu?"

Gloria shrugged with annoyance. "You, the medical people, the kids—is everyone on Bob's side?"

"No sides, here, Gloria."

Gloria sighed. "Well, yes. Of course he had a point. It's hospital food, for heaven's sake. But he almost died! He should take things seriously."

"I agree."

"But he's not! He complains about the diet plan. He's sick of oats, he's tired of beans, he hates celery."

"It's kind of funny," Alexa began, and then added quickly, "not ha-ha funny, of course. But, odd maybe, because you've always prepared very good food for the family."

Gloria drew her brows together. "Yes, it doesn't seem like much of a stretch from our usual menu. It's the sneaking." She nodded back toward the house. "Bob can't get around to sneak extras as well as before. Yet."

"Ah. Bob was embellishing the menu, so to speak."

"Right, and for now, he can't. But I can tell. As soon as he's driving, all bets are off."

"And you're worried about that."

"Of course I'm worried!" Gloria burst out. "Who wouldn't be? How would you feel if Joe almost died?"

"Terrified. Angry."

"Well." Gloria took a sip of coffee and looked sidelong at Alexa. "Well. Not really terrified, per se. Just … anxious. Of course." She shook her head. "Why would you be angry?"

Alexa half turned in her chair to better face Gloria. "Well, I'd be angry at Joe for neglecting himself and maybe cheating me out of years of a healthy husband. I'd be angry for the grandchildren he might never meet. I'd be angry at the situation—finding myself in your position, with everything chaotic and disorganized and feeling fairly helpless. I'd probably be angry at people who didn't understand and acted like I should be happy and looking for the silver lining." Alexa frowned. "I think that would piss me off most of all."

Gloria frowned. *What has gotten to into Alexa?* "I can't imagine being 'pissed off,'" Gloria said sharply, "just because other people were … encouraging."

"Just being honest. That would be me." Alexa paused. "But, truthfully, Gloria ... not angry at all? It sounds like you're plenty annoyed with Bob. And the boys. And Rachel. And all the professionals."

"Well, I am annoyed with Bob. Disappointed, you know. I mean, he's admitting now he felt like there were warning signs but he didn't want to 'think about it.' Well, here we are. Nothing else to think about but 'it.'"

"Oh, no. Really?"

Gloria nodded, lips pressed hard. "Yes. 'Brief' pains in his chest. His left arm, his left jaw. He was a walking billboard for impending heart attack. And let's not talk about the diabetes."

"I see." Alexa sighed. "Oh, Gloria! I'd be furious with him. Furious and scared."

Gloria's shoulders sank. "I am angry. And scared, too." She paused. "This isn't my first rodeo, so to speak. I've seen what long-term injuries do to a family." She paused, glanced at Alexa, who nodded encouragingly. "I mean, in my family. I've seen this. I just don't want to see a repeat."

"Of course. But Bob is supposed to recover, not be permanently disabled." Alexa paused. "But you've seen it go badly? In your family?" She paused. "Your dad, right?"

"Well, yes," Gloria said. She glanced back at the house. "I think we should go in. Bob probably needs something." She stood up slowly, rubbed her lower back, and headed back to the house without looking at Alexa.

Right behind her on the way into the kitchen, Alexa was trying to follow up. "What actually happened to your dad, Gloria? Did you want to talk about that?"

"Oh, Alexa. I don't have time for this," Gloria said impatiently, striding toward the living room. "Bob! How are you? It's almost lunchtime. Would you like your lunch in here? Outside?"

"Oh, outside would be nice."

"Maybe I should head out," Alexa said.

"No, no, join us for lunch," Bob urged. "It would be nice to have company. Gloria makes the best little lunches."

Gloria glared at him and said tartly, over her shoulder to Alexa, "See what I mean? The little dig. The *little* lunch."

Bob grinned. "Yes, Gloria. Little. I get it—I have to relearn how to have a healthy relationship with food. Blah, blah, blah. Got it. And it's hard, and I'm doing it. And you are quite ... diligent. Dedicated. In helping me with it."

Gloria nodded firmly. "Well. I'm glad you understand." She turned back to the kitchen. "Alexa, dear. Come give me a hand."

"Of course," Alexa replied.

Chapter 10

"Grandma! Grandpa's cheating!"

Gloria rolled her eyes. "Marta! How can Grandpa cheat at chess?"

She heard giggles, followed by Sean saying, "She's a bad loser!"

"I'm not losing!"

Then Bob piped up, "Nothing to see here! Marta wasn't keeping an eye on the knight and forgot he could hopscotch right over another piece."

"Ah, well. In that case ..." Gloria trailed off. She looked up from peeling potatoes to catch Cody's eye; he was grinning over his task of cutting up carrots for soup. He wiggled his eyebrows at his mother. "That's not like Marta," Gloria commented.

Cody shrugged. "Mom. She's ten now. Apparently, she's right on schedule."

Gloria snorted.

Cody shook his head. "I know. Ten years old. But we had to have the talk."

Gloria put down her potato and knife and stared at him. "The talk."

"Well, yeah. It was either me or have the first formal info come from the school." He sighed. "Family life. The guidance counselor talks to the girls. Since some of her friends have started … yeah, it was time."

"And Sean?"

"Yes, and Sean. But not at the same time." Cody shuddered. "Imagine that circus! It was hard enough without the unfairness of it being the central theme."

Gloria took up her potato peeling, frowning. "I don't like this. She's too young."

"Well, I'm not a big fan, either, Mom. But it was time. I mean—" He was interrupted by Marta stomping into the kitchen, complaining that Grandpa didn't let her change her mind after she took her hand off her rook. Cody gave her hair a rumple. "Marta! You know the rules. No surprises here."

She frowned and folded her arms. "I know … I just. I don't know."

"Why don't you go in there and tell Grandpa you're sorry you were a bad sport? How about that?" Cody paused. "You'll feel better if you take care of it now."

Marta nodded, wiped her eyes and headed in. They heard her soft murmuring and Bob's gentle, "Oh, little Marta—of course I forgive you. Give Grandpa a big hug!" Cody and Gloria smiled at each other.

"There you go," Cody said. "I guess the twins have been spending a lot of time with Rachel and Sandy. You missed the first steps of this." He jerked his head in the general direction of the living room, where giggling was once again bubbling.

"Hmm." Gloria wondered about that. Perhaps Rachel and Sandy were being a bad influence.

"Luckily Sandy took me aside and gave me a little guidance on this," Cody went on. "She mentioned seeing little changes, Marta complaining about some new mean girl behavior at school, needing to wash her hair more often." He gave the colander a shake. "Is this enough?"

"Yes."

"Because I would have been oblivious."

"Mm-hmm."

"Like, I didn't put two and two together. The complaining about her arms and legs hurting. Who thinks growing pains? But Sandy was all over it."

"Hmm."

"And I didn't really take the time to notice even Sean is getting a bit"—he glanced toward the living room—"stinky. Not that little-kid smell. It's daily showers no matter what now. And he and I had to have a little chat about the difference between getting wet and getting clean."

"Sandy certainly is around a lot." Gloria knew she sounded disapproving.

"And I appreciate her." Cody had turned to lean his back against the counter, arms folded. "I think Rachel is so focused on kid drama at her school that she didn't see the forest for the trees when it came to the twins."

"Well, I've appreciated the girls stepping up so I could focus on your father," Gloria said tersely.

"Me, too," Cody said. "And it's been nice to spend more time with Sandy."

Gloria slammed her knife on the cutting board and wiped her hands on her apron. She gripped the edge of the counter, feeling her fingers pressed too hard on the granite. She felt very warm. She turned to Cody, keeping one hand on the counter as if hanging on for life. "I don't like this."

"What?"

"All this time with Sandy. Cody, I think this is a very bad idea."

Cody looked right at her, calmly. "What, exactly, do you think is a bad idea?"

"This ... little thing ... with your cousin. I think this is a very bad idea."

"Mom, there's no 'little thing' and she's not my cousin." Cody shook his head. "What is it you think is going on?"

"I wasn't born yesterday, Cody. I'm your mother. I know you better than anyone." She saw his eyebrow lurch up. "And I saw that eyebrow. You know exactly what I mean. This dabbling in romance with Sandy Bonhall is a very bad idea."

"Mom, let's go outside. I don't think the twins need to hear this conversation."

"I don't have anything to hide."

"Well, maybe you do."

"What's that supposed to mean?"

Cody sighed. His voice was quiet and gentle. "Mom. Your face is bright red, you are practically putting dents in the granite, and your voice is a lot louder than you think. I don't want you blurting out something about Sandy that you will regret. I don't want the twins to hear that happen." He turned and went toward the sliding door to the backyard. "Mom. Come on. The soup will wait."

Gloria stomped out and turned angrily as he carefully slid the glass door closed. "Fine! We're outside! And I still think this is a bad idea!"

"Why?"

"Because I know what's good for you!"

"I'm not sure you do."

"Well, I do. You should listen to me."

"Mom, let's not go there."

Gloria opened her mouth, and then remembered Jenna. How she had pushed Jenna at Cody, relentlessly played matchmaker. She clamped her mouth shut, hard, eyebrows flaring up. "I see."

"Mom … how long has it been since you had a real talk with Sandy? Anything besides her and Rachel whizzing by with some cause-of-the-moment in the environment?"

Gloria sank into the nearest Adirondack chair. "Cody. I just don't want to see you hurt. Or the twins," she added darkly. "They don't need another disappointment."

Cody crouched to wrap his arms around his mother, his chin resting on her shoulder. "Mom. Trust me. There's no rushing going on, nothing crazy. We're just spending a lot of time together, with the twins, and a lot with Rachel and Aidan. We'll see what happens."

Gloria gripped his wrists, hard. "I'm just scared, Cody." She felt his nod.

"I know, Mom. But don't put that fear where it doesn't belong."

"Meaning?"

"You're worried about Dad, and the changes for you and him. Don't spread it around on the rest of us."

"But it's not just your father." Gloria leaned forward, half turning and breaking his hug. "Listen to you! Marta in puberty! Sean right behind! You're seeing Sandy! Rachel's dating a foreigner! Your Aunt Alexa's gone mad and Uncle Joe is a terrible influence on your father! Veronica's probably pregnant and … I don't even know what else."

Cody moved around to sit in the other chair. "Mom. Listen to yourself. You're acting like good things are bad. The kids are growing up—yeah, it's sad but it's also healthy, happy. Normal. I'm grateful. Rachel is dating a good man, a teacher, a Catholic." He nodded at his mother. "Aunt Alex—she's having a real rebirth. I think it's beautiful. And Uncle Joe is encouraging Dad. Dad has something to fight for—something soon, where he has to get better quickly and not just do his usual dilly-dally routine. He either gets better or he misses the big sabbatical trip."

Gloria snorted. "Fine, Pollyanna. And Sandy ..."

Cody leaned back, looked up at the blue sky, then, head still tilted back, turned to face his mother. "Mom, Sandy is everything I could want. She's kind, and smart, and so full of life ... She loves children. Really loves them, warts and all." He paused. "I have never felt like this about anyone. I've loved Sandy since she was a tiny kid. God, what a pest," he added, "but even then."

"Even then?"

He leaned forward, elbows on his knees, still looking straight at his mother's face. "Mom, I think I knew Sandy was the girl for me before she even started school. It was just too weird to talk about, but I knew." He shrugged.

"You never said anything. And you married Jenna. That seemed real enough."

He nodded. "Yeah, I just moved forward with life. And Jenna should have been wonderful. Maybe there was a part of me that wasn't completely in the game; maybe she felt that. Sometimes I struggle with that. Did she flip out in part because she could tell I wasn't really all in? Just lying to myself and her?"

"Oh, Cody, that's not fair," Gloria protested. "Jenna—"

Cody held up a hand to stop her. "No, Mom. I'm being honest. I'm not taking responsibility for Jenna. Just for myself. But I'm being truthful with you. I thought I was in love with Jenna, and maybe I was, for a while. But with Sandy, well, it's just different. It's more than that infatuation high. Sandy makes me feel like I'm a whole person."

"I see." Gloria's voice was clipped. She was unconvinced; she was sure he was on some sort of delayed rebound, brought on by the stress of Bob's accident and her unavailability to take time with the twins. She didn't like this situation at all. "Well. If that's the way it is. We'll see." She stood up with a grunt, putting her hands on her hips. "Is that all? Can I get back to my soup now?"

"Mom. I just didn't want the kids hearing this conversation." Cody stood up, but Gloria was already stomping into the house, slamming the sliding door open so hard that it vibrated on hitting the other edge of the door jamb. She was butchering the potatoes by the time Cody reached the kitchen. "Mom, is everything okay?"

Gloria closed her eyes, sighing, and then turned to face him. "Oh, yes, Cody. Everything's just fine, fine"—and she threw the potato into the sink; it hit a glass, which shattered as it fell.

Cody stepped up to the sink and began carefully picking up pieces of glass and putting them into a bowl. "I got this." He glanced at Gloria. "Mom. You've got to stop letting things get to you like this. Everything's going to be fine." He placed a few more pieces of glass into the bowl. He lifted the potato, looking it over. "There's some glass stuck in this. Into the compost it goes." He placed the potato into the compost bin next to the sink. "Ugh. Doesn't Rachel ever take care of this?"

"You might as well get used to it," Gloria snapped. "That's your future with Sandy."

Cody grinned. "Oh, she's got the twins alternating compost duty already." And then, catching his mother's eye, the grin faded. He shrugged and went back to carefully cleaning up the sink. "Mom. Seriously. This isn't like you. What's going on?"

Gloria sat down at the table with a sigh, elbows on table, head in her hands. "Everything. That's what's going on. Life is just one big crisis after another."

Cody rinsed his hands carefully. After putting the broken glass in the trash, he sat next to his mother and rubbed her back. Marta ran into the kitchen and froze.

"Grandma! What's wrong?" She went to Gloria and hugged her. "Are you sad?"

Gloria sat up, shaking her head. "No, no, sweetheart. I'm just ... tired." She shot an angry look at Cody. "Very tired. But now it's time to make soup! Would you like to help?"

"Yes. What can I do?"

Gloria got up slowly, saying, "Well, first, put on an apron. Then you can put the onion that your daddy cut up into the big pot." She turned to Cody. "Why don't you go see what your father and Sean are up to?"

"Sure," Cody said. "Thanks, Mom."

Gloria heard the three male voices, and then Sean appeared. "Grandma! Daddy said to come make myself useful! What can I do?"

"Oh, well," Gloria said hesitantly. She glanced toward the living room; she heard soft voices but their words were unintelligible. She frowned in their direction and then smiled down at Sean. "How would you like to be in charge of getting the spices down for me? I need oregano, cumin, and ... oh, let's see. A little black pepper."

"Okay!" Sean was enthusiastic, dragging the step stool over to the spice shelves.

"What next?" Marta asked.

Gloria settled into the familiar routine of directing the twins and praising their efforts, but half her attention was straining toward the quiet conversation in the other room.

Chapter 11

Gloria turned into the parking lot; it was crowded. She sighed. That meant a long wait in that ridiculous waiting room, listening to that endless loop of so-called health advice on the television. She gathered her purse, made sure her book was in it, and got out of her car. She locked the door and checked the handle; yes, it was locked. She nodded approvingly and headed in. She signed in, frowning; what was the point of all this so-called medical privacy if she was signing her name after all those other names right at the front desk?

"Good morning, Mrs. Quinn," the receptionist said. Gloria smiled tersely. She wondered if the woman even had a spine; she always looked and sounded as if she were a scared rabbit. "Just have a seat, please. They'll call you back soon."

"Thank you." Gloria glanced around the waiting room. Good—only four people. She sat down in a chair that faced away from the television and took out her book. The volume was set so loudly she couldn't concentrate; it was like trying to read at a football game. She sighed and slapped the book shut with disgust.

"Caregiver stress is real and dangerous," the anodyne female voice droned. "If you're a caregiver, talk to your doctor about your stress level."

"Oh, please," Gloria muttered. "What good would that do?" The woman across from her glanced at her and Gloria pressed her lips together. The woman looked away quickly.

"Signs of caregiver stress include poor sleep, temporary short-term memory loss, poor concentration, irritability—"

"Well, who wouldn't be irritated?" Gloria blurted out. She glanced quickly around the waiting room; that scared-rabbit receptionist was peeking at her over the countertop and the other patients were assiduously staring up at the television, as if she hadn't spoken aloud. Well, perhaps she hadn't; perhaps she was just a little anxious.

The door swung open and Doug, the PA, appeared, chart in hand. "Mrs. Quinn! How nice! Good morning." He stepped aside for Gloria. She was sure she heard a sigh—as if of relief—as the door closed behind them. She followed Doug into the exam room.

"Have a seat, please," Doug said. "Okay, let's just get a quick update. Any big changes?"

"Well, you probably can't say you know because of some sort of privacy rule, but you know my husband was in a very serious accident, he had a heart attack, and his diabetes is out of control. So that's the big change."

"Mm-hmm." Doug nodded. "Well, you're on his chart as his healthcare surrogate. So, yes, we know." He turned toward Gloria. "And how has that been? Being a caregiver?"

"I am fine." Gloria glowered at him. She stuck out an arm. "Can we get on with this? Blood pressure? Make sure I'm still breathing? That sort of thing."

"Of course." Doug took care of the essentials briskly and confidently; Gloria was weighed, her lungs listened to, her heart heard, her blood pressure measured. A small bright light was shone into her ears, throat, and nose, and Doug typed quickly into the electronic record. Gloria nodded with approval. *Someone who can do his job*, she thought, *that's nice. For a change. So much incompetence these days.* She pressed her lips together in disapproval.

"Everything okay?" Doug asked.

"Hmm?"

"You looked as if you were unhappy there for a moment."

"Oh, no, not at all." Gloria paused. "As a matter of fact, I was thinking what a relief it was to deal with someone who actually knows what they're doing and does their job."

"Well, thanks," Doug replied. His voice and face were serene. "Okay, Mrs. Quinn. I'll be stepping out. Doctor will be in shortly."

Gloria thanked him and took out her book. This part usually involved even more waiting than the waiting room. At least this time she was clothed and not wearing a ridiculous paper gown and a sheet. She had barely turned the first page before Dr. Meredith breezed in, smiling. "Gloria! How are you?" She sat, glanced quickly at the information Doug had typed in, and turned to face Gloria directly.

"Good morning, Doctor," Gloria replied stiffly. "I'm fine."

Dr. Meredith was about Gloria's age and had been the family doctor for thirty years. She was athletic, slim, and almost always wore a dress with her white medical coat open over it, and sensible, low-heeled shoes. She was used to Gloria's bluntness. "Gloria. You've definitely got a lot going on." She leaned a bit forward. "You're under a lot of stress and it's showing up in your bloodwork. And your blood pressure, too."

"Oh, that's just because I'm here," Gloria asserted. "And what about the bloodwork?"

"Your vitamin D is low, and your iron is a bit low. Not getting outside much these days? And cutting back on red meat for Bob, are we?"

"Of course."

Dr. Meredith stood up. "Have a seat on the table, please. I want to check your back and shoulders." She moved around to stand behind Gloria and moved her hands over the upper back and shoulders. "Okay. How does that feel?" She placed pressure in a spot on each shoulder; Gloria winced. "Mm-hmm. And this?" She prodded a couple of places on Gloria's upper back. "Okay, stand up, please. Now bend gently forward … let your back curve." She felt along Gloria's spine gently. "Thanks, Gloria. You can sit down." Gloria sat with a little grunt. Dr. Meredith looked at her sharply. "That's not like you."

"What's that?"

"The little grunt. You're usually the energizer bunny. Bob must be really wearing you out." Dr. Meredith paused. "More than all those beautiful grandchildren! How are they?"

"Oh, the children are fine," Gloria replied. "I'm just tired."

"You must be. And stressed." Dr. Meredith grinned at Gloria's indignant expression. "Please! Your back is so tense you've managed to make your scoliosis worse. Your shoulders and neck are just a series of knots. I barely touched you and you flinched."

"And what do you suggest I do?" Gloria was annoyed. *What do people expect?* she wondered. *Under the circumstances, what can I do?*

"I think you need to schedule breaks for yourself. Let the kids step up and take time with Bob. And leave Bob alone sometimes, for God's sake." Dr. Meredith was not above exploiting her long familiarity with the family. "Bob's not a toddler. He can be left alone."

"Hmph."

"Seriously. I want you outside for a walk every morning. Early, while it's cool. Get a little natural light to get that vitamin D level back where it belongs. Take your multivitamin. If you're not going to eat red meat to accommodate Bob's diet then get the ones with some iron, at least for now. I want you to take your blood pressure three times a week at home, same time every time, and keep a record of that. We'll get new bloodwork in three months and I'll see you after that. Before, if needed, of course."

"I'll try," Gloria said stiffly.

"Just do it," Dr. Meredith replied, kindly. "For your own good. And Bob's."

"Yes. I will." Gloria nodded. She reminded herself that Dr. Meredith had taken good care of their family for years.

"Oh, and you might want to talk to someone. About the stress," Dr. Meredith said.

"Talk to someone?"

"A friend. A mental health professional. Your pastor. Someone. It's a lot, being a caregiver, and then piling on just regular life and all its changes. And what will change about Bob's work. Well ... It's a lot to handle, and it would be helpful to have someone neutral to talk to."

"I'm fine," Gloria said firmly. "I have my family and close friends." And then she thought about Cody and Sandy, and Alexa's apparent insanity, and Joe's pathetic influence on Bob, and sighed.

"Well, I'm not sure you're as fine as you think," Dr. Meredith said cheerfully. "Give it some thought. Let me know if you'd like a referral."

"Thank you, I will." Gloria reached for her purse. "Anything else?"

"Warm baths. Gentle stretching. A massage if that suits you. Or use a tennis ball and the wall to try to roll out some of those knots. Go gently and just a little bit each day." Dr. Meredith stood up. "Please go on up; Suzanne will give you the bloodwork order and help with that next appointment."

"Thanks, Doctor," Gloria said sincerely. She appreciated a little concrete guidance, something clear and doable. She went out to the front. Suzanne tentatively slid the bloodwork orders across the counter and set up the three-month follow-up, avoiding eye contact. Gloria shook her head with disapproval as she left the office. Was it impossible to hire staff with less resemblance to a scared rabbit?

Chapter 12

Gloria nudged the door handle with her elbow; her arms were loaded with grocery bags. She always prided herself on her ability to take minimal trips to bring in the groceries. She knew her upper arms waggled when she waved, but she could still carry in at least twenty pounds of groceries at a time without difficulty. She swung open the door and stepped into the kitchen. Bob was standing in front of the refrigerator. He turned and smiled warmly.

"Sweetheart! You're home! How was Doc? Do we have any sliced turkey?"

Gloria put down the groceries with a huff. "What are you up to?"

"I'm not up to anything. I'm packing lunches. I can't find the turkey."

Gloria rustled into one of the bags and held up a paper-wrapped package. "The turkey is here. Why are you packing lunch?"

"For tomorrow." Bob sounded mildly surprised, as if she were supposed to know.

"And what's tomorrow?"

He looked confused. "I'm going fishing for the morning. With Joe. And the boys."

"And when were you going to tell me?" *Lord*, she thought, *look at him. That butter-won't-melt-in-his-mouth look doesn't fool me.*

"I thought I mentioned I would be seeing Joe at dinner yesterday. That we were going to the county park. To fish."

"I don't remember that."

"It was right after that argument you had with Rachel about whether it was a good idea for her to go to Ireland for a week with Aidan this summer."

"Ireland." Gloria began taking groceries out of the bags, slamming food items onto the counter. "I remember *that* part distinctly." She glared over her shoulder at Bob. "I also remember you didn't pipe up and take my side."

Bob shrugged. He had taken out the bread and cheese and was putting together sandwiches. "It's not a side thing, Gloria. Don't you think it's a good idea for her to get a sense of who Aidan is? When he's home, among his family? And what his family is like?"

"Well, of course," Gloria replied stiffly, slamming the cabinet after putting in the box of whole-grain breakfast cereal.

"They're in Ireland. The only way to do that is go there and be there. A week seems kind of short, but at least it's a start."

Gloria turned to stare at him. She wondered if he was insane. "You're kidding, right? She's going to another country. To stay with strangers. And what will they think, this American girl coming over without a ring? It looks terrible."

"I distinctly remember Rachel emphasizing she'd be in the sister's room." Bob carefully cut each of the four sandwiches into two triangles and reached for the waxed paper.

"Well, yes. But, still." Gloria put her hands on her hips. "I just don't like it."

"What don't you like about it?"

Gloria threw up her hands in disgust. Could the man not see the forest for the trees? "Bob Quinn! Think about something besides fishing for five minutes." Bob looked up at her, sighed, and straightened up, keeping his eyes on her. Gloria sighed with impatience. "Rachel's getting ready to leave us. Doesn't that matter to you?"

"And hasn't that been the plan all along? Weren't you proud of her last year when she announced she had nearly enough for a down payment on her own place?"

"Well, of course."

"And we don't want her living here forever, do we? Just being dependent and chasing sea turtles and complaining about our eating habits?"

"Of course not," Gloria said, folding her arms. "You just don't understand."

"Well, help me out here." Bob limped over to her and wrapped his arms around her. She felt his chest against her folded arms and reluctantly unfolded them to wrap around him. She let her forehead lean against his shoulder and, to her surprise, began to cry. Bob stroked the back of her head and murmured softly, "It's okay, sweetheart, everything's going to be okay," which only led to Gloria sobbing aloud. Bob kept one arm around her and kept gently stroking her head.

Gloria's sobs had quieted into soft hiccups and gentle shudders when Cody walked in and momentarily froze in the doorway before stepping in. "Dad? Mom? What's wrong?"

Bob smiled, winked at him and said, "Everything's fine. Mom's just having a ... moment."

Gloria pushed back slowly from Bob's embrace, wiping her face with her hands. "I'm fine. Your dad's right." She pushed the hair back from her forehead; she felt the length and made a mental note to get a trim soon, before she started looking like Alexa. "Just fine." Gloria wiped her hands on her clothes and made a weak smile. "We were just talking about Rachel's plans for the summer and I guess I got a little weepy. Missing her already. Until"—Gloria attempted a lighter tone—"until she comes home tonight and complains about the blend of salad greens being wrong for some reason."

"What's Rachel planning?" Cody was putting orange juice and apples into the refrigerator. "She going off to some faraway place to save polar bears?"

"She's planning to go to Ireland. For a week." Bob was wrapping the sandwiches. "And Mom's going to miss her. As will I," he added, "but I think it's a good idea. For her to go, I mean."

Cody nodded, gathering up cans of beans to put in the pantry closet. "Yeah, it would be good to meet Aidan's family and see how he behaves when he's back in that environment."

Gloria glared at Cody's back and then sharply toward Bob. "I agree. Can't a mother be a little ... emotional?"

Cody grinned and kissed the top of his mother's head. "Of course, Mom. I don't blame you." He grinned. "Wait until the twins are ready to go to college; I'll be over here crying on both of your shoulders."

"Don't rush me," Gloria grumbled. "I don't feel ready for any of this."

"Oh, Mom. None of us ever leaves for long or goes far. You won't lose Rachel. It's always a gain for you." Gloria looked up at him, brows flaring and lips clamped shut. Cody shrugged. "Okay ... yeah, Jenna. Well, I'll do better next time."

"Next time," Gloria echoed.

"Yup." Cody turned his attention to Bob. "Dad! Packing a picnic?"

"Going fishing at the county park tomorrow morning with Joe, Matt, and Tim. Nice and easy. A lawn chair for me. Just get out there, try my luck, enjoy the time with the boys. Swat mosquitoes. Look out for gators."

"Now, see there," Gloria interrupted. "You can't get out of the way of an alligator! What if that big one comes after you—what, that ten-footer that lives in that lake?"

"Gloria." Bob chuckled. "The King of the Lake doesn't want to eat me. That little rat dog that Jonah dotes on, that's the gator's preference."

"That's not nice," Gloria said flatly.

"But it's true," Cody offered. "Mom, seriously. It sounds nice. Very low-key. Fresh air, conversation." He leaned back against the counter, arms crossed. "You know what they actually do. They talk and drink coffee. Or stand around enjoying the scenery until the no-see-ums drive them crazy. It's not exactly demanding."

Gloria sighed and turned away from them, blinking hard. She wondered if anyone would ever be on her side. "Fine. Fishing it is. Will you want some fresh fruit or veggies?"

"Of course," Bob answered. Gloria was sure that if she could have turned quickly enough, she would have caught him and Cody grinning at one another at her expense.

Chapter 13

It had been a couple of months—sometime before Christmas, anyway—and Gloria was past due for a nice cup of tea with Miss Arlene. Gloria carefully arranged some homemade oatmeal-raisin cookies in a fresh tin: Five stacks of three fit perfectly. She pressed the lid on and nodded firmly. The cookies, and a few photos from the Christmas pageant to entertain Miss Arlene, and she was ready to walk over, through the gate at the side yard fence, and go for a visit.

Miss Arlene was ninety-three years old and had retired only five years ago from teaching art part-time. She had segued from a long career—over forty years—in the public school system into teaching part-time at two of the area art centers, and then cut it down to one of them at about eighty-five, and then wrapped that up just three years later. She was tiny, not even five feet tall, with white hair and a face lined with echoes of smiles. She had cleared off half her kitchen table to make room for mismatched mugs and a tea pot. Gloria reminded herself that artists were always eccentric, although she was not sure why the table had to be such a mess. A sketchbook, some colored pencils, a snapshot of a bird, a pencil sharpener, and what appeared to be a few days' worth of mail: Gloria pressed her lips together. *Unhygienic*, she thought. *How did Arlene manage to never get sick?*

"Oh, Gloria, it's so good to see you," Miss Arlene was chattering with excitement. "Sugar? Milk? Lemon? What would you like for your tea?"

"Whatever you're having," Gloria said. "Can I help?"

"No, no! Sit, sit." Miss Arlene came over with a small plate of lemon wedges and then rummaged around in the other half of the table to uncover a bear-shaped bottle of honey. "I love honey and lemon myself."

"And I brought the oatmeal cookies you enjoy," Gloria said, patting the tin and placing it between them.

Miss Arlene was gratifyingly appreciative, opening the tin, holding it about ten inches below her chin and breathing in. "Oh, Gloria. These cookies smell marvelous! It's not just cinnamon; what is your secret?"

"Ah, the secret," Gloria said, smiling with satisfaction. "I'll tell you, but you must promise not to share."

Miss Arlene wiggled a pinkie. "Promise!"

Gloria leaned forward, lowered her eyebrows, and said in a conspiratorial whisper, "It's a pinch of cardamom."

"No!"

Gloria nodded firmly. "Does it every time. Gives things that little subtle something."

"Interesting," Miss Arlene said, "and oh, so good." She took a bite. After she'd swallowed, she put her hands down firmly on the table. "Now, my friend. How is Bob? And how are you?"

Gloria paused, squeezing lemon into her tea. She pressed her lips together. "Bob is actually doing well. The treatment team is very happy with his progress."

"That's lovely. And his morale?"

"Except for being very unhappy with the dietary restrictions, he seems very good. He's quite determined to get back to everything as it was before."

"And you seem concerned about that."

Gloria shrugged. "Well, of course. Of course, I'm concerned. Bob has never been what anyone would call a good patient. I don't trust him to stay the course." Miss Arlene nodded empathetically. Gloria continued, "I'm concerned he'll be a bad patient and end up not recovering. Or relapsing."

"And yet the treatment team is pleased, you say."

"Well, sure, but they don't have to live with him. They don't know what it's like."

Miss Arlene tilted her head, her face even more crumpled in concern. "What has it been like, Gloria? For you, I mean. It must be a lot of work and care."

"Oh, you have no idea," Gloria blurted out, and then, "I'm sorry." Miss Arlene had, of course, some idea; her only child had been a little boy with Down syndrome and her husband had deserted them. Miss Arlene became a single mother of an intellectually disabled little boy, who had died ten years ago of heart problems after a long and difficult decline. Miss Arlene had never remarried, had never complained, and had bulldozed the way for little Charles to have the most robust life possible.

"Don't worry, Gloria," Miss Arlene said. "It's been ten years last month since Charles died. And raising a child is different than having a husband become disabled."

"No, no," Gloria protested. She sighed. "You understand how overwhelming it is."

Miss Arlene nodded thoughtfully. "I know how it was for me. There were times that were terrifying. Lonely. Confusing. And Charles was the light of my life. But I don't know how it is for you."

"I've been through this before, that's all. And I'm not in a big hurry to repeat the experience." Gloria frowned, eyebrows flaring.

"Before?"

Gloria shrugged and stared out the kitchen window. She frowned at the clutter on the windowsill: seashells, a bird's feather, a bud vase with drooping beach sunflowers. *How could the woman think straight in this chaos?* "It's chaos, having someone badly injured. Trust me."

"Is it chaos now?"

"No. But it could be. If Bob doesn't get better."

"You're really frightened about this."

"I'm not frightened. I'm ... concerned. That's all. As I said, I've seen this before."

Miss Arlene stirred her tea and took a nibble of cookie, watching Gloria carefully. Gloria averted her eyes from Arlene's pale-green gaze. Miss Arlene put down her hands again and cleared her throat quietly. "Gloria. Something bad has happened but you're not being clear. It sounds like something bad happened to you, and now you're concerned Bob will be a repeat of that. Is this about Jenna?"

Gloria snorted. "No! Definitely not about Jenna." She paused. Miss Arlene was silent and still. Gloria cleared her throat and stared at her tea. "Well, my father had a workplace injury when I was a child and of course that had a big impact on the family. As you can imagine."

"I'm so sorry. That must have been very frightening, especially for a child. Was he okay?"

Gloria took a sip of tea and studied the front of Miss Arlene's refrigerator—a riot of magnets from various state and national parks, medical appointment cards, and some old pictures of Charles. There was Charles at the Special Olympics; Charles in his work uniform at the first anniversary of his one and only job, the job he held successfully for twenty-five years as a bagger at the local grocery store; Charles in a wheelchair shortly before his passing. She turned to face Miss Arlene. "My father did not make a full recovery. He lived for a long time. Jerzy Grabowski"—she took a deep breath—"was never what anyone would have called 'okay.'"

Miss Arlene sat silently, nodding, waiting. Gloria studied her face for a moment, then pressed her lips together, smiled determinedly, and asked, "And what have you been doing lately? It looks as if you've been sketching birds."

Miss Arlene nodded in assent to the change in subject. She spoke of sketching some birds, just to keep busy, and asked about the children and grandchildren. Gloria spoke at length about the family. When she rose to leave, she bent to kiss Miss Arlene's cheek and the older woman placed a hand on her shoulder. "Gloria, things are going to be just fine. But when you feel like a cup of tea and a time to just chat, you just call. I'm here almost all the time."

Gloria blinked hard. She was, to her surprise, momentarily out of words. Then she thanked Miss Arlene, told her to enjoy the cookies, and headed home.

Chapter 14

It was ridiculous, Gloria thought, for parents to pretend they don't have a favorite if they have more than one child. She carefully finished folding the dish towel and reached into the dryer for the next item, shaking it out and folding. She'd heard that tired trope too many times—even Alexa, protesting she loved both her children equally, as if she never met her own son. Love for a child was one thing, but in Alexa's case, it was wrong to even pretend it was a close call. Sandy, as silly as she was, was at least a good daughter.

She patted the stack of dish towels and reached into the dryer. In her case, she thought with satisfaction, there was at least a plausible excuse to not have a favorite. Three good boys and her good daughter! She nodded with satisfaction. *And yet ...* She glanced at the time. *Yes, Matt should be here any moment.* She smiled and sighed. Matt and Tim would be here, and everything would be fine.

She wondered how they were doing. This time of year was so busy for them; late winter and spring were just a bottomless pit of work for accountants. She tilted her head, listening. *No,* she told herself,

Bob hadn't called me. She folded the last towel and loaded the piles of towels into a basket to bring to their various destinations. She peeked into the living room; Bob was reading. *A fishing magazine, of course. Will he never let it go? Just be content to heal up and stay safe. Why push his luck?* She put a stack of bath towels on the hall closet shelf and slammed the door.

"Gloria? Everything okay, hon?"

"Fine. Sorry to startle you," she called back. She rolled her eyes. The man could be oblivious to half of what she said and then have ears like a rabbit if she closed a door too hard. She finished her task and went to the living room, the empty basket dangling from one hand. "Reading, eh? Fishing again."

Bob looked up, taking off his reading glasses. "Yes, absolutely." He waved the magazine. "Rachel will have to look at this one. There's a long article about the impact of those invasive pythons on native animals in the Everglades." He grinned and added, "That will give her a little challenge, whether to root for the natives or be impossibly in favor of both. Ha!" He put his glasses back on and went back to his article.

Gloria shook her head. "Ah, mischief," she said. "Matt and Tim will be here soon."

"Oh, that's right. Good."

A few minutes later, the door to the kitchen swung open with Tim in first, then Matt. Tim was holding a plant and Matt had a bag of groceries. "Mom! We're home," Matt called out. She hurried over to them and hugged them each hard. She took the plant, a tall, pink-and-white blooming orchid.

"Lovely! Thank you," she said. "Look at this! Two stalks, ten—no, twelve flowers. Beautiful!"

"You're welcome," Tim replied, taking the carrots and parsnips Matt held out to him and putting them in the refrigerator.

"Mom, we picked up some fresh produce at the greengrocer," Matt said. "Do you want apples at room temperature or in the refrigerator?"

"Oh, this time of year ... room temperature will still work. Thank you."

"How's Dad doing?" Matt arranged a few apples in the bowl on the counter that already held bananas and a few tangerines.

"Oh, he's fine," Gloria said, shaking her head. "He's in the living room, reading about fishing. He's been looking forward to seeing you two."

"Likewise," Tim said. "We were thinking of taking him out for a little stroll. Just around the block, maybe."

"I don't know," Gloria said hesitantly.

Matt draped an arm around her shoulder. "Mom. He's going to be fine. He's been doing all his exercises; he has to push himself. Better to do that with us on each side of him than you having to do everything."

Tim rested one hand on her shoulder, on top of Matt's hand, and nodded. "Nate said it was time. So, let's have a go at it. Then he can come home and we'll have a nice healthy meal and he can tell us all about fishing."

Gloria clamped her lips together and watched her boys shoot each other a quick look. She took a deep breath. "Fine, then. You're right. Better to have one of you at each side." She jerked her head toward the living room. "You know where to find him."

Matt kissed her forehead. "Love you, Mom," he told her, and then they went in. She heard them greeting Bob, announcing it was time for a nice walk. She heard Bob's cheerful assent, and shook her head. *He is refusing*, she thought resentfully, *to deal with reality. He insists on behaving as if he is already, and is going to be, just fine.* She slammed her hand on the counter in frustration.

"Mom? Everything okay in here?"

Gloria turned; Tim was leaning around the corner from the living room. She rubbed her hands, and smiled, lips pressed close, before replying, "Yes! Everything's fine! Go on—enjoy the walk." She turned very deliberately back toward the counter, pretending to be fussing with the fruit bowl. She rotated a tangerine, listening for Bob's quiet "Umph" as he stood, Matt's jovial comment that he seemed a lot stronger these days, Tim's agreement, and Bob's attestations of how hard he had been working.

"Your mother," he said, "has been absolutely steadfast at keeping me on track." Gloria nodded with satisfaction, and then her jaw dropped open as he continued, "If it weren't for her, I don't think I'd be going to meet Joe along the way on his sabbatical trip."

Gloria squeezed the tangerine so hard that its dimpled peel seemed to become semi-smooth as it bulged between her fingers; the pain in her hand felt gratifyingly distracting. She had a brief flash of understanding for the young people who cut themselves to alleviate emotional pain, was horrified at her own thought, and hurled the tangerine away from her, toward the fruit bowl. It bounced off the backsplash, rolled off the counter, and came to rest, with a thud, next to her feet. Gloria flexed her fingers, stooped for the tangerine, and came up with an "oof." The boys had headed out for their walk. She shook her head in annoyance and paced the kitchen, only half attentive to what she was doing as she gathered ingredients to make dinner.

She decided that she would have to have another little chat with the boys. Surely, they could see that encouraging Bob was a bad idea; he needed to be satisfied with being "okay," nothing risky or excessive. She nodded approvingly at the thought. *Yes, what is needed is a bit of realism, a bit of accepting the limitations of Bob's age. He isn't getting any younger and the fact that Joe*—she frowned, eyebrows flaring—*is chasing his youth with this ludicrous road trip doesn't mean Bob has to join in the foolishness.* Yes, a chat with the boys—perhaps all three of them, over supper, this evening—was the thing to do.

Gloria smiled with satisfaction and put dinner together. When Bob, Matt, and Tim returned, she had chicken breasts baking, a salad made, and a rice dish—half rice, half a vegetable blend of peas, carrots, and onions—simmering on the stove. They all praised how nice the house smelled; Gloria waved them off with a smile.

Dinner did not go quite as planned. The walk had gone just fine; Bob seemed energized by it rather than exhausted. Gloria was concerned he was overdoing it.

"Just the opposite, I think," Bob said, taking a large scoop of rice and vegetables. He was reaching for a second scoop, caught Gloria's frown, sighed, put the scoop in the bowl and handed it to Tim. "I really think all the sitting is doing me more harm than good. Nate said I need to be active—that moving more will help."

"And you've been 'more' active." Gloria's voice was sharp. She caught Matt and Tim sharing a glance and a nod, and she frowned. "We've," she paused, "we've been very diligent about your exercises."

"It's not just exercising," Bob replied. "It's being more active in between. For God's sake, Gloria. Look at you! You never sit. You're constantly up and about. And look how healthy you are."

"We're not talking about me," Gloria said.

"Well, I'm able to be up and about and I'm going to start being up more. I'm going for a walk every day. And then I'm going to start going for two, to spread it out and build up my endurance."

"I don't know."

"The rice is delicious," Tim commented. He smiled at Gloria. "Hard not to worry about this guy, huh?" He nodded toward Bob.

"I just don't want him to overdo it and hurt himself."

"And that's exactly why I plan to take this on in small pieces. But I am done sitting in that damned chair all day like an invalid."

Gloria pressed her lips together. Before she could speak, Matt leaned forward and asked, "Mom? What's going on?"

Gloria paused. She pressed her hands on the edge of the table on each side of her plate and looked from one face to the next, all three of them gazing at her calmly. "Nothing's wrong. Of course. I just want your father to accept reality. Which he is not doing and which you are not helping him to do. All this blather about road trips and fishing! As if you"—she glared at Bob—"are ever going to be the same. You're not! You're sick, you're fragile, you have to be very careful so you don't end up in a wheelchair with your life ruined."

"That's not on the radar," Bob said. "Gloria, it's as if you haven't been paying attention. I'm fine! I'm almost completely healed. Now comes rebuilding my strength. And, yes, the diet. The medication." He gestured with his fork, tines piercing a piece of baked chicken breast. "Yeah, fine. Changes in lifestyle. But it's not as if my whole life is just tiptoeing around trying to not hurt myself."

"See! You're not fine. Honestly, Bob Quinn, I think you hurt your head in that accident."

Matt reached across the table to touch her hand. "Mom, Mom. Please."

She jerked her hand away and glared at him. "I thought you'd be on my side!"

"I'm on both your sides. There's no side to be on. Dad's having a great recovery. Something he couldn't have done without you. Sorry, Dad."

"No, you're right. I couldn't have done it alone, couldn't have done it without you, Gloria."

"You don't understand." Gloria heard her own voice wobbling and shook her head with impatience at herself. "He's got these pipe dreams, this ludicrous notion about Joe's so-called sabbatical. Your father," her eyes darted angrily toward Bob, "has got to accept reality."

Tim sighed. "Mom. Can't you both be right?"

Gloria stared at him.

Tim waited a moment and continued. "Dad's right. He's almost healed. It's important for him to get his strength back so he can exercise to strengthen his heart, manage his health better. He will have to keep watching what he eats. He's right; he's not fated to be an invalid. And you're right; the days of living on junk on fishing trips are over. He'll have to find a way to eat healthier on the road. I'm sure Rachel can help with that."

Gloria shook her head slowly. What was wrong with these people? Were men incapable of seeing the forest for the trees?

Tim went on. "And you're right, Dad's not as young as he used to be and he has to use judgment about pushing himself. But a little pushing is necessary to get better."

"And you've been doing such a good job at helping with that balancing act," Matt added.

Gloria nodded. "I see. You three must have been plotting this on your little walk." She frowned, lips pressed together.

"Actually, the boys kept talking about their house," Bob said. "I think we should get over there and see what they've been doing. It sounds like the office space has really shaped up well."

Matt smiled. "We'd love to have you over! It's been a while."

"Since before the accident," Gloria said, poking at her chicken.

"Right. So, it's past due." Tim glanced at Matt. "What about, say, next Tuesday? Tuesdays are a bit slower; we'll have dug through the flood of over-the-weekend calls and emails, and it would be nice to have the two of you over." He leaned toward Gloria. "Wait until you see the orchids! They've gone crazy this year."

"Distracting me with flowers and food won't work." Gloria stood up stiffly. The three men all gazed up at her.

"Gloria, sweetheart. Please. Sit down. Eat with us." Bob smiled at her.

Oh, that man, Gloria thought. *With that twinkle.* She sat down, a bit hard, reached out to pat Bob's arm. "Of course," she said.

"It would be a pity," Bob added, "for you to take the trouble to make this delicious meal and miss it."

"Hmph."

"And besides, you know it's always better for me when you're here."

"Then why," Gloria asked, her voice tight, "do you need to persist in this ludicrous idea of Joe Bonhall's ridiculous sabbatical?"

When she glanced up, she saw the three men again exchanging a look. She stabbed at a piece of lettuce and pretended not to notice. *They just need to be reasoned with; they need a few more facts. The boys are clearly so excited to see Bob feeling better that they are losing perspective on this. Perhaps,* she thought, *I need to talk with Kevin and Cody. They're more pragmatic. They will be my allies in putting a stop to this nonsense.*

Chapter 15

"Mom, I'm sorry. I just don't see it that way."

Gloria glared at Kevin, who was sitting with her at the small kitchen table, sharing a cup of coffee. Bob was in the bathroom, having a shower. Gloria insisted he not lock the door so she could get in if he needed help. He had reminded her, with only the slightest edge, that he didn't lock the door to the bathroom attached to their bedroom anyway, and he was unlikely to need any more help than she did. "I don't think you're seeing this at all." She put down her coffee mug, a little too hard. "He wants to go back to work at least half-time! Do you think he can handle it?"

Kevin shrugged. "Yes, actually. Could Dad retire and the practice roll along? Yeah, sure. I'd have to hire someone. But a nice, soft roll-out to retirement would be good for both of us. Dad could do the front store work: the eyeglass fittings, the checking how they work for people. He's good at it, he's patient." Kevin shook his head. "The agonizing over frames drives me bonkers. But Dad has his way. Well, you know."

"Yes, I know how patient your father can be. We're not talking about his virtues. We're talking about his health."

"Right. And I think it would be good for him. A part-time return would give him a reason to keep healthy and give him time to figure out what's next."

"What's next is retirement."

"Right." Kevin tilted his head. "And what about you? You went from the frying pan into the fire. You didn't retire; you did a second go-round of childrearing, basically. But the twins are getting older, and we always appreciate you, but we don't need that daily help like Cody did. Understandably, of course. So, what's next for you?"

Gloria stared at him, lips pressed together, collecting herself. She felt her face getting hot. "What's next? This!" She waved her hand at the kitchen. "Home! My husband! My family! That's 'what's next.'"

"Right. And what's going to be the thing that gets you out of bed and excited about life? Once the twins are bigger and Dad's all better?"

Gloria picked up her coffee mug and put it back down. She wiped her hands on her thighs, and then pressed her fingers down on the edge of the table. "For me? I have plenty to do. The Christmas pageant, grandchildren, my family. Chores. Keeping this household running. Being your father's nursemaid."

"He doesn't need a nursemaid."

Gloria stood up, picked up her mug, and went to the sink. She rinsed the mug, robotically put it next to the coffee maker for its next use. She stared out the window, wondering how even this son, the one who worked side by side with his father, could be so oblivious. *No doubt*, she thought, *this inability to notice things helps him cope with his idiot wife.*

"Veronica and I were talking the other day," Kevin went on, startling Gloria. "She was mentioning that the preschool at church is always looking for volunteers. People to come in and help with crafts, read stories, that sort of thing. She said she thought you'd be perfect at that."

Gloria turned, leaned back against the counter and folded her arms. "So that's the idea? Give me something to do so I don't care about your father's crazy scheme to go off on a wild, junk-food eating road trip with his best friend?"

Kevin gave her a pointed look. "No. Just saying, Mom. You need something to do besides be obsessed with Dad. He's fine."

Gloria frowned. "I'm very disappointed, Kevin. I thought you, of all my children, would be reasonable."

Kevin stood up and came over to Gloria, and hugged her. She slowly unfolded her arms and gave him a halfhearted hug in return; then she took a shuddering breath and buried her face in his shoulder. Kevin patted her back with one hand, the back of her head with the other. "Mom. This whole thing must have been absolutely terrifying. I'm sorry it's been so hard."

Gloria was quiet for a few moments, collecting herself, then she straightened and released Kevin. She looked at his calm, concerned face, his smattering of freckles, the early traces of dullness in his hair that meant gray hair was on the way. She sighed. "Thank you. I appreciate all you've done, all that all of you have done. But in this eagerness to cheerlead for your father, you are all losing sight of the big picture."

Kevin smiled gently and replied, "Mom, I think we all have a pretty good take on the big picture."

The conversation with Cody went just as badly. He had rubbed her back and listened while she complained about Matt, Tim, and Kevin. He had nodded and made all the right comforting sounds. Gloria had looked at him fondly. Her good, dutiful, oldest son; she had known she could count on him to see reason.

"Well, Mom," Cody had said after a short silence, "I get it. You're stressed out. But really, everything's fine. Dad's nearly all better; he's just taking advantage of all this to get to retirement earlier than he'd been saying before. That whole working part-time thing, that's a great segue for him."

Gloria stared at him, mouth agape, and then slammed her lips shut. "Have you seen him?"

Cody had leaned forward in the Adirondack chair, grinning. "Yes, Mom. Almost every day." He glanced toward the house. "He looks great! He's walking every day. Pushing the vacuum cleaner around. You must be ecstatic."

Gloria shook her head impatiently. "I am not 'ecstatic.' I'm ... worried. He's not pacing himself! He's going to end up having another heart attack, or having his blood sugar run amuck, or fall and reinjure himself. And then what?"

"Well, yeah, all those things would be bad. But actually, the odds of all those things are lower now than they were before the accident. Because now he's doing something about his health. With your help."

Gloria pressed her lips together. What Cody said was true, but he didn't seem to understand the urgency here. She could not deal with the obvious fragility of Bob's situation. Perhaps expecting the men in the family to understand was asking too much; they were likely to sympathize with Bob and his crazy dreams of a fishing adventure. What she needed was a good talk with a woman.

"You can't imagine," Gloria complained into the phone. She heard rustling and bird songs. "Alexa? Did you buy a bird?"

"I'm out in the backyard so I have some privacy while we talk."

"Oh, of course," Gloria said, mollified. "Well! I had a little talk with Kevin. I thought he'd be able to talk sense into his brothers but of course, he's on their side."

"Side?"

"You know! The Bob is fine side! The Bob should go fishing with your husband side!"

"Ah. Fishing with my husband. Are we talking the sabbatical trip?"

"Well, of course. But even these little Saturday morning outings!"

"But Joe tells me Bob's doing great. No trouble at all—a complete recovery, except he gets tired. But he was getting tired before the accident, before anyone knew how bad his heart was."

"Oh, sure, as if Joe would know. I'm the one who lives with him! I know what's going on!"

"What's going on?"

"He comes home and takes a nap, that's what."

"So does Joe. They get up before dawn to go fishing. Bob's what, sixty-five? Sixty-six years old? Is taking a nap something new?"

"Don't minimize this."

"Gloria, I'm sorry. I'm not minimizing. It's just that, well, a lot of people like a Saturday afternoon nap, especially if they were up before dawn and outdoors. You're seeing problems where there aren't any."

Gloria spent the next twenty minutes explaining to Alexa about Bob's fatigue after his workouts, his insistence on doing chores around the house, and his ludicrous obsession with returning to work the following week, half days, just three days at first. She reenacted part of the failed attempt to make Kevin see the light on this whole thing. Alexa was, Gloria reflected, not very helpful. She made little sounds as if she were going to interrupt and then, at a pause, Alexa said, "Gloria. I really think you need to talk to someone. Really. Someone who can help you ... cope with all these changes."

"I could cope better if everyone else would be realistic."

"But what if they are? Being realistic, I mean. Gloria, why are you so afraid that Bob's going to be fine?"

Gloria was stunned silent, and then said, loudly, "Fine! I'll go talk to someone!"

"That's a good idea," Alexa said. "I've done it myself. Makes a world of difference to have an objective set of ears."

It hasn't helped Alexa at all, Gloria thought. *Purple hair! Studying birds! Giving away half her clothes! The woman is a trainwreck, but she clearly means well.* Gloria felt the warm satisfaction that she was being generously charitable toward Alexa. "Well, thank you, dear. I'll see about it. But," she added with an edge to her voice, "I am not afraid of Bob getting better."

"I know," Alexa said comfortingly. "I misspoke. I guess you seem afraid he is going to be an invalid."

"Who wouldn't be?" Gloria asked.

Chapter 16

Father Anthony was leaning back in the oversized office chair, hands resting peacefully on the arms, head tilted. He had made a few attempts at speaking but Gloria had opened a floodgate of words. She was looking at him; she realized he had opened his mouth here and there, but she just kept talking.

Finally, Father leaned forward a bit, one hand gently raised. "Gloria. Gloria." He paused, and she was silent. "This has been a very difficult time. I remember well visiting you and Bob, with the children there, when this all first happened." Father had come in the early morning hours the day after the accident to give Bob an anointing. He had given the rest of them a blessing and a long explanation about how this anointing was no longer just for those about to die, it was a sacrament of healing, and to not think that the anointing meant Father thought Bob wouldn't make it. Gloria had breathed a sigh of relief and had been oblivious to the pointed glance between Father and Cody as Father left them.

"And now Bob is home and making a truly miraculous recovery, and the time has come for you to focus a bit on yourself."

"I don't have time to focus on myself," Gloria complained. "I need guidance. Spiritual guidance," she added pointedly, thinking of Cody and then Alexa mildly suggesting she "talk to someone."

"I agree," Father Anthony said serenely. "I'm in favor of that for everyone, as it happens. There just aren't enough spiritual directors to meet the needs of our people." He sighed and glanced at his wrist. "Gloria, I'm afraid I have to end our conversation. I suggest you pray on this and give the office a call in a day or two to set an appointment." He stood, and there was nothing to be done. Gloria stood obediently and bowed her head, hands clasped. She glanced up through her eyebrows at Father Anthony, who had raised both hands to embrace an invisible circle around her head.

"Father in heaven, bless your child Gloria." Gloria felt herself take a hiccup of breath at the word 'child.' "Give her the grace to feel the great love You have for her, and Your deep desire for her to be peaceful and happy. We ask all this as we do all things, in the name Jesus Christ, our Savior. In the name of the Father, the Son, and the Holy Spirit." His hand moved in the sign of the cross. "Go in peace, Gloria," he added kindly, and opened the door for her.

Gloria left the church office with barely a glance at Janice, the receptionist. She didn't think she could stomach the woman's perpetually anxious expression. She marched to her car and sat down, hard, staring out the windshield across the parking lot at the big statue of Mary standing, arms outstretched, over the prone body of her crucified Son. *Please help me*, she thought, *because no one down here is.* She jerked the seat belt into place, clicking it with extra pressure, and nodded firmly. At least something did its job. She headed through the errands of the day: groceries, the pharmacy, and then home.

Bob was napping in his chair, legs elevated. He barely stirred when she came in; she kept an eye on him as she put groceries away. He looked tired and pale. *He needs to get outdoors; he's been indoors too much. Not enough vitamin D from the sun*, she thought. That would help. What were they thinking in the healthcare industry, keeping people trying to repair bones indoors like a bunch of vampires? Gloria shook her head in disapproval. *Honestly*, she thought, slamming the refrigerator door, *do I have to think of everything?*

She heard movement and turned. Bob was awake. She hurried in. "Bob, dear. How are you? Did you have a good nap?"

Bob smiled up at her. "Gloria! How was Father?"

"Oh, fine," she said dismissively. "I've been blessed. Everything's fine." She adjusted the towel over the chair back. "There. It was bunched up."

"Ah. Thank you." Bob shifted. "I'm a little hungry. How about some lunch?"

"I'm just putting away groceries," Gloria said. "I'll make up our lunch as soon as I'm done." She glanced around the room. "It's dark in here! How about we go outside for lunch? I'll help you out and we'll get some fresh air and sunshine."

"That would be nice," Bob agreed. "I don't really need help." He smiled at her frown. "But maybe you could open the blinds some more? I think there's a nest being built in the holly tree there and when the blinds are open almost all the way I can see it from here."

Gloria adjusted the blinds. Good, he was showing interest in things outdoors. She just hoped he wasn't going to go from thinking about bird nests to talking about fly fishing. She was arranging their lunches on plates when Bob said, "Oh, Joe called while you were gone. He's coming over Saturday."

"Oh?"

"We're going to sit in the garage and tie some flies. Talk some fishing. You know," he added, "boy stuff, as you say."

Gloria vented her frustration on the apple wedges with a few decisive whacks. "Of course."

Bob said nothing. Soon Gloria helped him onto the deck despite his protestations, settling him in at the table, and then retrieved their lunches and tall glasses of water with lemon juice. *Nice and healthy*, she thought approvingly. She set up their plates and flatware, sat down with a satisfied plop across from Bob, and placed her napkin across her lap. Outdoors or no, Gloria believed in doing things properly. Sensible cloth napkins, white, so they could be bleached. She said grace for them, picked up her fork, and looked at Bob. He was staring at his plate, and then up at Gloria, and then at his plate. "Bob? What is it?"

He shrugged. "Gloria, this is ... ugh, I'm tired of so-called healthy eating. I want something that crunches! Something salty and crunchy!"

"The carrots are crunchy. And the celery. And the apples. And the hummus is sort of salty." Gloria frowned. "And the little dish of almonds and pistachios—"

"Are a serving the size for Gina, not me." Bob shook his head. "I know it's not your fault, I know you're doing what you think is best."

"For you." Gloria frowned at him. "I'm doing what is best for you."

"Well, yes, I'm sure you are," Bob said, "but it doesn't feel like it's best for me. It feels like you're treating me like I'm five, just putting food in front of me. Like that rehab center, except they gave me a choice. 'Dr. Quinn, would you like Greek yogurt for breakfast today? Or oats with fresh fruit?'" Bob sighed.

Gloria carefully dipped a celery stick into her hummus and crunched down on it. She chewed carefully, taking her time before responding. She thought about taking his plate away and letting him be hungry and then decided that wouldn't be good; he was diabetic and who knows what would happen if he went around skipping meals? She sighed with frustration. "So, what do you want me to do, Bob Quinn? Kill you with food?"

Bob reached over and stroked her face. "Gloria. My Gloria. Everything's okay. I just ... I want to feel like a man and not a baby." He thumped his cane on the patio. "This thing! The chair in the shower! The grip bars in the bathroom, the portable toilet you insist I keep next to the bed even though I never use it. I don't know if I'm five or ninety-five. And I just want to be me again."

"You being you caused all that," Gloria said angrily, waving her hand in circles at the cane. "How about being something different?"

"Fair enough," Bob said mildly. "You're right. Me being me was self-destructive. I've got a new lease on life ... like my dad got. And I intend to use it and I want, I need, for you to help me. But not by infantilizing me, Gloria. Help me."

Gloria nodded slowly. "And what would that be? Because this is me helping. Providing healthy meals. Keeping track of the appointments. Helping with your exercises."

"And I appreciate every bit of it," Bob said firmly. "Gloria, you're a saint. And I know you're worried, I know you saw what your mom went through."

"We're not bringing my mom into this," Gloria retorted. "Don't change the subject. This is about you. And your terrible habits."

"Which I am changing," Bob said. "I would like to have a little more ... variety, shall we say?" He paused. "I would like to have a couple of diabetic cookbooks."

Gloria felt her shoulders drop. "Oh. Diabetic cookbooks. That's a good idea."

"We could go through them and then pick out some new things to try, maybe some versions of things we like that are more diabetic-friendly." Bob paused. "I would like that, Gloria. For us to be team on this."

"Agreed," she said, nodding and rearranging her napkin. Gloria lifted her glass with a smile. "To us, Bob. To being a team."

Chapter 17

"So, Mom."

Gloria tensed her shoulders as she stirred the vegetable soup. Rachel had been yammering about some problem at her school—they needed to do more training in peer mediation and anti-bullying, and the teachers were resisting giving up classroom time with standardized testing just around the corner. This was a change of subject, and "So, Mom," always meant something Rachel had been saving up for a while.

"Mm-hmm?" Gloria asked, pressing her lips together and not turning to face Rachel just yet.

"So. Mom. I have a question."

Gloria sighed, carefully placed the spoon in the spoon rest that sat between the burners on the stove, and turned, wiping her hands desultorily on her apron. Rachel was in the dining room, leaning across the breakfast bar counter on her elbows, twirling a long strand of hair. "Did you go to school like that?"

Rachel looked down, looked up at her mother, and grinned. "Yes. I did. Mom, we don't do pantsuits and blouses anymore." She looked down again and back at Gloria, shrugging. "I think this is fine."

Gloria sighed. A button-up shirt as a jacket over a pink polo shirt with the school logo and a pair of khakis did not seem professional, and neither did the long, straight hair. Rachel insisted on looking more like a college student than a guidance counselor. "Fine, then. What's the question?"

Rachel pulled her lips in briefly and then asked, eyes darting toward the living room, "So ... you and Daddy. How did you know?"

"Know," Gloria echoed flatly.

"How did you know Daddy was, well, the one?"

Gloria sighed. "Is this about Aidan? Already?"

"Mom. It's been almost a year. I think if we're going to be serious it's either now or never." Rachel smirked. "As you keep pointing out, I'm not getting any younger. So, how did you know it was Dad?"

Gloria checked the soup and turned down the flame, then went to the breakfast bar, facing Rachel, slipping onto one of the stools. "It's not a quick answer, Rachel."

"Okay. I have time."

Gloria pressed her lips together and studied Rachel. She looked toward the living room, where Bob was reading, this time about campgrounds in North Carolina. She sighed and turned back to Rachel. "Well, he was one of the only men my height who was interested in me," she said tartly.

Rachel laughed. "Mom! That's not true. You used to look like a model."

Gloria flinched a little inside. *Used to*, she thought. *Well, of course, I'm a grandmother and can't run around fussing over my appearance; it would be pathetic.* A thought flashed, suddenly, of Alexa and her recent changes—the updated wardrobe, the exercise routine—and she reflexively ran a hand over her belly and sighed. "Fair enough," she managed. "Well, you know, we met at school, at the school where I worked. But not like you and Aidan."

"Right, eye exam day," Rachel said. "But meeting on eye exam day and knowing Daddy was the one are two different things."

Gloria gazed past Rachel toward Bob and smiled.

Bob had been a very young optometrist, working at a local practice, and had been sent to do the cursory eye exams for the elementary school children. The number of children who, it turned out, had been unable to read the blackboards and had to be moved to the front of the room was a surprise each year. Occasionally teachers would wonder aloud why the children hadn't just piped up that they couldn't see what was on the board and had to have it explained that, for the child in question, it was normal. They didn't know anyone could make out what was on the board from the desks. Bob was there, doing eye exams, and Gloria, who was barely twenty-two, was a fairly new teacher and already successfully managing her kindergarten class. She had barely spoken to Bob; she had noticed him, of course, with that red hair and kind face, but twenty-five kindergarten children required careful oversight.

The next day Bob was back, for the upper grades, and, according to the story, he had asked, circumspectly, about the kindergarten teacher. Marlene, the school secretary, retold the story for years. She had replied, wide-eyed, "Oh! Mrs. Schultz. Of course. Don't tell me—you were one of her students, weren't you?" According to the tale, Bob had turned bright red, stammered, and explained he was just sort of wondering about the other teacher. Marlene pretended he actually meant elderly Mrs. Brown, the second-grade teacher, and then kind-faced but very plain middle-aged Miss Hazel, the first-grade teacher. She worked her way through almost the entire lower grades' faculty, until Marlene swore Bob was so brick red that his freckles were lighter than the rest of him. He finally blurted, "No, no. I mean the tall, young one, with the long, shiny brown hair." Marlene never told one part of the story; the part in which, after being tormented, somehow Dr. Bob Quinn knew that young Miss Gloria Grabowski usually stopped at the public library and then the local grocery on her way home each Friday. It took about three weeks for, as Bob would later describe it, the stars to align, before he was able to nonchalantly encounter Gloria in the produce department, pretend to be surprised to see her, and reintroduce himself over the acorn squashes. She was polite but distant; the conversation was short. A week later, he managed to arrange to be at the same grocery yet again, this time where he could solicit a bit of advice on whether it would be better to broil his pork chops or pan fry them. Gloria had suggested broiling, but the next day, of course—it being a Friday. Bob had said, "Of course!" Another two weeks passed, and he managed to encounter her in the child psychology section of the public library; the conversation went better because he asked advice on how to have young optometry patients cooperate, and the librarian came over to shush them when Gloria, telling a story about an unnamed pupil, began waving her arms excitedly. Gloria blushed and Bob suggested they meet at the diner, just for a cup of coffee, perhaps. They did. And somewhere between the turkey club sandwich and the apple pie a la mode Gloria felt, deep in her bones, that this tall, athletic, gentle-faced man with a shock of unruly red hair was the one.

Gloria sighed. She did not want to tell Rachel, who knew the general story, that it was basically love at fourth sight and a done deal on the first date. There was just the formality of courtship and an awkward first kiss, and a marriage just twelve months later. She knew Rachel was older than she had been; Rachel was twenty-seven years old, for God's sake, but really, children just took longer to grow up now.

"I know you think I'm too young," Rachel said, startling Gloria, "but Mom, seriously. I'm five years older than you were when you met Daddy. So, how did you know?" Rachel leaned forward conspiratorially, shooting a glance in the direction of the living room. "It wasn't the fishing stories, so, what?"

"If you must know," Gloria said, straightening up, "it was ... everything. Nothing. I just knew."

"When? How?"

"Oh, Rachel, it's not science, it's love. How can I know? It was just everything. Your father is, was, everything anyone would want in a husband. Even if he is a bit too much with the fishing."

"I heard that part," Bob called out.

"Daddy." Rachel leaned back to see her father. "How did you know? That it was Mom?"

Bob turned in his chair and gazed at them both, his daughter and his wife, and shook his head, smiling. "I knew when she strolled into the school gym with twenty-five five-year-olds as if she was walking down a runway, oblivious to how beautiful she was, that I would be happy just to be near her for the rest of my life."

"Oh, you," Gloria said, waving a hand at him as if shooing a mosquito.

Rachel, however, was intrigued. "Seriously?" She glanced at her mom. "So just love at first sight?"

Bob grinned. "Absolutely."

"Isn't that sort of superficial? Just because Mom looked pretty?"

"That, and her ... competence. Her kindness to the children, her refusal to be flustered by all those fidgety little kids." Bob shifted in his chair. "Rachel, you studied psychology. You know how important attraction is. And for a man, well." He shrugged and opened his book again. Before he settled into reading, he added, "Any man who denies that beauty matters isn't a man worth having."

Rachel shrugged and turned, smiling, toward her mom. "So. Wow. That's Dad. How about you?"

Gloria stood up and went to stir the soup. She glanced at Rachel. "It was everything. His kindness, his sense of humor, his eyes, that red hair." She shrugged. "I'd like to tell you something more helpful."

"Oh, that's very helpful," Rachel said. "Very, very helpful."

Gloria was going to ask exactly how that generality could help, but Rachel twirled away and headed off to her bedroom, leaving her mother with her mouth open and the spoon midair over the soup. Gloria sighed, clamped her lips together, and tried to turn her attention to dinner. She paused and went in to the living room to talk to Bob. She stood near his chair, hands on hips. He glanced up and nodded, eyes shooting toward the hall and back to Gloria.

"Yes," he said. "I think so."

"That's what I thought, too." Gloria sighed, and sank onto the ottoman next to Bob's feet. She rested a hand on one of his knees. "Has he talked to you yet?"

Bob shook his head. "No. But I guess now it will be any time." He sighed with a half-smile. "You weren't here to hear it, but Cody and I had a similar conversation the other day."

"No."

"Yes. Obviously, it's a different situation entirely."

"To say the least," Gloria said tartly. And then, after a pause, "And?"

Bob shrugged. "I think Cody's ... appropriately gun-shy, let's put it that way. I don't expect any super-fast movement, but I wouldn't be surprised if we're dealing with an announcement there by the end of the year."

"What do you think of it?"

Bob reached out to touch Gloria's face and her heart felt a little flop. "Gloria. He described feelings for Sandy that sound just like ... just like what I felt that first day I laid eyes on you. If that's how he feels about Sandy—after knowing her and all her quirkiness and that ridiculously overcharged brain all these years—then I will be very, very happy for both of them."

Gloria placed her hand over Bob's, holding the warmth against her cheek. She blinked hard and smiled. "Then I will stop being afraid," she said. Bob smiled at her. They both knew she was lying.

Chapter 18

Two days later, Gloria phoned the church office. The receptionist, Janice, answered the phone. "Blessed Sacrament Catholic Church. How may I help you?"

"This is Gloria Quinn."

Gloria was sure she heard a bit of a sigh. "Yes, Mrs. Quinn. How may I help you?"

"I'm calling to make an appointment with Father Anthony."

"For …?" Janice had a way of sounding as if she was about to be bitten by a large and vicious animal.

"To meet with him," Gloria said firmly. "He asked me to call soon."

"Oh." There was a pause and some rustling. Gloria rolled her eyes. Couldn't anyone just be efficient? Janice came back on the line. "Mrs. Quinn."

"Yes." Gloria pressed her lips together. The woman was trying her patience. *Doesn't she realize I have a sick husband at home? Do I have all day to remind her who is calling?*

"Father Anthony left word in case you called back. For when you called back." The voice on the other end of the line was wobbly; Gloria wondered when Janice would see a doctor about that. Perhaps she had some sort of tic. "Father said ... He said that he recommends you make an appointment with Father Jack."

"Father Jack?" Gloria's voice cycled up. "What about Father Anthony?"

"He recommends Father Jack. Father Ringling. Father Jack Ringling." Janice's voice went a half-octave higher, quivering. "He says Father Jack is just the person. Father Anthony has prayed on it," she added, as if that were the final word.

Gloria sighed. *Father Jack. That cranky Capuchin.* "Fine. When is he available?"

"Well, I checked with Father Jack for you, just in case," Janice announced, "and he said he can meet with you on Fridays at ten a.m. or else at one p.m. He has the nine and the noon Masses on Friday."

Gloria glanced at the calendar. She wondered what that meant, that Janice had checked with Father Jack. Perhaps she did that right after that initial meeting with Father Anthony. That would be surprisingly efficient of Janice. There was nothing on the calendar for Friday; she agreed to the 10:00 a.m. Better to get it over with, she thought. All was confirmed. She was sure she heard a faint "Whew" before the line clicked.

Father Jack Ringling was a Capuchin, part of the Franciscan family of religious orders. He usually wore the rough brown robe with a hood and sandals, although in the summer he would show up to vest for Mass in khaki shorts and a polo shirt—usually bright blue. He was semi-retired, living in the small house that served as a friary with three other priests in the same neighborhood as Matt and Tim. He had worked in psychiatric hospitals, street ministries, and done some hospital-based work. He had gray hair, a permanent tan, and dark-blue eyes that seemed to cut through everything in front of them. When he gave the homily, he would push up his sleeves and lean on the ambo, looking more as if he should be at the bar with a beer in front of him than like a proper priest breaking open the scriptures for the people. Gloria couldn't quite place a finger on what she disliked about Father Jack; he was friendly with Matt and Tim, even though Father knew their situation. He was known to be gentle and encouraging in confession, and almost everyone had a story about a friend who was reluctant to go and was talked into seeing Father Jack, and came out tearfully smiling and peaceful.

But he annoyed Gloria for reasons she could not quite put a finger on; she just trusted her gut. Yet Father Anthony had said Father Jack was the one.

Gloria arrived at the church office five minutes early. She pushed open the heavy glass door. Janice, perpetually anxious-looking, peered up at her. "Oh. Mrs. Quinn. Good morning." She pushed back in her rolling chair, reaching for the phone and keeping her eyes on Gloria. "Father's just gotten in from Mass. I'll let him know you've arrived." Her eyes darted around the foyer. "Please, have a seat."

"Thank you," Gloria replied. She sank into one of the waiting chairs, glancing around the office. Prayer cards and brochures were in a basket on the small end table; she picked one up and put it back quickly, frowning. *Prayers for widows and widowers.* She lifted another. *For those in a spiritual desert. Well. Perhaps.* She was frowning at the card when the door to the offices swung open. Father Jack nodded to her. "Gloria. Welcome. Come on in."

She rose. "Good morning, Father." She followed after him. She had not noticed he was shorter than she was, but then, so were a lot of people. Father Anthony was, of course; he was Irish. Then, on the other hand, Aidan was Irish, and he was tall. Gloria wondered fleetingly if she needed to reconsider whether Irish were mostly short or mostly tall, but then Father Jack was offering her a chair and sitting in the other chair, on the same side of the desk. She glanced at the chair behind the desk and at Father Jack.

He gestured toward the desk chair. "I know. The big chair behind the desk. I'm not a big fan of that, I don't think it makes for good conversation." He tilted his head. "Are you comfortable? Or would you rather be outdoors?" Gloria's eyebrows came down. He shrugged. "Some people prefer being out in the prayer garden. Or walking around the grounds. It's your call."

She nodded slowly. She thought about being outdoors and everyone seeing her, seeing that she was consulting with Father Jack. She imagined people thinking, oh, Father Anthony didn't want to talk to that one, he shoved her off on the cranky Capuchin. "Maybe we'll just stay in for today," she replied.

Father Jack nodded. "So, Gloria. What brings you here?"

"What brings me," Gloria muttered. "Well, my husband almost died. And now he's home and still all banged up and I can't get him to cooperate and the kids are driving me crazy. My daughter's dating an Irishman, my oldest son is falling in love with my best friend's flaky daughter, another son is going to have a nervous breakdown if my husband doesn't get back to work soon. My daughter-in-law is probably pregnant again, and she's a complete idiot when it comes to children. My best friend has gone bonkers and her husband wants to take mine on a fishing trip. That's what brings me here." She sat back, arms folded across her chest, lips pressed together.

Father Jack nodded thoughtfully, gazing at Gloria. He glanced up at the San Damiano crucifix on the wall and back to Gloria again. "So, a lot of life going on; some beautiful things, some terrifying things, some a bit of both."

Gloria pressed her lips together, squinting. "I'm not seeing beauty."

"Gloria. Your daughter is in love. What about this Irishman?"

Gloria's mouth twisted. "He's a teacher. History teacher. Very nice. Handsome. His family's in Ireland. He spends summers there."

"Is he kind? Thoughtful?"

"Yes. And Catholic," she added. "His uncle is Monsignor Seamus. The pastor over at St. Stephen's."

"Well, that helps," he agreed. "Makes marriage a little less complicated. And your oldest son?"

"He's divorced. His wife went crazy and abandoned him and the twins. And now he's apparently besotted with Sandy."

"And Sandy is …?"

"Rachel, my daughter's, best friend. And my best friend's daughter. She volunteers here, I think. She's a nice enough girl, fairly bright, but just wacky. She and Rachel are both little environmental activists."

Father Jack's eyes twinkled and Gloria remembered with a wince that he was a Capuchin, one of the Franciscan orders, and they were as wacky a group of nature lovers as Sandy and Rachel. "Okay, so far, we have two young couples falling in love. That sounds beautiful."

Gloria shrugged. "Well, then there's Bob."

"Ah. That's a big deal." Father Jack leaned forward. "If Bob were fine—still healthy, still working—would we need to have this conversation?"

"No." Gloria was firm. "Well, he is working. A few days a week. A few hours. But it's the accident and Bob's health problems." And, with little encouragement, Gloria poured out a river of words. She described managing Bob's diet and his medications, overseeing his glucose meter and his learning to manage his diabetes, bullying him through his physical therapy exercises. She discussed how Bob was just starting to go back to the office for a few hours, a few days a week, just to oversee things and help patients with eyeglass fittings; he wasn't up to the eye exams yet. She talked about suspecting this was going to be it—that he would never really go back to work as he had, but would cede the clinical work to Kevin and work in the front, where eyeglass selections and fittings were done. Father Jack listened carefully, asked a few thoughtful questions, repeated a few things to be sure he was understanding.

Gloria paused, feeling as if she'd said enough. A glance at her wrist showed her it was nearly eleven; no doubt the appointment was nearly done. Father Jack caught her glance. "We'll wrap up soon," he said cheerfully. "No doubt you have a lot waiting for you at home." He paused. "Gloria, I'd like to give you a bit of something to reflect on, to pray on. A bit of spiritual direction homework, if you like. Then, in a few weeks, we can meet again. You can set that up with Janice," he added.

"All right," Gloria said. She reached into her purse and pulled out a small notebook and pen. "Ready."

Father Jack paused. "Okay. I think there's a lot of focus on yourself in all this, Gloria."

She stared at him.

Father Jack gazed back peacefully. "I heard a lot of how all these things affect you, or how they displease you, in the case of your son and the flaky friend, for example. But you really don't seem to be taking in where God is in this, or even what all this means to any of the other people involved."

Gloria found it difficult to speak.

"I can see," the cranky Capuchin continued, "that you are a woman who is very good at organizing things. I know you keep the Christmas pageant going for us, year after year. Even that camel." He sighed, shaking his head. "And no doubt all these things make it feel as if life is spiraling out of control."

Gloria nodded, blinking hard a few times. She wondered why her eyes were picking now to be watery.

"So perhaps you need to reflect a bit on where that control really lies. I'd like to you to start reading Matthew's gospel. Slowly. Just a bit at a time. Rest in it. See what speaks to you. If you like, write about what comes up. For example, when you get to the part about not worrying ... don't rush that. Sit with it. Let come what will; write it down. See what you hear from our Lord in your heart. We'll talk about it."

Gloria jotted down his instructions. "Read Matthew. Go slowly. Write about reactions." She tucked the notebook and pen back into her purse. "Thank you, Father."

Father Jack nodded. "You're welcome." Still seated, he raised a hand and blessed her, and then stood up to open the door and see her out. As he opened the door to the foyer he leaned around to speak to Janice. "Janice, could you set something up with Gloria to see me again? In three weeks or so?"

"Yes, Father," Janice said, nodding, and then turned to look up at Gloria.

"Thanks again," Gloria said. She and Janice set up the next appointment and Gloria stepped outside. It was a beautiful day—clean-aired, high sixties, and the birds were singing. She wondered, briefly, if perhaps next time they could sit outside for this ... spiritual direction, she supposed. Yes, spiritual direction. She nodded firmly with satisfaction, smiling a bit at the idea of herself as the kind of woman who, with all this chaos to manage, still found time to seek spiritual direction. She waved beatifically to the maintenance man as she made her way out of the parking lot, nodded to the young mothers pushing strollers past the church parking lot.

She felt warm and peaceful. Perhaps she had underestimated that cranky Capuchin. She almost forgot to tick off the stores to stop by if she could get Rachel to take half a day to go shopping. Gloria fairly floated into the house, savoring a sense of hopefulness.

Which ended sharply when she swung open the door from the garage to find Bob eating ice cream out of its gallon container at 11:15 in the morning.

Chapter 19

"Gloria, calm down."

Gloria did not want to calm down. She wanted to dump the bucket of ice cream on top of Bob's balding head. She threw her purse down and began waving her arms wildly. After that, it became a blur. Bob escaped to the backyard. She followed him, still shouting.

Bob kept repeating to her, "Gloria. Breathe, Gloria. Gloria—everything is fine."

"Everything is not fine," she shouted. "You're sabotaging your own recovery. You're going to end up dead. You have to follow the instructions. You have to watch what you eat. You can't—"

"Gloria, stop. I can't talk with you like this."

A third voice cut through the shouting. "Gloria? Bob? Everything okay over there?"

Gloria and Bob both whipped their heads toward the fence along the west side of the property. Their neighbor, Arlene, was calling to them. Her silver hair was visible in a gap in the fence.

"Oh, crap," Bob muttered. Louder, he called, "We're fine, Arlene. Arguing over the ice cream."

"Ah, ice cream. That's nice. Well, as long as you're both okay. Gloria?"

"Fine, Arlene, thank you," Gloria managed to say. She felt her chest shaking and hoped her voice was steady enough to keep Arlene from wandering over.

"That's nice," Arlene said. "Well, you kids have fun arguing about ice cream. Share nicely," she added with a chuckle.

Gloria waited until she heard Arlene's back door shut and then, through clenched teeth, continued her verbal assault on Bob. "You will *not* sabotage yourself. You *will* follow your diet. You will *not* do this to me."

Bob sighed, sinking into an Adirondack chair and placing his cane across his lap. "Gloria. I'm not doing anything to you. I was having some ice cream. For God's sake, honey, I'm a grown man. I understand about the diet. And I have to have a treat once in a while." He held up one hand to silence any rebuttal. "You're not going to be along when I meet up with Joe on his sabbatical. You're going to have to trust me to take good enough care of myself."

"You can't go."

"Well, that's a matter of opinion, Gloria."

She stared at him. Bob looked calm, even slightly amused, as if his disobeying doctors' orders was nothing at all. *He's not taking this seriously. He could have died in that accident. He could have died even without the accident, and here he is, planning on going on some overgrown boys' adventure.* She would have to call Alexa and put a stop to this nonsense. "You can't go. You're injured, you are diabetic, you are an invalid."

"The hell I am." Bob sat up straighter. "Yes, I have diabetes. Yes, I banged the heck out of myself in that accident and I have heart problems. But I am not, and I will not live like, an invalid. The accident isn't going to ruin my life, Gloria. And it isn't going to ruin yours, either." He sat back, nodding in apparent satisfaction. "I have no intention of letting it ruin either of our lives. But you," he paused, "you seem intent to have this be the story, the big story, of our life together. That's not right."

Gloria sat down in the other chair, gripping the armrests and shaking her head slowly back and forth. He didn't seem to understand. This was the defining event of their lives. She'd seen this before, she thought grimly. Bob didn't know; his father was lively and healthy. He didn't know what it was to live with an invalid. She sighed, blinking hard. "You don't understand, Bob. You don't know what it is to live with someone who's been ruined by an accident."

"I'm not ruined, Gloria. And I'm not Jerzy Grabowski, either."

Gloria was half out of her chair, arms waving, when they heard the back door slide open and Rachel burst into the backyard. "Mom! Dad! What's going on? Miss Arlene called me and I couldn't reach you."

Gloria stared at Rachel and then at Bob. Bob shrugged. Rachel was clearly upset. "Rachel. What are you doing here?"

"Miss Arlene called and said she thought something was wrong. She heard crashing and then yelling and said there was some crazy story about ice cream. So, I let the principal know I was going home for lunch. What's going on?"

"Well," Bob said slowly, "as it happens, it was about ice cream."

"That's hardly fair," Gloria interrupted.

"Your mother came home from an appointment and found me eating ice cream and had a meltdown. I guess you saw the kitchen."

Rachel nodded. "Yes. I saw the kitchen." She stared at her mother. "Mom? Are you okay? What happened?"

"I guess you can see what happened," Gloria snapped. "Yes, I was quite upset. Your father"—she glared at him, brows drawn sharply together—"was eating ice cream right out of the container."

"The container you threw at the wall? Or did Daddy throw it?"

"The wall?"

Rachel sighed. "Yes, the wall. Mom, there's Neapolitan ice cream all down the wall and in a big puddle on the floor. There are dishes ... well, pieces of dishes, all over the place. Dad, are you okay?"

Bob waved his cane. "Behold, my dish deflector. I played baseball in school, remember?"

"This isn't funny," Gloria said angrily.

"No, it's not." Rachel folded her arms. "I think this has gone far enough."

"I quite agree." Gloria nodded. *Good.* Things were falling into place. Rachel would help her get Bob to comply with the rules.

"Yeah. I'm calling the boys. Seeing when we can all meet here."

"I'm glad to hear it." Gloria's smile quickly faded as she caught Rachel's glance at Bob and Bob's barely perceptible nod. He wouldn't be so smug when all the children explained to him that he needed to do better as a patient. Then she shook her head, straightened up. "Well, since you're here for lunch, can I make you a sandwich?"

"I have the lunch I packed for school; I'll just eat while I work this afternoon. No student meetings scheduled." Rachel sighed. She hugged each of her parents. "Okay. Call me if you need anything. See you later." She left quickly, phone up to her head as she hurried into the house and out of sight.

Gloria watched her and then sat down again. She leaned back, closed her eyes. She still felt shaky, and now there was the kitchen to be cleaned up. She opened her eyes and saw Bob watching her, his face serene. "Well, it seems Rachel's going to see about the boys coming over tonight," she said. "I guess I had better get the kitchen straightened up and put something together."

"I'll give you a hand," Bob said. He hoisted himself up and headed in ahead of her. "It sounds like it will take some doing."

She noticed, frowning, that he didn't use the cane; he was almost twirling it.

Rachel had, of course, arrived first, inspecting the kitchen and then the rest of the house, going from room to room—even her brothers' old bedrooms—looking for Gloria could not imagine what. She had glanced at her phone often. Gloria was in the kitchen, finishing up homemade soup. She wasn't sure if everyone would be there; Rachel had been unusually vague on details, so Gloria had decided a good vegetable soup with a salad and some bread would be just right, and in compliance with Bob's diet. She glanced through to the living room; there he was, reading. She sighed. Another book on the Lenni Lenape tribe; no doubt he was thinking of that ridiculous fishing trip. Gloria hacked at a pepper with annoyance.

She heard a tap at the front door and then Bob's warm welcome, followed by what sounded like ... Alexa and Joe? Gloria stepped out of the kitchen, wiping her hands on her apron. Alexa came over, smiling tentatively, and hugged her. Joe was right behind her. Gloria returned the hugs, and then stepped back, confused. "What are you two doing here? Not that I'm not glad to see you, of course, but ..."

"Oh, Rachel called us to see if we were free this evening," Alexa said. *That sounds a little too casual*, Gloria thought. *Good. They're keeping Bob in the dark*. "Oh, here." Alexa reached into the tote bag over her shoulder. "I brought along some veggies and hummus. You know, healthy stuff." She nodded toward the living room.

"Thanks, perfect," Gloria said, taking the plate she was holding toward the dining room table. "I made soup and salad. Didn't know what Rachel had planned. I'm expecting the boys."

"Ah." Alexa nodded. "Well, in the meantime, what can I do to help?"

Gloria shrugged. "There's not much left to do. How are things at work these days?"

Alexa told a story about students who thought research assistance meant writing their outlines for them and Gloria commiserated. Before long, Matt and Tim arrived, followed by Kevin, and then Cody, with Sandy in tow. Matt and Tim carried in the desk chairs in from Matt's and Kevin's old bedrooms and soon everyone was seated around the table. Gloria sighed in satisfaction, scanning the tableau: all the people who knew Bob best, except his father. This would help. He surely would take all of them seriously.

Bob said grace, they all toasted one another with their water glasses a little too enthusiastically, and then Bob starting interrogating Joe about the arrangements for his sabbatical trip, wondering which parts would be the best for the two of them to enjoy, and dragging the boys into the conversation so their availability to be a companion for Bob, and enjoy the trip, could be discussed. Gloria stabbed at her salad with annoyance. *What a waste of time and energy. He can barely navigate the house yet without a cane or putting out a hand to the wall or furniture. What does he think is going to change?* She rolled her eyes, remembering the physical therapist, Matt and Tim setting up the canoe in the backyard and then Bob being taught how to get in and out. In and out of the canoe, over and over. Gloria gritted her teeth just thinking about it.

"Mom?" It was Matt. "Mom, everything okay?"

She glanced up. Everyone was looking at her; she felt the gaze of all those faces. She drew her eyebrows together, pressing her lips. "I am fine. I am not the one with a problem." She jerked her head toward Bob, sitting at the other end of the long table.

"Mom ... Mom." Rachel sighed. "Mom, we're not here for Dad. Nothing personal, Dad," she added. "But, Mom. We're all here for you."

"Me?" Gloria pulled her head back, raising her chin in the air. "I don't have a problem."

Cody, at her right, put a hand on her shoulder. "Mom. Look at your plate."

She looked down. Somehow there was food all over her placemat, as if a toddler had taken over her fork. She looked at Cody, perplexed.

"Mom, you are just about at the breaking point. And we're all here because we love you, and we want to help you. But that?" Rachel pointed toward the placemat. "And the kitchen today? Mom, you need to get some help."

"Oh, one messy meal and that little kerfuffle in the kitchen." Gloria shook her head with annoyance. "Rachel, we are not twelve. Stop being dramatic."

Rachel pursed her lips and then said, quietly, "Mom. I took pictures. The boys have seen it. It wasn't a little kerfuffle." She tapped her plate. "Don't you think we all noticed the dishes are mismatched? That you dragged out the plastic picnic plates and bowls for half of us?"

Gloria tried to argue. The conversation went downhill from there. She heard each person, one by one, tell her that they loved her, that they were worried about her, and that they insisted she get help. Kevin talked gently about her impatience with the children. Matt spoke softly about the circles under her eyes, the deep exhaustion in her voice. Tim voiced compassion for her lack of sleep, her worry for Bob. Cody talked about her obvious overload, trying to manage everything with so little assistance.

"I have plenty of help," Gloria retorted. "I am handling things here just fine."

"Not the emotional piece," Rachel said. "You're not accepting the emotional help. Except from Aunt Alex." Alexa had looked embarrassed. *She should be, with that remark about me needing to talk to someone the other week*, Gloria thought with annoyance. Rachel droned on; she was using her professional voice, as Gloria called it, the one she pulled out for argumentative parents as well as administrators. Gloria had overheard it on the phone often enough. "You're not handling it fine. Breaking dishes and scaring the neighbors, and Dad, are not things people do when they are fine."

It was quiet for a long time. Gloria stared around the table at the kind, calm faces. She felt Cody's hand on one shoulder and Matt's on the other. She watched Sandy rubbing Cody's back supportively; she saw Kevin with an arm draped over his father's shoulders. She shook her head slowly, placed her hands on the table and pushed back. She stood up, put her hands on her hips, and looked down at all of them. She pressed her lips together, sighed, and then spoke.

"I can see you all think you're clever, having this little ... what would you call it, an intervention? But none of you understand. You can't know what it is like, to be in my position."

"You're right, Gloria." Alexa nodded. "We can't. And that's why we think you need extra support. Maybe you could see Father a little more often?"

"I don't need a priest!" Gloria roared. "I don't need anything except you to understand. All of you. You don't understand what it's like.

But I know! I know just what it's like! I've been through this—the accident, the lives ruined."

"Oh, Mommy," Rachel sighed. Gloria stared at Rachel; she had not said "Mommy" in years. Rachel wiped the tears off her cheeks and said, "Oh, Mommy. It's not like that. Daddy's not Poppa."

Chapter 20

"Daddy's not Poppa."

Rachel's words—which the boys had echoed, each in their own way, bounced off Gloria's world for the rest of the evening. She wandered around the house after Bob was asleep. Rachel was in her room, the light off. Gloria sighed and heated up water for another cup of herbal tea. She carefully tore the packet of sweetener, poured the fine grains into the mug, and put the packet in the trash. She took out a tea bag and placed it into the mug, mindlessly shifting the mug so that the handle was exactly parallel to the edge of the counter as she gazed down on it.

Well, of course, Gloria thought. *Of course, Bob's not Poppa. Good God.* Was there anyone like her Poppa? Hopefully not, but she suspected the world was overflowing with people similar to Jerzy Grabowski.

Jerzy Grabowski was a second-generation Polish American, tall and athletic, with unruly wavy hair and pale-green eyes. He was smart, and a skilled stonemason; he figured out young that the world was kinder to skilled craftsmen than it was to lower-class boys with aspirations of white-collar work. He could excel in the world he knew, and he did. He wore his confidence in his competence like an old, worn-in sweatshirt, almost as if he forgot he had it on. He had little patience with others on the best of days; he refused to acknowledge any distinction between "cannot do" and "will not do," and would roar with frustration at anyone—his wife, his children, the men who worked around him—if they did not understand something or were unable to do what he happened to be able to do. If it were something out of his purview, he regarded it as barely useful, if at all, and was dismissive of whatever expertise it took to achieve that particular skill.

"Stop being a stubborn fool and just do the homework," he had bellowed at Gloria. She was seven years old at the time, and struggling with fractions. Her mother, Nora, had attempted to intervene.

"Jerzy, she's only seven."

"The damned kid has been reading chapter books for two years. She can do math."

"Jerzy, darling. That's her sister's math book; Lorena's two grades ahead."

Jerzy had thrown the workbook at Gloria. She caught it; his tossing things in disgust was not new. She had looked at her mother, who smiled at her and nodded toward the bedrooms. Gloria gathered up her books and school supplies and hurried off to the room she shared with Lorena and Anna.

The five children had learned to avoid their father as much as possible, keeping their eyes down and their exits quick and quiet. Construction work kept him busy sixty hours most weeks, and Nora managed to have them in bed or studying in their rooms most evenings when he came home. Even so, the children could not escape Jerzy's tirades. When Josef, the oldest, reached fourteen, he suddenly found quiet yielding harder to do. He would not give in, would not admit to being in the wrong when he felt he was not. For Josef, Jerzy moved from throwing things and the occasional slap to a few well-placed, full punches. Nora started to insert herself between them; once, she took a hit, which Jerzy claimed was an accident and entirely her fault. All five children had encircled Nora and walked her out of the living room to the kitchen. Josef threatened to kill his father; twelve-year-old Lorena put an icepack on her mother's already-swelling cheek; ten-year-old Gloria had gone into a frenzy of trying to find something to do for her mother, putting together a crooked peanut butter sandwich. Seven-year-old Micah and five-year-old Anna had each clung to one of their mother's sides, and she draped an arm around each. She had gazed around at her children and, her eyes settling on Josef, had spoken calmly and quietly.

"There will be no talk of killing in our home." She paused. "Josef, I love you. Thank you for protecting me, for wanting to defend me. Remember that it is also my job, as your mother, to defend you." Josef began to speak and she said, "Ssh!" She turned to face Lorena. "Lorena, my good big girl. Thank you." She looked at Gloria and smiled. "My Gloria. Always eager to help, to make things better." And then she tightened her embrace on Micah and Anna. "Micah! Anna! My little ones. Such joy."

The children seemed, to Gloria, to all have breathed out at once. Jerzy was quiet in the other room. They glanced at the doorway. Quiet could be good; perhaps he had fallen asleep? Lorena tiptoed to the doorway, holding the ice pack. She peeked out and came back, frowning. She did not speak. She held her hand as if holding a glass and then lifted it to her lips, tilting her head back as if drinking rapidly. Gloria watched her mother's shoulders fall a little, but then Nora smiled and said, "Well! The afternoon looks sunny. Why don't all of you go outside? Maybe a nice bicycle ride. Get some fresh air." She looked around, standing, taking the ice pack from Lorena. She pressed her lips together, glanced at the doorway to the living room and added, "Go. Now. All of you. Everything's fine."

Of course, Gloria thought, dunking her tea bag, *everything wasn't fine*. She sighed. It wasn't long after that day that the "accident" happened. That was how it was described, and that was how the lawsuit had been settled. When the children were adults, Nora confided that she did not believe it was an accident; she thought it was deliberate, but intended to frighten Jerzy, not permanently injure him or kill him.

Jerzy bullied the men with whom he worked as much as his wife and children. No one had a name; they were, at best, labeled by their nationality. The Germans were Krauts or, if he really disliked them, were called by names of Nazi leaders. "Hey! Goebbels! Get up here with that mortar. Moron," he would bellow. Likewise, he abused the Italians, the Mexicans, the African Americans and the Irish.

One spring day, Jerzy went to work as he always did, leaving before the sun rose to make the most of daylight, and shortly after lunch the call came to the house. Jerzy was in the hospital. There had been an accident. A load of roofing tiles had, inexplicably, fallen on top of him while he was on his hands and knees, putting in a custom fieldstone hearth. No one could explain how it happened. There was a multitude of suspects and no one to blame. No one from work ever came to visit Jerzy in the hospital. Nora, of course, was dutifully there each day; Lorena and Gloria took over managing the home on the inside, and Josef the outside. For little Micah and Anna, their mother was absent for a while after they came home from school, but, except for that hour or two when the neighbor, Mrs. Shanahan, brought them to her home to have snacks, do their homework, and play with her large, boisterous dogs, their day-to-day lives were largely unchanged until Jerzy came home from the hospital.

He was in a wheelchair for a long time, but gradually was able to walk, a little, with a cane. He could no longer work in construction; his provision for the family came from the large settlement awarded for the accident. The case had been resolved very quickly. Jerzy settled into a routine of ordering his wife and children around more than ever, and drinking even more than before the accident. What had been barely tolerable when he was out of the house sixty hours a week became uninterrupted misery. Once Jerzy was able to get around with a cane, Nora went back to the volunteer work she'd been doing at the elementary school. The staff had suggested she apply for a part-time job and, after a few evenings of heated arguments at home, and cleaning up things Jerzy had thrown in a temper, Nora had applied and begun working four mornings a week. Jerzy later claimed to anyone who would listen that it was his idea, get her out of the house and doing something useful for a change.

Gloria eased her head back in the chair, glancing up at the photo of her parents on the bookshelf. It had been taken shortly before the accident. Jerzy, big, handsome, and arrogant; and little Nora, with her thin, pointy face, big eyes, and frail shoulders. She was wearing the shapeless dress and tired cardigan she seemed to have adopted as a uniform before the younger children were born. Gloria's eyes roamed to the smaller photo beside it; it was Nora, alone, ten years ago, five years after Jerzy died. His last years were spent in alcohol-fueled dementia and heart problems. Nora seemed barely changed, except in the smaller photograph her smile was broader, her still-pointy chin lifted a bit. She had a good decade before she passed away, a decade in which she somehow managed to blossom after years of abuse.

Momma was a cipher, Gloria thought, half smiling and taking a sip of tea. She recalled, shaking her head, the Tallahassee weekend, as Gloria took to calling it in her mind.

Gloria had graduated from high school just weeks before. She had won a scholarship to the state university in Tallahassee, but Jerzy was adamant: Her mother needed her here. She could go to the junior college. Gloria begged, she pleaded, she began to cry.

"See, look at that. You can't have a discussion without waterworks. You don't belong in college," Jerzy sneered. "Just get a nice, simple clerical job. Like your mother."

"But, Jerzy," Nora had said, her voice soft and gentle, "she wants to be a teacher."

Jerzy snorted. "She's a monster," he announced, eyeing his daughter up and down. "Look at her! She's as tall as a man. She'd scare the children."

"But, Poppa," Gloria tried to interject.

"The girl stays here," Jerzy announced, his fist slamming down like a gavel. Nora had looked at Gloria and given her the usual glance toward the door. Gloria, choking back tears, went to her room. Her mother had checked on her later, stroking her hair and telling her things would be fine. Really. But Gloria did not believe her. She cried herself to sleep.

The next couple of days passed in a blur; Gloria had gone through the household chores robotically, barely answering anyone who spoke to her. She retreated to her room early each evening, unsuccessfully holding back tears, trying to be silent. Anna, fairly oblivious to anything but the drama of early adolescence, did not pay any attention to her seemingly sleeping older sister, turned toward the wall in the other twin bed, her legs folded up, as always, to keep her feet from sticking out over the end.

It was not even daylight yet, the morning her mother slipped in to wake her. Anna was sleeping soundly in the other bed. "Gloria. Ssh." Gloria turned on the pillow, confused. Nora smiled and stroked her face. "Sweetheart, get up, throw on some clothes, and come out to the kitchen. We have plans for the day."

Grumbling in her mind, but careful not to wake Anna, Gloria dressed. She could not remember any plans; no doubt this was some complicated chore to keep Poppa from being even angrier than usual. When she stepped into the living room, she found her mother standing on the ottoman in front of the bookshelf, taking something out of a book, then putting the book back, selecting a different book, and pulling something out of it. Nora smiled mischievously at Gloria's confused face and stepped down lightly. That's when Gloria realized her mother was holding money—a lot of money, which had apparently been hidden in the seldom-touched books.

Nora waved the money once, and then nodded toward the kitchen. In the cozily lit room, Gloria watched her slip the cash into her purse. "Momma. What's going on?"

"Well, Gloria, today's a big day. You and I are going out." Nora's voice was quiet and matter-of-fact, as it so often was, even in confusing times.

"The money?"

"I've been putting money aside for years." Nora sighed. "Josef didn't need it; he just ran off and joined the Army. Lorena left to go to college on scholarship whether Poppa liked it or not." She paused. "But you. You're our good girl. And I figured you would need a little push."

"A push?"

"Just eat your breakfast. We have an appointment at eight."

The appointment was at the salon in the rich part of town. Gloria turned to her mother in surprise; Nora shrugged. The stylist's name was Vanessa. Nora explained that Gloria was out of high school and getting ready to go to college. She needed just a little something to celebrate a new start. Vanessa had nodded thoughtfully. She recommended just a trim, and changing Gloria's part from the middle to slightly off-center. She also tweezed just a little bit. "Just the hair between the brows," she said firmly. "You have nice, strong, natural brows. If you overdo it, you lose them and then you're stuck drawing them on for the rest of your life." She had taken out a dark pencil and smudged just over the top of Gloria's lashes and under her eye, stood back to admire her work, and nodded approval. She turned Gloria to see her reflection. She was the same, but different, as if a suddenly slightly more attractive version of herself had shown up. The off-center part emphasized her eyes.

"Thank you."

"My pleasure," said Vanessa. Gloria tried to not pay attention as her mother paid for the haircut and an eyeliner, but couldn't avoid it; the simple trim had cost twice what their usual salon charged.

"Thank you," she said gratefully to her mother after they had left.

"You're welcome," Nora said, starting the car. "Off to our next stop."

"Next stop?"

"Gloria. You need clothes for university."

"But Poppa said I'm just going to junior college."

"Don't argue, Gloria."

Nora had driven to the shopping mall and parked in front of the most expensive department store. She got out of the car. Gloria sat frozen, staring at the entry to the store. "Gloria. Up. Out of the car. Let's go."

The store had just opened. A saleswoman, probably thirty years old, with long, straight brown hair, wearing a kaleidoscope-print tunic and flared black pants, was leaning on the counter. She straightened up as they approached, smiling. "Good morning!"

"Good morning ... Eileen," Nora had replied, peering at the name tag. She placed her hand on Gloria's shoulder. "My daughter is getting ready to leave for university. I'd like her to have a few nice pieces she can mix up. Maybe a dress, a jacket, a couple pairs of slacks, and tops. Maybe ten items, give or take? Not old-ladyish, but not looking like a leftover from Woodstock. Modern. Like you, perhaps," she'd offered.

Eileen had nodded thoughtfully, coming out from behind the counter. She looked Gloria up and down a couple of times. Gloria felt herself slouching, waiting for the criticism. Instead, Eileen grinned. "It will be a pleasure. Follow me." She strode off toward the racks of clothes. It didn't take long for Eileen to pile a number of things into Gloria's arms. "I know you won't be taking all of them," she commented, "but we want to be sure about fit."

Gloria had pursed her lips, thinking of her father's words—*she's a monster*. But Eileen was oblivious to the change in expression. "This is such a joy. Seriously." She had paused on the way to the racks of jackets. "I was a fashion major. I hardly *ever* get to dress someone built like a model." She had glanced around and added, more quietly, "Well. You know. Rich older ladies. You are making my day." And she was on the move again. Gloria had whipped her head to look at her mother, who seemed not surprised to have Gloria described this way.

In the dressing room, Gloria tried on clothes, came out, turned awkwardly for her mother and Eileen, and tried to participate in their lively conversation about what did and did not fit, and what pieces would work best together. Eileen suggested a skirt—something black, perhaps, that could be dressed up or just be worn for class. It would be more flexible than a dress. Nora acceded to this, although her eyebrows went up a bit when Gloria came out in a black pencil skirt, well-tailored but not snug, that ended a full inch above the tops of her knees. Gloria looked at her mother's face, concerned, but Nora had recovered to say, "You look beautiful, Gloria. I just got used to the Catholic school uniforms and, well, I forgot how nice and long your legs are." Gloria looked down at herself and then at the mirror and, just for a moment, saw herself that way: that she was tall and slim, and her legs were long. Her dark hair was shiny and smooth.

"You look great," Eileen had affirmed.

"Now, the jacket?" Nora wondered. Eileen held out a suede blazer. It was the color of caramel, and Gloria touched the sleeve tentatively. She looked at her mother, questioning.

Eileen lifted the blazer. "You said modern, not old-ladyish. This is suede—it's fashionable, it will be warm when it's cool outside, but it's not so 'this year' that it won't be wearable next year. You could wear this for years," she added, "provided you take care of it properly."

"Try it on, Gloria," Nora said.

Gloria slipped on the jacket. It eased over her shoulders. She stretched out her arms. The sleeves were long enough. She looked in the mirror. The warm, caramel color seemed to make her skin look better. "The color is perfect," Eileen remarked. "Which I thought." She tilted her head. "You need warm colors, honey. Keep the cool colors, the blacks, the blues, away from your face. You can wear jeans great—wouldn't I like to look as good in jeans as you do—but keep the blue for the bottom half. Golds, warm browns, warm greens, peachy colors—those are great for you. You'll glow."

Gloria stroked the sleeves of the amazing jacket. Her mother, meanwhile, was ticking off the items they had selected: the skirt, the jacket, two pairs of jeans, a beautiful cream-colored cable knit crew-neck sweater, and five different tops. "Okay, we are set. Eileen, thank you."

"Thank you," Eileen said, helping gather things to bring to checkout. "Honey, just meet us up front after you change."

Gloria heard them chatting as they went toward the front of the store. "Beautiful girl," Eileen was saying. "Aren't you worried about her being away from home?"

"Gloria's got even more brains than she has beauty," Nora answered. "I think she'll be fine."

They had stopped at the diner for milkshakes after the morning's adventures. Nora had a few instructions.

"Gloria, when we get home, I want you to put the new clothes into the trunk of your car." Gloria didn't have her own car, exactly; it was the old family car that each child had driven in turn. "I don't want Anna or Micah … or your father, to see what you have. Just don't mention it." She had taken a sip of milkshake, closed her eyes, and savored it. Opening her eyes, she added, "Anna is going to a birthday party this evening. While she's gone, I want you to pack up a few things and get them into your car. A few of your favorite books, your notebooks, pencils. A few other clothes, your underwear. Not enough for Anna to notice."

Gloria opened her mouth to speak but Nora kept talking. "Be sure your bicycle is in good shape. Check the tires. Be sure the lock is in working order. The basket, too; be sure it's solid."

"Bicycle." Gloria felt stupid, trying to figure it out.

"Just leave it in the garage for now. You can put it in the car Monday morning."

"In the car?" Gloria repeated, confused.

"We're leaving for Tallahassee Monday morning, four a.m. It's our little secret for now. I'll explain more when we're on the road." She had grinned up at Gloria's perplexed face. "Sweetheart. You're going to university."

By 9:00 a.m. Monday, they were at an adviser's office in Tallahassee; Nora had set the appointment in advance. Gloria's scholarship was activated. A work-study program was put into place that would cover the dorm and meal plan. She would start with a couple of courses in the summer term and then segue into the fall semester with two weeks off in between. At the end of the day, Gloria was in a dorm room, with Nora helping her make up the bed. The roommate wouldn't be there for another week. Nora sat on the bed and they talked a while. Nora had slipped a little cash to Gloria after the meeting, on the way to the dorm. "This won't cover much, so use your bicycle whenever you can. Keep the car for long trips. Like maybe coming home for Thanksgiving?"

"But, Momma, how will you get home?"

"I'm taking the bus back to Jacksonville."

"Poppa's going to be mad."

Nora had sighed and nodded. "Probably so. But don't worry about it."

"But what will you say?"

Then Nora had turned to face Gloria full-on, and Gloria watched her mother's face change. Somehow, her chin became even pointier and more childlike. Her eyes widened just a bit. Her head tilted slightly and her voice came out, quiet, and smooth as butter. "But, Jerzy, darling. You remember. We talked about it."

Then Gloria saw. She saw that so many of the times when she had heard her mother say that, Momma had been exploiting Jerzy's memory lapses and alcohol-fueled blackouts.

"You mean—"

Nora had held up a hand. "Gloria. You're an adult. You know your father drinks too much. And people who drink too much forget things. And when they forget things, they fill in the blanks with things they make up. This is a work-around. I can't leave him. He needs me. So, I do what I can to help you children."

Gloria nodded, remembering.

Jerzy, darling. You remember. Josef set up that summer job on the fishing boat with that nice man from church right after that little chat you had with him about earning money.

Jerzy, sweetheart. Remember, you had the idea that Lorena would be such a good nurse. How nice she was able to get that scholarship.

Jerzy, honey. You remember. Micah won that award in science and gets to go the marine science camp for a week this summer. You were so proud of him.

Jerzy, darling. You remember. Your sister wanted to have Anna come visit for a month this summer to get to know her cousins. You know how important family has always been to you.

And now, *Jerzy, darling. You remember. Gloria won that scholarship to study teaching.*

Nora had hugged Gloria tight and then gazed up at her with tears in her eyes. "Gloria, my good girl. You wring college dry, sweetheart. Live every minute of it. There are a few stamped envelopes in the satchel with your books; write to me and let me know what number to call at the dorm and when. And call collect if you need anything."

"Yes, Momma. Momma, I love you. I hope—"

"I love you, sweetheart. Don't worry. I'm going to be all right, Gloria."

Chapter 21

Gloria fidgeted with the collar of her blouse. She held up first one pair of dangling earrings and then another, turning her head. She thought the red would work; something cheerful to assuage all these concerns about her mental health. She rolled her eyes as she smoothed her hair, wondering briefly when it had gotten so long. It was practically a bob. Then she touched up her lipstick and stepped out of the bathroom. Matt was in the living room, chatting with his dad. They looked up.

"Gloria! You look lovely. All dressed up, eh? You two hitting some fancy restaurant on the way home?" Bob smiled, standing with just one hand on the chair, Gloria noticed with disapproval. *When will he learn to be careful?*

"Mom. You ready?" Matt stood up.

Gloria nodded. "Bob, you rest." She gave him a perfunctory kiss. She frowned, first at Bob and then at Matt. "Well. Here I am." She sighed. "I hope everyone's happy, because I am not. I can't believe I have to waste time seeing a therapist."

"Mom, we agreed," Matt said mildly. "You know Andrea; she's been at church forever. It will be fine." He paused. "Besides, she knows a little about, you know, caregiving." He glanced at Bob. "No offense, Dad."

"None taken," Bob replied. "I know I'm not the best patient."

Gloria snorted at that, and then grew thoughtful. Andrea had been practicing as a church-based counselor for years; over the past few years, she had been working just a few hours a week, as she was caregiver to her husband during his decline into dementia and then his death. Thomas had passed just a year ago. Andrea still saw just a few patients a week and had agreed to meet with Gloria. "Well then. Let's go."

The ride was short. Matt chatted about his and Tim's house projects and checked in about Bob's most recent appointments. Matt parked in the church parking lot. He turned to Gloria. "So, Mom, Andrea works out of the parish center building. Just go in, head down the hall to the left, and her office is the last door on the right-hand side. She said to just come on in." He paused. "I'm going to go hang out in the chapel a bit and then walk around the grounds. I'll be back here at the car in an hour." He rubbed his mother's shoulder. "It's going to be fine, Mom. You'll see."

Gloria got out of the car, straightening up and scanning the parking lot. There were, as always, a few cars; the crew of volunteers that cooked a meal for the homeless in the local shelter each Tuesday would be in the kitchen. She hoped she wouldn't see anyone. How could she explain being there? She hurried in and down the hall to the right, looking for a sign with Andrea's name. She frowned, then turned back and headed toward the other side. Ah, there it was: The door was ajar, with a discrete sign, *Meeting Room C. No mention of it being for crazy people.* Gloria nodded. *Good.* She raised her hand to tap but the door swung open and there was Andrea Cotton, smiling serenely up at her.

"Gloria. So good to see you." Andrea stepped aside, opening the door fully. "Come on in. Sit anywhere." Gloria looked at the shabby furniture, draped with colorful throws and scattered with toss pillows. Pictures of nature covered the walls. There were lamps on, no glaring overhead fluorescent lights. There was something a bit hippie-ish about it, Gloria thought with a flash of distrust. She glanced at Andrea, who was standing near the living room–style grouping of furniture, hand extended toward the seating in welcome. It would help if Andrea looked professional. She was about five feet tall, extremely frail, with long wavy gray hair. How she managed to find clothes was anyone's guess, Gloria thought, settling into the middle of the sofa. Andrea sat on the armchair perpendicular to the sofa, folding her legs up as if she were five instead of a woman in her late sixties. "So, Gloria, you have the paperwork I sent?"

Gloria nodded, taking the folded paperwork out of her purse and handing it over. Andrea scanned it quickly. "Any questions on this?" she asked.

"No. It's straightforward enough. Just a lot," Gloria said pointedly.

Andrea nodded, smiling. "You are right about that! And we have to do a few things now." She launched into what she assured Gloria was a standard explanation about the limitations of privacy and confidentiality ("Danger to yourself or others," Andrea had emphasized) and then together they signed off on pages indicating this conversation had taken place. Then Andrea had neatened the papers, put them aside, and sat up straight, facing Gloria, hands in her lap. "Okay. Good. Now. Gloria ... what brings you here?"

"I think you know." Gloria pressed her lips together. She did not like game playing.

"I know what Rachel told me. And then what—" Andrea paused. "Cody? Kevin? Matt? And of course, Bob, all told me." She sighed and grinned at Gloria. "It was a lot. But I don't know what *you* want."

"I want everyone to understand."

Andrea nodded. "It must be a lot, having Bob be so seriously injured, finding out his health was so impaired, wondering what's going to happen next."

"Yes." Gloria nodded firmly. "You understand." Gloria looked over Andrea's shoulder at a picture of a barn owl. "I'm sorry about Thomas."

"Thank you." Andrea hesitated. "It's been hard, harder than I expected. I guess I lost him twice, or maybe hundreds of times. The dementia took parts of him and then death took the rest." She squeezed her hands and then looked at Gloria. "Now. Tell me about you."

Gloria paused. She put her purse on the sofa beside her and then glanced at her lap and up at Andrea's tilted, peaceful face. *Andrea*, she thought, *will understand. Finally, someone will see my side of things and not try to poo-poo my feelings away with platitudes about how well Bob is doing.*

"You'll understand," Gloria sighed. "You know what it's like. And I know what it's like," she added, drawing her brows together. "I've been down this road before."

"What road?"

"You know. A big injury. The way it—" Gloria hesitated. "The way it changes everything."

"Oh," Andrea said, leaning forward. "Has Bob been hurt before?"

"No, no." Gloria shook her head. "No, not Bob."

"One of the children?"

"No."

"Then who, Gloria?"

Gloria hesitated. She pressed her lips together, studying Andrea. She looked like a little aged elf, sitting there, earnestly gazing back at her. She did not seem ... serious enough. That was it. Gloria straightened up, leaned back, and nodded. It was no good to go jumping into things with this virtual stranger. Granted, she'd known Andrea, superficially of course, through church activities over the years, but Gloria saw no need to go rushing into details. Better to paint a big picture, and let Andrea see just what Gloria was up against.

"Well," Gloria said slowly, "of course, my father was seriously injured in a workplace accident when I was a child. He lived for years afterward, but sort of went between a wheelchair and cane. It was a lot for him, and my mother."

"And you children, too, no doubt," Andrea said quietly.

"To some extent, but my mother really held things together well. I had a good role model."

"You must have learned a lot from her."

Gloria nodded. "I certainly did."

"So of course you're concerned that Bob may not make a full recovery."

"Well, he's doing well as far as the injuries. Down to a cane sometimes, mostly when he's tired. And, frankly, I'm not sure how much of that is just for show. To convince me he's being careful. The physical therapist is quite pleased, as are the physicians."

"That sounds great."

"Yes."

"And?"

"And what?"

Andrea tilted her head slightly to one side. "And yet you are very ... stressed out. Concerned. What else has been going on? Anything else new?"

Gloria snorted. "Anything else? Everything else."

"Oh?"

"Let me go through the kids first. Okay, my oldest son, Cody—the divorced one, with the twins—I am pretty sure he's dating my best friend's daughter."

"That sounds lovely; what's the concern?"

"You know Sandy Bonhall."

"Oh, Sandy! Yes, very well. She's very active here, supporting the youth and young adult activities."

"Yes, well. She's a bit ... flaky, shall we say? And my son is being quite discreet but he's not fooling me."

"Okay, so Cody dating Sandy is a concern. And that's something new?"

"New? Yes. It's Bob's fault, so to speak. Everything is Bob's fault."

Andrea nodded, waiting. Gloria stared at her and added, "The accident! Everything got messed up with Bob's accident. I had to spend less time babysitting Cody's twins, and so Rachel and Sandy pitched in and the next thing you know, Cody's going on beach cleanups and guarding sea turtle nests."

"Ah. So, the accident led to them spending more time together."

"Exactly." Gloria pressed her lips together and nodded firmly. *Andrea is seeing the situation*, she thought. *Good*.

"So, what else? You said 'everything' is changed."

"Rachel is dating an Irishman." Gloria paused. "Okay, he's a teacher. A history teacher at the high school. And he's very nice. But he goes home every summer. And she's talking about going there with him this summer for her month off! To meet his family and go exploring."

"And this is because of the accident?"

Gloria shook her head. "No, this started months ago." She frowned. "I was all for it at first, of course, but then I realized it meant traveling and being away from home."

"But the young man?"

"Aidan? Oh, he's delightful. Smart and good-looking. Very tall, which was a surprise. I thought the Irish were short but I guess that was due to Father. And Bob's father isn't particularly tall, although Bob is my height …" Gloria trailed off. "Yes. So. Well, it's just one more thing."

"Do you like him?"

"Well, of course. And he's Catholic. Did I mention that? His uncle is Monsignor Seamus."

"Lovely." Andrea smiled, but Gloria just stared impassively. "So, Cody might be dating Sandy, and Rachel's been dating Aidan and that one sounds serious, too," Andrea said. "Anything else?"

Gloria sighed. "My son Kevin has been working extra hard at the practice. Because of Bob's accident, you see," she added. "And every time there's some sort of stress, he and Veronica … well. Bobby was conceived right after my mother passed away, and Kevin had been very close to my mother. And Gina … Gina was conceived … oh, I don't remember, but something was going on. Maybe on Veronica's side? Anyhow, between Bob's accident and the extra work—and Veronica's got that look."

"Look? Is she showing already?"

"No. That smug look, like she's got a secret no one else has." Gloria rolled her eyes. "As if the rest of us haven't had children."

"Everyone hasn't," Andrea replied gently, and Gloria suddenly remembered that Andrea and Thomas had been childless and had thrown themselves into the life of the church community in lieu of the family they could not have.

"You're right, of course," Gloria said, softly. She looked past Andrea and then right at her. "And even my best friend seems to have gone a bit mad, although that started even before the accident. She's changed her hair, changed her wardrobe, and she's planning some crazy year off to paint and study birds, I think. Yes, birds. Right when I need her most."

"So, she's been unavailable to you?"

"Oh, no. Not so far. But in the fall, she will be."

"And Bob's not expected to be recovered by fall?"

Gloria rubbed her temples. The woman was dense. "Yes, Bob will be recovered. As far as the injuries. But the other conditions. You don't understand. There's just so much ... going on. Too much. And Bob thinks he's going off on a fishing trip with Alexa's husband, Joe, who is, possibly, even more crazy than his wife. Taking a year-long fishing trip and calling it a research sabbatical."

"I see." Andrea nodded. "There *is* a lot going on. Gloria, would you mind filling me in just a little more on each of these things?"

Gloria took a deep breath. She explained more: how Rachel and Sandy had been best friends since they met, and how Cody dating Sandy seemed to threaten the families' unity. How Kevin was so wonderful but his wife, what could you say? She was a terrible parent and poor Kevin couldn't do everything. Not that Veronica did anything terrible, she was just weak. Passive. All that fussing over feelings. Matt and Tim were wonderful, of course—she studied Andrea when she mentioned them, because, well, you never knew how people would be, she thought—but Andrea just kept nodding and making small affirmative sounds and asking a few questions that were not, Gloria considered, all that dumb. She explained her concerns, about Rachel and Aidan and the morbid meeting after a fatal accident had taken the lives of a carful of students on prom night. Somehow the time flew by, and Andrea unfolded her legs, straightening them slowly in front of her and grinning. "Oh, I should know better than to sit so still for so long! At my age, especially." She rotated her feet in circles, then planted them on the floor and leaned forward.

"Gloria, I'd like to see you again. Perhaps in a couple of weeks, since you're so busy? Unless you think sooner would be better."

"I think two weeks would be fine but I think my children and husband expect me to show up sooner." Gloria sighed. "Let's find a time next week."

An appointment was agreed upon, payment was made, and then Andrea added, "Gloria, for homework, I'd like you to take some time here and there to make a list. Make a list of all the things that have changed, all the things you're concerned about, and bring that with you."

"A list."

"Yes, please. You're right; a lot has happened. It's helpful to write it all down—see it in black and white, so to speak—and then we can sort of dig in, one at a time, and see what could be helpful."

"Fine. A list." Gloria hoisted herself up with a slight grunt. "Thank you for your time," she said perfunctorily.

"Thank you," Andrea replied. "It was good to see you, Gloria. I'll be praying for you."

"Thank you."

Gloria left the building quickly, glancing toward the back. The kitchen crew was at work and she hoped no one noticed her. She stepped into the sunlight, blinking; the day was so bright compared to Andrea's quiet office space with its subdued colors. She looked around. She saw Matt's car, but not Matt.

"Mom!" She turned. Matt was approaching, smiling. "Mom! Sorry. Were you waiting long?"

"No, I just walked out."

"Oh, good. I was over in the prayer garden. Beautiful there. Ran into Father Jack. He's coming over to our place for dinner next Saturday after the vigil Mass."

"Your place?" Gloria's mind raced around, and then remembered that Father Jack knew about their situation. *Of course, how could I forget?*

"Yes, somehow we haven't had him over in a while. I'm looking forward to getting some advice from him on what to put in that weird shady spot in the back that never gets sunlight."

"Oh. Nice." Gloria felt the relief flow through her. Perhaps she had underestimated Father Jack. "I don't remember you mentioning that he visits you boys often."

"Mom. Everyone knows you don't like Father Jack." Matt grinned, opening the car door for her. "Why kick that anthill?"

Gloria waited until Matt settled into his seat to reply. "Perhaps I just haven't gotten to know Father Jack well enough," she said firmly. She waited. She hoped Matt wouldn't ask how everything went, or what she and Andrea talked about, or if she liked Andrea. Matt did not let her down.

"He's quite the character," Matt said. "Interesting guy. Did you know he worked with mentally ill street people in London for twenty years? Imagine that! He's got some amazing stories."

"Impressive," Gloria said flatly, staring out the window. *Mentally ill street people in a big city*, she thought; *no wonder he wasn't impressed with me and my concerns.*

"So, ready for an early lunch? Or would you like to go straight home?"

"I probably should check on your father," Gloria began, and Matt chuckled. "Fine," she said, drawing her brows together. "A lunch would be nice."

"I agree," said Matt, smoothly turning into the family's favorite diner.

Chapter 22

At the end of the day, the only satisfying thing about it was the bitter taste of having been right about it all.

Gloria sat in the Adirondack chair, exhausted, her head tilted back, eyes shut against the waning light. She did not see the spectacular golden glow of the trees in the last bright light of sunset, the violent orange reflecting off tree trunks as the sun left and Sunday evening settled in. She shook her head, eyes still closed, wondering how everything in life could be so disorderly at the same time.

As day ended, the temperature dropped. The house windows were open and she could hear the quiet voices of her family, the occasional louder laughter, the clank of dishes being cleaned. She heard giggling. *Any moment now*, she thought, *the children will be out to see what I'm doing*. She was half waiting to be interrupted, but thus far, no one had come out to join her.

Well, of course not. They're happy enough, all of them. Isn't that nice? Gloria stamped one foot on the ground without opening her eyes or otherwise changing position. With all that chaos in their lives, individually and as a family, how could they be in there, laughing and joking and talking about their ruinous plans?

Happy Mother's Day to me, she thought darkly, and for a moment, yearned for her own mother, for her guidance. What would Nora say? Against her will, Gloria for a moment imagined she could hear her mother's voice, soft and smooth.

"Gloria, darling, you remember; it's all going to be all right in the end."

Gloria opened her eyes. Perhaps she'd been dozing off; yes, that would explain it. In that strange place between awake and asleep all sorts of odd things could seem to happen. Certainly, it did not seem like everything was going to be all right, ever.

Oh, the afternoon had started well enough: the entire family over for Mother's Day dinner, all there by 3:00 p.m. Balloons and cut flowers and another orchid, the sideboard was strewn with handmade cards from the children, a handprint plate from Bobby, "gift coupons" for fun from Marta and Sean they had written and illustrated themselves, and a small stuffed animal, a little bear with an apron on it, from Gina. "It wooks wike you, Gwandma," Gina had explained, and Gloria had made a fuss over it and all the other gifts.

Earlier in the day, she and Bob had wrestled the extra two leaves into the table so everyone could fit: Cody, Sandy, Marta, and Sean; Kevin, Veronica, Bobby, and Gina; Matt and Tim; Rachel and Aidan.

"Why aren't you with your mother today?" Gloria had asked sternly, and Sandy had blithely replied that she, Cody, and the twins had gone to Mass and breakfast with her parents. Gloria had said that was nice but had frowned when she spoke.

Dinner was supposed to be a wonderful event: all of them gathered, like a Norman Rockwell painting. Bob saying grace, a toast to Gloria, of course, and to Veronica, also a mother. Bobby did spill some of his milk during the toast but Gloria had been prepared for that and had a dish towel ready on the back of his chair for his mother to mop things up. Kevin had mopped up, and Gloria's eyebrows flared. Things just went from mildly annoying to terrible. With each new step of descent, Gloria watched in dismay as her family, having all apparently gone mad, acted as if things were just getting better and better.

Rachel announced that she'd be visiting Ireland for two weeks this summer, the first two weeks of July. She would fly into Dublin, where Aidan's sister, Elizabeth, lived now. Elizabeth led tours in Dublin and also hiking tours in Wexford, Cork, and Kerry for a company specializing in small-group tours. Aidan would come over to meet them and have a bit of a mini-tour to show off Dublin and the eastern part of the country to Rachel, and then the last nine days would be spent with Aidan's family where, Rachel clarified, she'd be in Elizabeth's old bedroom, Elizabeth now living in Dublin. Bob was pleased and full of questions. *God help us*, Gloria thought with a shudder. *He's asking about the fishing.* The other children were full of excitement and interest.

That led to Bob discussing his plan to meet Joe Bonhall up in Rhode Island in late August. He didn't want to be away the same time as Rachel; he wanted to have a little of that empty nest feeling with Gloria. He had lifted his wine glass to her as he spoke and she had attempted to smile despite her clenched jaw. He would fly up and spend two weeks with Joe, and then fly back. The boys were particularly enthusiastic. Cody said he'd like to go along, but he was committed to a trip with Sandy Labor Day weekend, where she was speaking at a conference. Bob thought that he and Joe could make that work. Aidan wondered if they couldn't go a bit earlier, just before school began in mid-August, so he could go, too. Bob agreed that made sense and said he would ask Joe. Gloria had asked if Alexa was aware of this nonsense and everyone had turned to look at her.

"Nonsense," she had repeated flatly, as if they had not understood.

"Mom, I think it's a great idea," Rachel said. "I mean, I know you're worried about Dad being off his diet and all, but he'll have three people looking after him." She'd glanced at her father, who shrugged like someone accustomed to being spoken of in the third person.

"I don't think it is a great idea," Gloria said. But everyone else had gone back to the topic of Bob's fishing trip.

The descent into madness continued. During a pause, Kevin had cleared his throat and said he and Veronica had an announcement to make and today seemed a good day to do it. Veronica had looked up at him with that adoring Nancy Reagan look that Gloria hated, and rested one hand on her belly. Rachel and Sandy started squealing before the words were fully out of his mouth. They were expecting a baby, due in November. Bob had shouted his congratulations, as did Cody. Matt and Tim had joined right in with enthusiasm. Gina and Bobby giggled and Bobby said, "So it's NOT a secret? We can tell?"

"Oh, Bobby, you did such a good job keeping a secret," Veronica had said. "I'm so proud of you! Yes, now you can tell—we kept it a secret just to tell Grandma and Grandpa, and everyone else in the family, today."

Gloria had to admit, a baby was wonderful. "I thought so," she had said, smiling a bit. "You had that look."

"Yes, she's glowing even more than usual," Kevin had replied, beaming and putting an arm around Veronica.

"Yes," Gloria had agreed, even though that was not the look she meant; she meant that smug look Veronica had early in every pregnancy. She sat as if she were in a trance, listening as the dishes were passed around again, the glasses refilled and clanked as everyone seemed to toast everyone else. She took part, of course, robotically eating and lifting her glass. She imagined she was smiling and nodding and making appropriate sounds.

"Honey? Are you okay?" Bob's voice cut through the heaviness of her head.

"I'm fine."

"Mom, you look tired. Maybe you need to rest? How about a nice sit in the living room, and we'll take care of cleaning up." Matt looked concerned. As Gloria looked around the table, she saw all those faces, perplexed, pink-cheeked with excitement. She imagined the months ahead: Rachel scampering off to Ireland; Bob, Cody, and Aidan off trying to get hurt in the woods, drowned in some river, eating junk food and biscuits with gravy; Cody dancing off to spend a weekend with Sandy. Veronica becoming more beautifully pregnant and even less able to manage the two she had; the twins, leading up to what would be, for Marta at least, the very edge of puberty. She imagined the engagements no doubt on the way; Rachel and Aidan, Cody and Sandy. That all of them could look into that mess and seem happy was maddening.

Gloria had pushed herself back from the table. "I'm … fine. Really. But yes, I'm tired. Perhaps I need a bit of fresh air. I think I'll go sit outside and rest a while."

Tim had commented that sounded good, and then the conversation had quietly turned back to all the plans for the summer. Gloria had walked outside heavily, slammed the screen door, and settled with a grunt into a chair. The ham, the pierogies ("Only two, Bob, remember your sugar"), the salad and the mixed vegetables seemed to be a rock in her stomach. Her mouth felt sour.

Gloria sat and listened and waited. She waited for someone to come out and ask her to come in, or perhaps sit with her and listen to a bit of reason. When it was dark, Cody had come out to let her know he, Sandy, and the twins were leaving, and Kevin and Veronica and the children, too; wouldn't she come in to say goodbye? She had gotten up awkwardly, ignoring his proffered arm, and followed him into the golden light of the house. No one had asked anything about her long time outdoors; they had been solicitous about whether she would like a cup of decaf and some cake, or perhaps some tea, but no one seemed to want to know how she was.

Gloria sat stiffly, feeling like an awkward guest in her own living room, holding a cup of decaf and feeling more as if she were watching a family visit than the recipient of one on this horrible Mother's Day evening. Cody, Sandy, and the twins left, with hugs all around. Kevin and Veronica took longer, of course, to get Bobby and Gina together. Aidan had glanced at the time and announced it was a school day tomorrow, and his first class began at 7:05, so he'd be heading home. Matt and Tim left then, and then Rachel had kissed Gloria and Bob good night and headed off to her room.

Gloria and Bob were left alone in the living room. It was so quiet that Gloria could hear the hum of the refrigerator in the kitchen. Bob had headed off to the kitchen, announcing he was going to have a cup of chamomile tea, and did she want one, too?

"No, thank you."

"Well, I think it will do you good." Bob's voice was mild. He'd come back in a few moments with steaming mugs of chamomile tea, set one down before Gloria, and then taken his seat across from her in his chair. He placed his mug on the coffee table, leaned forward, and looked straight at her. "Gloria. We need to talk."

"Yes, yes, indeed we do."

"Good." Bob had straightened up. "How about if I go first this time?"

"Go right ahead."

"Okay." There was a pause. "Gloria, honey. You are perhaps the most unhappy person in the world. Or at least the most unhappy person I know. And, well, you're spreading it around."

"Unhappy? Who wouldn't be unhappy?"

"Oh, for God's sake, Gloria. There! That's the issue. What, exactly, do you have to be unhappy about?"

"You, the accident. Your health. The kids—the mess they are all making of their lives."

Bob had rubbed his temples, sighed, and was briefly silent. "Okay, here goes. Right. I had a horrible accident. And it was my fault. And I've made a miraculous recovery—I'm healed. I can do what I want. I'm back at work part-time; I'm watching my diet; my sugar's been under control. Can you not wrestle up a little happiness about that?"

Gloria had begun to protest she was happy about that, but Bob went on.

"And this issue you have with the kids making messes of their lives—what the hell is it you want? After all your kvetching about Rachel not growing up, she's met a very nice man, whom we all are growing to love, who checks off every item on your checklist for an acceptable son-in-law. Matt and Tim are settled and stable. Kevin and Veronica are happily married despite having two kids, and a third on the way, in what are usually the roughest years for a marriage. Kevin's taking over the practice—something we both had hoped for. Veronica's working part-time for the church preschool—what else could you want? And Cody—Cody, after that disaster of a first marriage, looks to be ready to settle down for real with someone we both know and love. What the hell are you so scared of, Gloria?"

"What makes you think I'm scared?"

"Oh, please. You're either psychotically self-absorbed or terrified. I'm going with fear because you're not Jerzy Grabowski."

"Thanks for that, at least."

Bob had taken a sip of tea. "Gloria, sweetheart. I love you. I want us to have lots of happy years. And it looks like we could have those, after all, in spite of my criminal self-neglect. And I'd like for you to stop being so petrified that if you aren't running it, it's going to go to hell. Let go of other people's wheel, Gloria."

Gloria felt herself shaking. She felt as if she might throw something. She put her mug down very carefully, shifting its handle to the right angle. She turned and looked straight at Bob. "Is that all? Can I 'go' now? Is it my turn?"

"Of course."

"Fine." Gloria had stood up slowly and looked down at Bob. "I'm not afraid, I'm not a control freak. But in case you haven't noticed, this family is not exactly overrun with people who can manage their own lives."

"I disagree. I think almost any problems we can point to usually have to do with other people trying to run their lives."

The specter of Jenna hung heavily between them. Gloria had pressed her lips together, eyebrows flaring, and managed to say, "I see." Then she had picked up her mug very carefully, gripping it with both hands as if it might fly across the room of its own accord. "I'm very tired. It's been a long day. I'm going to get ready for bed. I'll be out to say goodnight in a few minutes."

Bob had not argued or tried to dissuade her. He had nodded and said gently, "I love you, sweetheart."

Gloria had managed to squeeze out "And I love you," but her back was already turned.

Chapter 23

Alexa had always been a bit of a mess, but Gloria had not noticed until that moment how much more, of late, Alexa seemed even more out of order. She had the appearance of a woman in late middle-age who kept being surprised that she was not, in fact, at home, but out in public, where there were expectations to be … respectable. To put one's best foot forward. Not that Gloria hadn't tried her best over the years, dragging Alexa along for manicures and being careful to praise those long, sensible dresses with matching cardigans she had worn for a while. Alexa was almost as impervious to feedback as her son had been back in kindergarten. Praising anything Jonah did would usually result in a pint-sized sneer followed by an enthusiastic enactment of the opposite action.

Gloria shifted in her seat, wondering when the waiter would come by with that supposedly bottomless pot of coffee. Meanwhile, Alexa was droning on, as it happened, about that same Jonah.

"I don't know," Alexa said slowly, and then looked straight at Gloria. "I really think something is seriously wrong in that marriage. And

I don't think there's anything I can do about it, besides be there for each of them."

"Mm-hmm," Gloria said. "And what makes you think there's trouble?"

Alexa shook her head. "Just a feeling. Something about how Beth looks. The woman always looks sad."

"Well, she's married to Jonah."

Alexa raised her eyebrows and shrugged. "Well, yes. But it just seems worse. Sandy feels it, too. We've been reaching out more. To Beth, I mean."

"And?"

"She's pretty guarded. There's some sort of secret but she's not talking."

"Well, you know how marriages are. Always different behind closed doors."

"Oh, I don't know about that. I think healthy marriages are pretty much, what you see is what they've got. Yeah, there are discussions and negotiations behind the scenes, of course, but I don't believe that all relationships have big, dark secrets."

Gloria frowned. "Well, of course, not 'big, dark secrets.' That seems a bit … dramatic, don't you think, dear?"

Alexa did not look abashed or get quiet. Instead, to Gloria's surprise, she laughed and said, "Oh, Gloria! Everything that's not bland vanilla isn't 'dramatic.' Can't life have any normal ups and downs without you seeing disaster or hysteria?"

"I don't understand your point."

"Oh, I think you do."

Gloria's lips pressed shut and her eyebrows flared. She began to regret ever having encouraged Alexa to come out of her shell. A couple of manicures and a new haircut, and now she was embracing that artistic temperament that Veronica had. She pursed her lips and then managed to say, tensely, "I think you mean some sort of 'artistic' temperament. You know, everything big—big highs, big lows."

"I don't know what you mean by an artistic temperament, but I don't mean big highs and big lows." Alexa took a sip of coffee. "I mean ... Bob's accident was a big low. But he's recovered, just about as good as new. In terms of his heart and diabetes, maybe better than before. But the normal ups and downs of life just are ... normal. You know, navigating into semi-retirement, for Bob. Kevin figuring out how to manage the practice with his father around less. Matt and Tim developing deeper roots in their neighborhood. Just the ups and downs of life, and in those cases, all normal ups."

"Fine. Normal ups and downs." Gloria poked her fork at a cold French fry. "What's the concern about Jonah and Beth?"

"Like I said, she seems sad all the time."

Gloria frowned. *I'd be sad if I were saddled with Jonah: either sad or doing hard time for manslaughter.*

"I mean, I'd be sad if I were married to someone like Jonah," Alexa went on, startling Gloria. "But I think there's something more than that."

"Well, if there is, I'm sure it will come out." Gloria put her fork down with a clank, closing that topic. "What about Cody and your Sandy?"

"What about it?"

Gloria frowned. Alexa looked serene. How could the woman be oblivious? "I mean it appears they are spending a lot of time together."

"Yes, my hunch is that we'll be hearing an official announcement by the end of the year."

"Aren't you concerned?"

"About?"

"Well, about the appropriateness. Of," Gloria circled one hand vaguely over the table, "this relationship."

Alexa shook her head. "No, I'm not. I was a little surprised, for about five minutes. And then it made perfect sense."

"Perfect sense?" Gloria realized as she spoke that she needed to stop the words, but could not. "Have you ever met your daughter? How the hell could this make perfect sense?"

Alexa put down her coffee cup and placed her hands carefully on each side of her plate. She pulled her lips in, blinked a few times, took a deep breath. "Wow." She paused before repeating, "Wow." Alexa paused again, looking at Gloria expectantly, and then added, "Maybe … maybe you'd like to reel that in, Gloria?"

Gloria just stared at her.

"Ah. Okay." Alexa picked up her napkin, wiped her mouth, and placed the napkin on her plate. She waved one hand to the waiter for their check. She turned back to Gloria, her face a mask of neutrality. "I have to get back to work. I'll get the check this time." She stood up and then, placing a hand on Gloria's shoulder, added, "You can get lunch next time, when you're ready to apologize." Gloria felt the gentle squeeze and, too late, lifted her hand to place it on Alexa's. Alexa had walked away to the cash register. She heard the quiet, warm voice praising the meal, thanking the staff, and heading out. Gloria imagined herself standing up and going after her, but felt unable to move, just sitting, feeling heavier and heavier, as if she would sink through the seat and into the diner floor.

Gloria sat staring out the diner window. The waiter had come over three times to see if she "would like anything else, more coffee, maybe?" before Gloria realized she's been sitting far too long. She drove home in a half daze. Bob would be home from the office; he would understand. She found him puttering in the garage, organizing his fishing supplies. Gloria frowned at his back, and tried to erase the frown as Bob turned around, smiling. She watched his smile fade and wondered what was wrong.

"What's the matter?"

"I was going to ask you the same thing. Is Alex okay?"

Gloria sighed. "Yes. No. Well, she's fine, I suppose. But," she paused, and put her hand on the door to the kitchen, "I am not." She went in, expecting Bob to be right behind her. She was halfway through explaining how Alexa had just taken offense and run off with some excuse about having to get back to work when she realized Bob was still in the garage. She stomped back to the door and yanked it open. Bob looked up with mild surprise.

"Gloria? What's going on?"

"I thought you were right behind me."

"Well, no. I have some things to take care of here. Going fishing with Joe tomorrow morning. Did you need something?"

She rolled her eyes. "No, I don't 'need' anything. Just wanted to … talk about some things."

"Sure. I'll be in in five minutes. Any chance we could have some iced tea?"

"If there's some left from yesterday, yes. Otherwise, I'll just put on tea." Gloria slammed the door shut.

They sat down with iced teas. Gloria stretched what was left with a little lemonade. Bob gently swished his drink and took a sip. He looked at Gloria quizzically. "Okay. What's going on?"

Gloria's mouth felt unaccountably dry. The words she had blurted out so easily when she first came into the house seemed more and more terrible as she heard them echoing in her head. She shook her head, lips pressed together, and looked past Bob at the photos on the sideboard.

She took a deep breath, looked straight at Bob and managed, "I said something a little hurtful. Honest, but hurtful. And Alexa just ... left."

"I'm sorry?"

"I said something she didn't like and she just left."

"That doesn't sound like Alex. Good God, Gloria, you say things she doesn't like all the time!"

"What's that supposed to mean?"

"It means you talk to her like she's an idiot. You boss her around. You talk over her. If you saying something she didn't like could make Alex just leave, the friendship wouldn't have even begun."

"That," Gloria said stiffly, "hardly seems fair."

Bob shrugged. "Gloria, I love you. But you're a kindergarten teacher and you tend to treat most people as if they were five years old. And most people don't put up with it as gracefully as Alex Bonhall." He took another sip of iced tea. "So, what actually happened?"

"Oh," Gloria said impatiently, waving her hand. "She was babbling on about Jonah's marriage and that insipid wife of his looking too sad and I just changed the subject."

"To?"

"Hmm?"

"What did you change the subject *to*, Gloria?"

"Cody. And their Sandy."

"Ah, yes." Bob smiled. "That's like a dream come true, isn't it?"

"You, too?" Gloria gaped at him. "Have you gone insane? Have you even met Sandy?"

Bob put his glass down, putting his elbows on the table and leaning forward a bit. "That's not, by any chance, what you said to your best friend?"

"I didn't ask her if she was insane." Bob was silent. Gloria looked past him again and went on. "Well, I did ask her if she'd met her daughter."

"And then she just left?"

"Well, she did pay. And before she left, she asked me if I wanted to take it back. Reel it back, she said, I think. And she said I could pick up the next tab, when I apologize."

"And you said …"

"Nothing. I said nothing." Gloria rubbed her temples. "I can't believe she would just leave like that."

Bob leaned against the chair back, arms folded. "Oh, I can. Gloria. What the hell did you think she would do? You just insulted her, you insulted her daughter … what did you think she would do?"

"But, Bob, you know Sandy."

"Yes, I do." Bob put his hand on Gloria's arm. "I do know Sandy. She is sweet, and warm. She's very smart—clearly much smarter than Jonah, and so careful not to rub it in his face, even though he's chronically obnoxious to her and it would be so gratifying to see her do that. Even for me, and I'm just her honorary uncle. When she's not working, she's volunteering—at church, cleaning up the beach. She's been a real gem since my accident, helping with the twins."

"Well, clearly with an ulterior motive."

"Oh, for God's sake, Gloria." Bob stood up. "That's going too far. I don't know what you're so afraid of here. Cody's a grown man. Sandy's a grown woman. If he doesn't mind that she can think circles around him, and she's willing to step up and be the mom the twins need, I am grateful."

Gloria stared at him, wondering if he, too, had gone insane. Didn't he see the chaos ahead—a lifetime of beach cleanups and composting and the twins subjected to the whirlwind of energy of life with Sandy Bonhall? "And you think this is all just fine."

Bob lifted his iced tea as if to make a toast and then lowered it for a sip. "Yes. Yes, I do. Better than fine. I see my oldest son, who has been through relationship hell, looking as happy as I was when I first won the heart of Gloria Grabowski." He sighed. "I'm going to go get some more chores done in the garage and then trim around the driveway. It's a little ragged."

"Fine. That sounds like a good idea."

"You might want to think about apologizing to Alex sooner rather than later. It's not going to get easier." Bob went out to the garage, the door shutting gently behind him.

Gloria stared into her glass and wondered what he meant by 'was.'

Chapter 24

Some people are just too sensitive, Gloria thought. She carefully pulled the canisters away from the backsplash under the cabinets, dusted the counter and the canisters, and carefully lined them up again. She moved them so that they all lined up in the front, stepped back, frowned, and then pushed them back against the backsplash so that the larger ones stuck out further. She shook her head. Neither looked … right. She sighed and looked out the window. Bob must have finished trimming around the driveway and had taken on the overgrowth along the fence in the backyard. She frowned at the sweaty expanse of his T-shirt. *He should not be out working on this hot afternoon.* She thought about bringing him out some water and then frowned, thinking about that little dig about how happy he 'was.'

Still, no use letting him have another incident, she told herself, filling a glass with water and heading out the back sliders. She stood near him, waiting for a pause in the racket of the trimmer. He caught sight of her and turned it off, smiling. She held out the water.

"You're an angel of mercy," Bob said, and took a long drink. He handed the glass back to her. "Thanks, sweetheart."

Gloria pressed her lips together and then took a deep breath before blurting out, "What did you mean by 'was'?" Bob looked confused. "Was," she repeated. "You said how happy you were. Back when we were first in love. Meaning what? That you're not happy now?"

Bob sighed. "Gloria, sweetheart. For someone who is so oblivious to other people's feelings you sure do take offense easily. I love you. I have always loved you. And I'm happy with you." He mopped sweat off his forehead and wiped his hand on his damp shirt.

"Thanks," Gloria said stiffly. "But I don't think I am oblivious to other people's feelings."

Bob kissed her gently. "I don't think this is the time for this conversation." He nodded in the direction of Miss Arlene's yard. "Let's have a nice chat later. After I cool down and clean up."

"Fine," Gloria replied, and headed inside. She wondered what Bob meant about her obliviousness to others' feelings. She felt as if she were very sensitive. It seemed to her that, if anything, the rest of them were either unable, or unwilling, to see that chaos was encroaching at every moment. She felt her heart beating in her throat, felt a bit disoriented. She sat down on the ottoman and stared around her living room; it seemed suddenly unfamiliar. She had the strange sense of knowing the place without really knowing it, as if she were there and not there at the same time. She pinched her left forearm, hard, trying to anchor herself into the reality of the sting. She felt herself begin to tremble and, to her surprise, she felt tears well up in her eyes. The unreality of the living room persisted. She stared at the pictures, the books: Yes, that was her mother, her in-laws, the portrait of all the children the year after Rachel was born. She felt her heart pounding. It felt as if her insides were quaking. She put her hands on her thighs, surprised she could not feel the vibrations she felt in her bones. She was still sitting there when Rachel strolled in, yelling, "Mom! Dad! I'm home!"

Gloria tried to call out a greeting but her voice came out in a kind of squeak. Rachel came through the kitchen and dining area. "Mom? Dad?" She saw Gloria and said, "Mom! What's wrong?" She came over, touched her mom's face. "You're crying! Mom, what happened? Where's Dad?"

"He's outside. Wrapping up chores," Gloria managed. "And I'm just resting." She put a hand over her heart. "I think … yes, I'm fine. Just a little emotional and tired, that's all."

Rachel squeezed onto the ottoman next to her mother. "BS, Mom. What's going on?"

Gloria squeezed her eyes shut and then opened them. The room seemed to be familiar again. "I don't know. It's the oddest thing."

"Tell me."

"Well, I came in from bringing water to your father. I didn't want him to overheat. And then I came in here. And it was very odd. My heart was pounding and everything seemed very strange." She shook her head. "It was as if I didn't recognize my own home, but I knew where I was." She gestured at the photos on the wall. "I mean, I could see those were all of you. But it all seemed strange."

"Anxiety attack. Panic attack, maybe."

"Oh, for goodness' sake, Rachel. Don't diagnose me."

"Not diagnosing. You described it. Disoriented, heart pounding, feeling strange. Maybe tearful?" Rachel wiped her mother's cheek with her hand. "Mom, what happened today? Weren't you going to have a nice lunch with Aunt Alex?"

"Yes, and that has nothing to do with this," Gloria said firmly. She did not want to discuss the lunch with Rachel. She wondered if Alexa would tell Sandy about the conversation, and then assured herself that

Alexa, good and loyal Alexa, would never go running to her daughter over a little misunderstanding between friends.

"Ah, well, good." Rachel stood up. "Can I get you something? Mom. Stand up. Come to the kitchen with me. Sitting still in a panic attack just makes it last longer. Feeds the fight-or-flight. Come on." Gloria heaved herself up. She wondered when it had begun to be so hard to get up out of a chair as she followed Rachel into the kitchen.

Dinner was over, Bob was reading, and Rachel was on a walk on the beach with Aidan. With June nearly here, all the educators in the family—Joe, Alexa, Rachel and now, it seemed, Aidan—were anticipating summer. Gloria rustled uselessly around the kitchen, straightening out the spices so they were lined up with their labels centered properly.

"Gloria?"

She sighed. She knew he was going to ask her about calling Alexa. "I'm going to. Now. I think I'll just step outside."

"You'll feel better."

You mean you'll *feel better*, Gloria thought with annoyance. *Honestly, he's making a big deal out of this.* She stepped outside and called the Bonhall home number. She wondered if maybe they would be out for a walk and was just mentally rehearsing the message to leave when Alexa picked up.

"Hello, Gloria."

Hello. Not "Hey there" or "Gloria, how are you?" but just a cool "hello." Well then, the thing to do was to get it over with. "Alexa." Gloria cleared her throat. "I was just calling to … to clear the air." There was silence; Gloria felt her heart pounding and wondered if Alexa would be able to hear it.

"Okay. I'm listening."

Gloria thought regretfully of all the times she had urged Alexa to speak up for herself; she didn't see why the woman had to pick this moment to put all Gloria's good advice into action. Gloria pressed her lips together, counted to ten, and then continued. "I wanted to apologize."

"For."

"For accidentally implying that Sandy wasn't ... good enough for Cody." The words didn't sound as convincing out loud as they had when she'd practiced them earlier. "I mean, I know that's how it sounded. And I'm sorry. I was worried about, you know."

"I'm sure I don't. Know, that is."

Gloria raised her eyes to the evening sky in prayer. "I was worried that, you know. After Jenna. That Cody would be on a sort of rebound and with Sandy being someone so familiar that maybe he was," Gloria paused, "you know, confusing comfort with romance."

"Okay. That's reasonable enough as a concern. But it doesn't look like that to me."

"So ... can we, oh. Can we have lunch again soon? And talk a bit?"

"Sure. I think the boys are fishing tomorrow. How about we make it breakfast instead?"

"Sure. The diner?"

"Absolutely. Let's say eight o'clock. I'll meet you there." Alexa sounded serene.

"Thanks, Alexa. I appreciate it."

"Sure, Gloria. See you then." There was a soft click. Gloria stared at the phone and then up at the darkening sky. She locked her gaze on a bright star and wished that breakfast was already over.

The door slid open behind her. Bob settled into the chair next to her and put a hand on her shoulder. "So? Get the dirty deed done yet?"

Gloria waggled the phone. "Yes. We just hung up. We'll be having breakfast at the diner tomorrow while you and Joe go fishing."

"Good work. You'll see. It will be better after breakfast tomorrow. Alex isn't the type to hold grudges."

Gloria sighed. "But I've never insulted her children before." She had barely finished speaking when Bob burst out laughing. She stared at him. "And what's so funny?"

"Oh, honey. You've got to be kidding. You do nothing but insult her children. You've been insulting her children since Matt and Jonah were in kindergarten. You insult her, almost constantly. God love her, she's been the perfect patient friend with your constant criticism."

"I do not constantly criticize," Gloria argued. "I try to be helpful. Any idiot can see that."

"And you just insulted me and everyone else who disagrees with you," Bob replied. "Gloria, I love you, but the constant berating even gets to me sometimes. I know you adore your mother but, sweetheart, maybe you need to stomp the Jerzy out of yourself."

Gloria stood up quickly, felt a bit lightheaded, and sat down with a thump.

"Are you okay?"

"I," she replied stiffly, "am fine. And what exactly do you mean by that remark about stomping out my father?"

Bob shook his head. "Seriously. You need to go talk to Andrea more often. If you're not in control you just start tearing things down. With your words."

"I don't know what you're talking about."

Bob sighed. "Today, you have rolled your eyes at me at least five times. You implied I was an idiot. You insulted your best friend and her daughter, and criticized yours. Three times over dinner, as it happens: her clothes, her hair, and her bedroom. You complained that the trash pickup was early and the mail was late, you pointed out three places where I needed to touch up the edging. And you didn't even notice, did you?"

Gloria sat, stunned. She unwound the reel of the day: the complaint about the brownness of the fries at lunch, but of course, one expects the food to be properly prepared. Of course she griped about the heat; it was late May in Florida. Perhaps she had dismissed Alexa's apparent concern about Beth, but really, how could Alexa be surprised that marriage to Jonah would be, well, challenging, even for that insipid daughter-in-law? She recalled her own comments on artistic temperaments and heard her voice blurting out "Have you ever met your daughter?" with a cringe. She recalled the remarks to Rachel at dinner but they seemed, to her mind, to be in the purview of a dutiful mother, trying to drag her immature daughter into adult comportment. Apparently other people did not see it that way. She wondered how Andrea would be helpful with other people perpetually misunderstanding her.

"Seriously, honey. I think you need to go talk with Andrea regularly for a while. Or Father Jack. Or someone. And maybe do some hard thinking about how you talk to people and exactly what it is you think is going on when you constantly tear people down and tell them what to do."

"I see," Gloria said quietly. "I'm getting mosquito-bitten. I'm going in." She heaved herself out of the chair and headed into the house. Bob followed behind her but she did not speak to him. She headed off to their bedroom without a word.

Chapter 25

Gloria had debated canceling breakfast. Her head hurt; she needed to be available if Bob had any incidents when he was out fishing with Joe; she had errands to run. She had started reciting the litany of rationale over coffee with Bob and he had raised his eyebrows while taking a sip of coffee, his eyes locked on hers. She had shrugged, sighed, and taken a long drink of coffee. She felt the need to be fortified for breakfast with Alexa.

She stepped into the diner and saw Alexa sitting in a booth, facing the door, waving to her. There was already a pot of coffee and two mugs on the table. Gloria told the hostess she was going to join her friend. The young woman nodded and Gloria, lips pressed into a tight smile, walked up to the booth. Alexa smiled up at her.

"Good morning! I ordered us coffee."

"I see. Thanks. Good morning." Gloria slid heavily into her side of the booth. She noticed Alexa was, as always these days, dressed as if either an art lesson or a hike would break out at any time. Today, it was hiking: the khaki shorts, the walking sandals, the casual T-shirt type top with long sleeves. Her hair was, as it had been for a few months now, an absolute mess. Still, Alexa had shown up, early, and did not appear angry.

"How are you? And Bob?"

"Fine. Bob's fine. Of course he's grateful to go fishing with Joe." Gloria pursed her lips as she put some creamer into her coffee.

"And Joe's grateful for Bob," Alexa said lightly. She glanced up at the waiter, who had just arrived. They ordered breakfast and, when the waiter had gone, Alexa leaned forward on her elbows, hands resting on her upper arms, and said, "So. Gloria. About yesterday."

"Yes," Gloria said, looking past Alexa's head to the back of the delivery man having breakfast in the next booth. "I realize I was pretty harsh."

"Yes."

"And I'm sorry if I offended you."

Alexa smiled, shook her head, and took a sip of coffee. "Well, I appreciate that, Gloria, but it doesn't help clear the air very much. We need to talk. Really talk." Gloria just stared at her. Alexa waited a moment and then continued, "I mean, it looks very much as if Cody and Sandy are an item, and quite serious. If you have serious reservations about Sandy—about our family—I think we ought to clear that up between us. Because the kids are going to do what they want, and we are going to have to figure out how to either get along, or just tolerate one another for their sakes."

"I don't have ... reservations about your family."

"Well, it certainly sounded so yesterday."

"I didn't mean quite what I said."

"What did you mean?" Alexa asked. She sat, gazing right at Gloria. Gloria felt annoyed. What was wrong with Alexa? Couldn't she just let such a little misunderstanding go? And since when was Alexa so feisty?

So willing to take things on directly? Gloria regretted ever encouraging Alexa to be more outgoing.

"I meant ... I mean, well." Gloria kept staring at the back of the delivery man's head, avoiding Alexa's direct gaze. "I meant, well."

"You meant?"

Gloria pressed her fingers onto the tabletop. "I meant, well. Sandy, and Rachel, too, seem so immature. Flighty." Gloria's eyebrows flared. "Believe me, I have the same 'reservations,' as you say, about Rachel and her romance with Aidan." Gloria stared down at her coffee cup and then up at Alexa. "You have to see what Rachel looks like when she goes to work! How can anyone take her seriously as a professional? She needs to grow up."

"I see what she looks like because she stops by so often with Sandy, and she looks fine. Like a modern guidance counselor in an elementary school." Alexa pushed her hair off her forehead and Gloria held back a sigh of annoyance when it fell right back over her eyebrows. "Gloria, do you even know what your daughter does all day?"

"Of course I do! I worked in the elementary schools, I know what the counselors do."

"And exactly how do you expect her to dress when she's doing arts and crafts and puppets with kindergarten and sitting around in a circle on the floor with third graders whose parents are going through chemo? In a suit and high heels?"

Gloria stared at her.

Alexa nodded as if Gloria had spoken. "Right. Her job is not what you necessarily think. Times have changed since you left to help raise the twins." Alexa took a sip of coffee. "So. Enough about Rachel. What's your beef with Sandy?"

Gloria pressed her lips together and took a deep breath. "I think we can both agree that our girls are a bit childish in their preoccupation with ecology and that you have expressed some concern about Sandy's difficulty in landing full-time employment."

Alexa tilted her head thoughtfully. "Yes, we have had our share of laughs about the insistence on all-organic and the endless public education efforts and the beach cleanups. And yes, Sandy has thus far chosen to stay close to home rather than take one of the very interesting positions in her field that would take her far away. And," she grinned, "apparently 'your' Cody has had a lot to do with that over the past few months."

Gloria pulled her lips in. She was surprised that Sandy had had job offers from far afield and declined them, choosing to stay close to home. "I had no idea. About the jobs, that is."

"Well, right. I didn't bring it up. Apparently, she's in talks right now for a very interesting position, mostly distance, in which she'll be teaching and part of a research team."

"Oh."

"Yes, she'll be giving a talk on the topic at a conference over Labor Day weekend. I'm sure she mentioned Cody would be her guest this time. Instead of me going," Alexa added.

"Oh."

"And, you know, Gloria, Joe and I are very proud of Sandy. She's a good girl. Woman. Well, whatever. In any case, she lives out what's important to her. She doesn't just talk about it or slap a sticker on her car. She gives up her free time to go give talks to kids' groups about ecological concerns, she volunteers at church, she's smart and doesn't rub it in everyone's face."

"I know," Gloria managed to say.

"Well, I'm not sure you did." Alexa leaned back as the waiter brought their breakfasts. After he'd left, she added, "And, Gloria, considering the circumstances, you could have been grateful that Sandy has been there for Cody. And, in fact, the concern ought to be on our side. Joe's and mine."

"And what's that supposed to mean?"

Alexa shook her head, spearing her fork into some scrambled eggs. "Because, on paper, Cody's the concern—a messy divorce, a complicated ex-wife, two half-grown kids. No annulment yet." She winked at Gloria and added, "And a pretty critical potential mom-in-law. But that's on paper. I know—Joe knows—the real Cody, the real you and Bob, those wonderful twins. So, even if Cody's not 'perfect on paper,' we're willing to accept that he could be very, very perfect for Sandy. And vice versa."

Gloria wondered where her voice went. It had never occurred to her to think about what the Cody and Sandy romance looked like from the other side. From Alexa's side, yes, her clean-living, church-going daughter had taken up with a divorced man with a crazy ex-wife and two children. Gloria felt queasy. She put her fork down and twisted her hands in her lap, looking around the diner. It seemed very odd that the place was bustling with people all acting normal—as if nothing in particular was happening at all. It felt as if she were in a snow globe, being violently shaken around and then watching bits of her reality swirl around her and settle into something confusing.

"Gloria? Are you okay?" Alexa sounded concerned.

Gloria trained her eyes on Alexa, squinting. She thought that perhaps squinting would help make the surrealness of the diner begin to look normal. "I don't know, dear. Does it seem to you that everything here seems a bit off?"

Alexa looked around. "No. My breakfast is fine. The place looks pretty typical. Busy, but, hey, it's Saturday morning."

Gloria rubbed her forehead with one hand, shaking her head slowly, and then put her hand down. "Alexa. I appreciate." She cleared her throat. "I appreciate you saying that. About Cody. Because it never even occurred to me that, well—"

"That there was more than one way to look at all this?"

Gloria nodded. She felt like a fool. Suddenly she imagined someone else looking at all this—her pastor, looking askance at sweet, innocent little Sandy, who volunteered with religious education and never missed a young adults' meeting, taking up with a divorced man! Teetering on living in sin, burdened with parenting two children who were not hers. She thought about the rest of her family: Kevin and his crazy wife, their incorrigible little son and hapless little girl; Matt and Tim—angels, to her, but she was well aware that a lot of people looked down on them and their quiet life together; and then of course, Rachel, always off saving manatees or turtles or insisting on the "right" vegetables. Her shoulders drooped. She startled; Alexa had leaned across the table to put a hand on hers.

"Gloria, stop it. Everything's fine. Let it go."

Gloria shook her head, lips pressed together. She was surprised to find she felt like crying. She looked at Alexa, who was serene, looking as if she understood how upside-down Gloria was feeling. "It's not fine. Alexa, dear, I'm not feeling terribly well."

"Ill?"

"No. Not exactly ill." Gloria hesitated. "It's as if things are all sort of upside-down. In my head, maybe."

"Oh, well. That's normal."

"It most certainly is not."

Alexa took a bite, chewed, swallowed, put down her fork. "Well, I disagree. Life is full of changes, and when a lot of changes are happening, Gloria, we get ... discombobulated. It's what Dabrowski called positive disintegration."

"Positive ..."

"Well, just, things have to sort of fall apart for the new things to get put together. Like"—Alexa paused—"you need to be able to step back and look at Cody's situation objectively sometimes, not just see your wonderful son—who we all love—through the lens of beloved son and victim of Jenna. Like I have to see my Jonah as potentially someone who is emotionally abusing his wife. Does any mom want to see that? No. But I have to let go of my notions about Jonah to let the truth start to gel."

Gloria cleared her throat. "I see."

"And I think that's enough on this topic," Alexa announced, opening a small container of raspberry jam. "Tell me about Rachel's plans to go to Ireland this summer. That sounds like such fun."

Gloria did not like that subject, either, but it was preferable to a longer discussion about the fact that, on paper, it appeared that Cody was getting the better end of the deal. "Ah, yes. The Ireland trip."

"She's flying into Dublin, right? And meeting Aidan and his sister, I think, before heading off to the west where his parents live."

"That's right. Aidan's sister is a tour guide in Dublin."

"And the parents have a shop, if I recall?"

"Yes."

Alexa took a sip of coffee. "Gloria, you don't seem very happy for Rachel to be taking this trip."

Gloria frowned at her. "Alexa, dear. It's not that I'm not happy. I'm concerned. Yes, concerned."

"What about?"

"Well, about her traveling there, of course! Being around strangers. Overseas travel. A young woman alone."

Alexa shrugged. "It's Ireland, for God's sake! Not some awful place. And Rachel's not a child. Besides, she'll only be 'alone' until she gets to baggage claim."

"Still," Gloria said with a huff, "I don't like it."

"Ah." Alexa nodded slowly.

"And what does that mean?"

"What?"

"The cryptic little 'ah' sound." Gloria tried to mimic the "ah" but realized she sounded peevish.

"It means, well, I think I understand. But perhaps I don't." Alexa paused, and added, "Gloria, it seems like you're annoyed at Rachel for having a life. Moving forward."

"That's a pretty awful thing to say."

Alexa shrugged. "Gloria, you're my best friend. But if something isn't your idea, and you're not the boss, you're just never satisfied. Never just okay with letting life happen."

"Oh, I've let life happen, as you say, and now look at it!"

"Are you trying to take responsibility for Bob's accident again?"

Gloria stared at her, brows drawn down. "No. Of course not."

"Well, what else? What else have you supposedly 'let happen' and now it's something bad?"

Gloria almost said "Cody with your Sandy," but caught herself. She pressed her lips together and said, "Well, if I had done a better job of managing Bob, he wouldn't have had that accident."

"Managing Bob? What, is he six? Or Sixty-six?"

"You know what I mean."

"Yes, I do. And you're talking as if a husband was a project to be managed."

"Well, aren't they?"

"No. At least mine isn't."

"Well, in my experience," Gloria said stiffly, "a husband is to be managed. It makes life go better."

"Your husband? Husbands in general? Whose?"

Gloria stared at the back of the delivery driver's head. Her head echoed with her mother's soft voice saying "But, Jerzy, darling, you remember," and she shook her head slowly. She turned her eyes directly to Alexa's questioning look and said, "Well, of course, not all husbands require a lot of management. But some do. That's clear to be seen."

Alexa pushed her hair off her forehead and said, "If I ever thought Joe was talking about me that way—that I was some sort of troublesome problem to be managed—I'd be, well, angry wouldn't do it justice."

"And you don't think a little discreet coaching, perhaps, to get out of your shell, out of that rut, wasn't useful? That a little management did you some good?"

Alexa rubbed her forehead, and then grinned at Gloria. "Oh! Is that what you were doing, with all that extra advice last fall?" She laughed, shaking her head. "Okay! Wow! Well, I guess I knew that. But, still, wow."

Gloria frowned. "What's so funny?"

"You don't see the humor in all this? Seriously?"

"I most certainly do not."

"Well." Alexa shrugged. "I do. I feel badly for you, too, of course, because it's got to be miserable thinking that if you don't keep everything 'just so' it will all spin apart. And I can see that with kindergarten classes, for sure! But, Gloria, that is just going to make you miserable if you don't get a whole lot more selective on who and how and what you try to control."

"You don't know what it was like, having the father I had," Gloria blurted out, surprising herself. "He was a control freak—terrorizing the family. I'd know controlling if I saw it. Or did it."

Alexa nodded. "But your mother. She was a bit of a controller, too—just a whole lot more subtle, and a lot more well-intended. And she probably had to be, to get all you kids through childhood and out of that house. Maybe you need to look at whether you're channeling your mother more than you need to, Gloria."

"I would be happy to be like my mother. You can't imagine, dear. What she was up against!"

"No, I can't. But I see you, and I see you terrified that any wrong move—or something you see as wrong—will lead to all kinds of disaster. And that can't be a good way to live, Gloria."

"I suppose," Gloria said. "I suppose you could be right. Now," she drew herself up, "what's the latest with Jonah and Beth?"

Alexa had smiled just a little, nodding, and went with the change of subject. *The rest of the breakfast was peaceful enough*, Gloria thought on the way home. *It's good to have it over with—to have straightened everything out with one of my best friends. Surely now Alexa will see how important it is for me to keep a sharp eye on my currently chaotic family.*

Chapter 26

Gloria thought of her mother often, and missed her. There were times when the longing to pick up the phone and hear her voice was as sharp as it had been right after Nora had died. Gloria sighed and carefully dusted the books, pulling them forward so that the spines were a smooth row across the expanse of the shelf, recalling how Nora had tucked cash into those books, knowing that the money would be safe from Jerzy. Gloria had been taken aback after Momma's death, when her siblings had been surprised about the money. They'd had one whole evening of sitting together, riffling through the pages of every book and laughing at the fives, tens, and occasional twenties that fluttered into the pile on the old coffee table. They'd decided to divide it evenly among them, with no quibbling.

Her older sister, Lorena, asked how Gloria had known about the money; she had hesitated and just said she'd come into the living room unexpectedly one day and found Momma standing on the ottoman, putting money into a book. Momma had explained she was just putting it aside for the future. Gloria felt that was close to true enough. It had unleashed a flow of "Momma" stories from each of them, and the picture, at the end, was of their mother as a woman who had carefully orchestrated things to facilitate each child's escape from life with Jerzy Grabowski.

She had carefully helped Josef get things set up with the Army recruiter and never let on that she was not surprised when he simply left home. She had helped Lorena find scholarships, bought the bus ticket, and smoothed Jerzy's ruffled feathers such that he began bragging to anyone who would listen about how he had helped Lorena see how healthcare was the right field for her. She had helped Gloria escape to college and then south to Sunflower Beach, far from Jerzy Grabowski; she had likewise helped Micah get away to college, and stealthily arranged for Anna to make her escape to art school. They were all amazed at the depth of Momma's secrecy, her deep commitment to each of them.

Gloria smiled and lifted a small porcelain mouse, a memento from Momma's curio cabinet full of the kind of gift shop items children give to their mother on holidays. She turned it carefully before placing it back gently. That had been quite a day, the day after Momma's funeral. A day in which Gloria—and, she supposed, her siblings, too—grappled with the similarities in their circumstances and the raw fact that Momma had not played favorites. She had, however, the gift of making each of them feel particularly loved.

Gloria wondered if she was doing the same thing for her children. She grimaced, pressing her lips hard. Probably not. She supposed that Kevin and Rachel saw Matt and Cody as the clear favorites. She assured herself she didn't have any favorites. Matt was, of course, just very lovable. And Cody was her oldest. And Kevin, such a good boy, and taking after his father! And then Rachel, her only daughter.

She shook her head and wondered if she were somehow scarring her children.

"Mom?"

Gloria startled out of her reverie; it was Rachel, arms full of groceries. Gloria saw what looked like leeks peeking out of the top of one reusable canvas bag. *The organic grocers*, Gloria thought. "Hello, dear. Home already?"

"Yes. I stopped at the store. Everything okay here?" Rachel started unpacking the bags, placing the groceries on the counter.

"Oh, we're all fine," Gloria said. She gave a last careful wipe to the side of the book shelf and headed into the kitchen. "Your father drove himself to the dentist. Past due for a checkup."

"Oh, yeah, that kind of took a back burner for a while. Nice to be back on a normal routine," Rachel commented.

"Mm-hmm."

Rachel turned to look at her mom, eyebrows raised. "Mom? Is something wrong?"

"No, of course not." There was silence, so Gloria continued. "But I'd like to ask you something, if I could."

"Sure." Rachel was leaning into the refrigerator, making room for the vegetables. "What?" She looked around the refrigerator door and added, "About my trip?"

"No, not about going to Ireland," Gloria said, a little too quickly. "It's something else."

Rachel nodded. "Sure."

"I was wondering," Gloria said slowly. "I was thinking about my mother." She watched Rachel smile. Nora had that effect on people, even in memory. "I was thinking," Gloria repeated, "and wondering. My mother. Your grandmother," she added, and wondered what happened to her ability to speak. "My mother had the ability to make everyone feel special."

"Yes, she did, didn't she?" Rachel said. "That was something. I think everyone always thought they were Nana's favorite." She laughed and said, "And maybe we all were, in our own way!"

"Mm-hmm." Gloria sat heavily on a chair. "And I was wondering, dear, if I was anything like that."

"Oh," Rachel said with a little surprise. "Wow. Okay." She looked quizzical, and leaned back against the counter, arms folded. "Well, in some ways you're a lot like Nana. Like how you talk to us sometimes like Nana did to Poppa—you know, telling us stuff we should know or telling us what you think. Like Nana saying, 'Oh, Jerzy darling, you remember,' and then telling Poppa whatever he needed to know." She paused. "Except you say 'dear.' Like the other day when you said to me, 'Rachel, dear, don't you think you ought to do something a little more professional with your hair?'"

Gloria frowned. "Well, I do like to be helpful. And encouraging."

Rachel sat down across from her mother. "And you are. Both helpful and encouraging."

Gloria cleared her throat. "And do I … make everyone feel like they're my favorite? Like your Nana could?"

Rachel tilted her head, thinking. "Well, everyone knows Cody's your firstborn and special. And that Kevin is taking after Dad and so he walks on water. And that you have a special soft spot for Matt. And that I'm your precious baby girl," she added with a grin. "So, yeah, I think we each feel special in our own way. Is that what you were worried about?"

Gloria nodded. "Yes. Thanks, dear. You've helped me a lot." But Gloria knew that Rachel had not told her what she wanted to hear: that Gloria made each child feel loved in a particular, special way. She had instead told Gloria what Gloria seemed to think was special—for Gloria—about each of her children.

Chapter 27

Brenda Shimski seemed, in every way, to be Gloria's opposite. She was short and a little plump in elementary school, which translated to petite and curvy by the end of middle school; she had dimples and bright-green eyes, and two doting parents who could afford braces and summer camp and pretty clothes. Everyone wanted to sit with Brenda at lunchtime; she was never picked last in gym class despite her complete inability to do anything athletic successfully except walk around the track. Every volleyball serve went into the net. She nearly decapitated the gym teacher while flailing at a softball and was given permission to be the "bat girl" for the next two weeks until they moved on to field hockey, at which time the PE teacher decided preemptively that Brenda could earn an A by handing out and collecting field hockey sticks. "Carefully." She announced this while rubbing the side of her head as if it were still sore. But Brenda was cheerful and kind to everyone, cheering on all the other students who got to play.

And, strange as it seemed, even in retrospect, she was Gloria Grabowski's best friend.

They became best friends the way children often do: They were randomly assigned to sit next to each other in kindergarten. Brenda had offered Gloria one of her pieces of celery with peanut butter, and Gloria had reciprocated with a handful of raisins. Then Brenda asked if she wanted to be best friends, and, not even sure what that meant, Gloria had said yes.

They sat together at lunch; they played together at recess. They hugged each other goodbye each Friday and hugged each other hello each Monday morning. They held hands nervously in line for their first confessions and squeezed each other's hands in breathless anticipation before queueing up for their first Holy Communion. They whispered about boys at the few sleepovers that Gloria was permitted to go to—Jerzy didn't believe in children being away overnight and besides, he argued, she was needed at home. They researched saints and picked the same confirmation name, Bernadette, which made all the grandmothers very happy. Their friendship continued through high school, and they had kept in touch while Gloria went to college in Tallahassee and Brenda went out of state to study chemistry. Their friendship had survived all these years, although Brenda now lived in Massachusetts. She came to Florida to visit her family two times each year, and always made time for Gloria.

"You're my best friend," Brenda always said, hugging her tight and never embarrassed to be affectionate in public. "I'm always there for you, no matter what."

"No matter what?" Gloria had mused aloud once in response, wondering.

Brenda had given a crooked smile and said, "Yup. If you ever tell me you murdered someone, I'll just show up with a shovel and ask where we're digging the hole," and laughed at Gloria's shocked face. "Seriously, Gloria—no matter what."

Gloria suspected she was only kidding about the shovel and hole, but she always felt Brenda would be there, no matter what. It never failed to amaze Gloria that little Brenda Shimski, whom everyone loved, seemed to like Gloria best of all.

The long summer vacations, all through school, were largely times of separation. Brenda's family took a vacation, and then she went to stay with family in Illinois, where there were a lot of aunts and uncles and cousins, southwest of Chicago, and even a family farm with pigs and chickens, and some ducks around the pond next to the old farmhouse where an aunt and uncle lived. Most summers, Brenda also went to camp for a couple of weeks. She would write to Gloria, and Gloria wrote back. Gloria was, of course, at home, doing chores and trying to avoid her father's attention.

"The girl is just lying around all afternoon reading," he would grumble to Nora, who would nod and gently remark on all the chores Gloria had done, adding that she'd taken the younger children for a bike ride in the morning, and now it was so hot and a good time to try to stay as cool as possible and read a good book. If Gloria tried to slip into the kitchen for a glass of water and Jerzy saw her, he would invent tasks for her to do.

"Make yourself useful and go weed around the tomato plants," or, "Go hose out the trash bins; they probably smell terrible," he would grunt. Gloria would head outside, but usually Nora was right behind her, finger over her lips, shaking her head and nodding toward the shade. They would rest in the shade on the cool grass and talk for a while about the book Gloria was reading, or whether it might rain a bit and cool things off so they could get some decent sleep. Then Nora would say, "Well, if your father asks, tell him I needed you and that I said to do those things afterward. As in, after supper, when it's less hot out here."

Every morning that was not rainy, Gloria would hop on her bike, sometimes with Micah and Anna in tow, and go for a ride, the wind blowing her hair back and evaporating the sweat as quickly as it came, her long legs pumping, the morning sun brushing pale gold on everything. But the precious freedom of the bicycle rides could not offset the dismal cloud of summer in the Grabowski house. Summer in Florida was always long, stickily hot, full of mosquitoes and no-see-ums; stir in the constant, often alcohol-fueled misery of Jerzy Grabowski, and it was almost unbearable.

The letters from Brenda would arrive, full of bubbly news and always closing with love for Gloria, and as welcome as they were, they seemed to underscore that summers were everyone else's time, but not hers. Even her siblings seemed better able to wrangle slivers of freedom, but Gloria felt trapped, fearful of Jerzy's temper and afraid to leave her mother alone.

And today, Gloria thought, wiping the sweat off her forehead with the back of her gardening glove, didn't seem much different. She rested her hands on her thighs, kneeling on the gardening mat, and squinted up; it was only 9:00 a.m., but the sun seemed so high in the sky, the shadows shortening, the birds already growing quiet from the heat. She had hoped to get some weeding done before it was too hot but of course, in late July in Florida, no time of day seemed not "too hot" to be doing outdoor work.

The twins were at vacation Bible school. Rachel was in Ireland with Aidan. Bob was going to be at work until lunchtime, and then he'd be immersed in his fishing equipment. Alexa was taking a bird class online and a painting class. Matt and Tim were busy with end-of-quarter reports for their self-employed clients but had taken up open-water paddleboarding. Tim was a surfer and found it relaxing, while Matt kept falling off. Kevin and Veronica were on vacation with Bobby and Gina, doing the Orlando parks before the new baby arrived and things would be complicated.

Gloria struggled up to her feet, slowly unfolding her legs and shaking her head. She removed her gloves, tucked them into her apron pocket, and flicked a mosquito off her arm. She picked up the gardening mat and left it beside the back door. She'd be out again tomorrow morning—better to just pace herself.

She sat in the shade and thought about those lazy, quiet talks with her mother and wiped at one cheek. For some reason today felt very much like almost every day of summer vacation, all those twelve long years of school, until her mother launched her secret plan to help Gloria escape to college. Everyone else was off having fun; everyone else was free. Meanwhile, here she was, stuck here, only there was no Nora to gently make things just a little softer, a little better.

"I wonder," she mused aloud, "what Momma would think of all this."

Oh, Gloria, darling, I think you know.

Gloria startled; the thought had popped into her head almost as if her mother were there, sitting with her in the flesh, speaking to her. She shook her head, hard. Momma's voice, in her head, clear as day. It must be the heat, Gloria thought, pressing her lips together. Just imagining things.

But Gloria, darling, you remember.

Remember? Remember what, Gloria wondered. She closed her eyes and leaned her head back. Memories popped up. Momma sending her out of the house on errands to the library with a few coins for a chocolate bar. "Have a little fun, Gloria." Momma wrangling a sleepover at Brenda's house and whispering, "Go have fun, Gloria; a good friend is golden." The way Momma would hug her when she came home from one of the long summer bicycle rides despite Gloria's sweatiness, kiss her forehead and whisper, "Doesn't it feel good to be free, Gloria?" The images came, over and over.

Gloria opened her eyes and looked around the yard, at the half-weeded flower bed, the little gardening implements still lying in the grass. The Adirondack chairs, the table between them with the candle that was supposed to repel mosquitoes, the birdhouse that Matt and Tim had carefully hung within easy sight of her kitchen window: her beautiful backyard. She tried not to tick off the list of tasks that needed doing as she hoisted herself up and made her way into the house. She wondered why she felt so tired.

The house was cool and dry, and Gloria gave a silent prayer of thanks for air conditioning. She had a drink of water, and then refilled the glass to take into the living room. Perhaps she would sit, just for a moment, and rest before she began vacuuming.

She sat down and her eyes landed on a pile of newspapers and magazines. She sighed and began shuffling through them, making piles: recycle, donate to the library, keep for now. She lifted a brochure on Favorite Fishing Spots on the Central Atlantic Coast, sighed, and, after a moment's hesitation, put it in the keep for now pile. She put the recycling into the garage, the donations into the canvas bag that hung in the foyer, waiting to go to the library with the borrowed books and donations. Coming back into the living room, she emptied the trash can next to Bob's chair, frowned, and put the remote back into the basket on the coffee table, then plumped up the toss pillows on the couch.

An hour later, she was still neatening and had not yet gotten to vacuuming. Somehow one little task led to another. She retrieved her now room temperature water from the living room and took a few sips. *How the time goes*, Gloria thought, glancing at the clock. *Before you know it, Bob will be home and I'll have to get lunch ready.*

The phone rang, startling Gloria. She checked the number: Brenda Neumueller, the former Brenda Shimski.

"Brenda! I was just thinking of you."

"And I was thinking about you, so here we are! How are you?"

"Fine," Gloria said, a little quickly. "And you? How are you?"

"Very well," Brenda replied. "Everyone's healthy. How's Bob's recovery going?"

Gloria sighed. "Officially, he's fine—a few aches and pains, but to tell the truth, he had those beforehand. He's working part-time, enjoying it, and doing a lot of fishing."

"Praise God!" Brenda paused, then said, "And you? What about you?"

"I'm fine. A bit worried, of course."

"No, I meant you. How *are* you, what are you doing these days?"

"Oh, you know. I keep busy. There's always something to do."

Gloria settled into a kitchen chair and they got caught up, as if it hadn't been just a week or two since their last chat. She laughed aloud as Brenda described the shenanigans of her college students: the woman who wanted credit for a missed test because she was protesting a school board decision three towns away that concerned whether there should be chocolate milk available in the cafeterias; the man who turned in the same paper his wife had turned in two semesters ago, remembering to change the student's name but forgetting to change the professor's name and the date on the cover page—as if the anti-plagiarism software wouldn't have found the problem, anyway. They chuckled over Marta and Sean's ideas on what Kevin and Veronica should name the next baby, and agreed that time was passing far too quickly.

"Which brings me to the reason for my call," Brenda said. "Marty's got a conference in two weeks; he'll be gone for a solid week and I'll be off. So why don't you come up here and we'll have a nice, long girls' vacation? Go to a museum, walk around the city, maybe spend some time seeing some historical places and walking the coast?"

"Oh, Brenda, I just couldn't," Gloria began, when to her surprise Bob's voice piped in.

"Whatever Brenda's asking, yes, you can." He closed the door behind him. "Brenda! Hello!" he said, louder, so Brenda could hear.

"Tell Bob I said hi! Looking forward to seeing him when we're down to visit my parents in November," Brenda replied. "So, Bob says yes."

"I can't possibly come to Boston for a week. I have things to do."

"Which can wait," Bob and Brenda said in unison, nearly 1,400 hundred miles apart.

Gloria sighed, and then her mother's face flashed in memory. "Well, what are we talking about?"

"I've got a ton of air miles, so if it's okay, I'll just use a few of them to set you up. I think I can get a direct flight." There was a pause. "Okay, I'm looking at it. How about a nine a.m. flight two weeks from tomorrow up, and then a week later home?"

"I'll check with Bob."

"Whatever it is, is fine," Bob announced.

"What about the twins? In two weeks?"

Bob glanced at the calendar. "They start school in fifteen days. Go, Gloria."

"I heard that," Brenda said. "So, what do you say?"

"Veronica's pregnant. I can't possibly leave."

"She's not due until November. Go, Gloria."

"I heard that, too." Brenda's smile came through the phone. "Gloria?"

"Yes," Gloria said with a sigh.

Brenda laughed. "Oh, Gloria! You need to have fun, get out, get some fresh air. I'll have the bicycles ready."

"I'm a bit rusty."

"Well, nothing heroic—just some easy rides with the wind in our hair. Just like the old days."

Gloria nodded slowly. "Like the old days." She paused and said, "Thanks, Brenda—I'm really looking forward to seeing you."

"And I you," Brenda said happily. "Give my love to Bob and the kids, and thank Bob for backing me up. Pinky promise, I didn't rope him into this in advance."

"Love to Marty and all," Gloria replied. Putting the phone down, she looked up at Bob, who was making sandwiches. He brought the plates over, and sat down with her.

Bob put a hand on hers, grinning. "See, honey? I can make lunch. I won't starve, Rachel will be back, the twins will be in school—and you can go have a little change of scenery with Brenda. I can't imagine better medicine for you."

"I don't need medicine," Gloria grumbled, but Bob just grinned, shrugged, and folded his hands for grace.

Chapter 28

Gloria felt as if she had always been more than a little in awe of Brenda Shimski. She was so little and curvy and sweet-tempered, and yet she just did what she thought was right no matter what anyone else thought. Just thinking about Brenda's life amazed Gloria.

Brenda Shimski had gone away to study chemistry, and married Martin Neumueller, a math major, at the end of her sophomore year. To her parents' mixed relief and dismay, she had stayed in college, having a baby during Christmas break of her senior year, and then another at the end of her master's program, and a third two months after wrapping up her dissertation. Marty, meanwhile, had likewise finished up his doctorate, moving into the rapidly expanding field of information technologies, and the two of them settled outside of Boston, where she could teach and he worked in the corporate world. They first lived in an apartment too small for them, and then found a house in a small town that was, they agreed, perfect.

It was, of course, far from perfect. It had begun its life as a small Cape Cod, and the first three owners had each added to it in some way or another, giving it the appearance of a small house, an even smaller house, and a random square add-on all jammed together. Brenda had taken pen to napkin while they were out for pizza with the children and convinced Marty that, as the house needed a new roof anyway, they could extend the roof, build a wraparound porch, and turn the strange little square add-on in the back into a sun room, to be a screened-in room in the summer. Marty agreed. The oldest child, then eight, a girl named Alicia, had announced plans for a bench swing on the porch and the next child, Aaron, had asked if there would be a fence so they could have a dog. Baby Artie, who was two, began chanting about dogs, and the deal was basically sealed.

They had now lived in the house for thirty years. It surprised Gloria, as she thought about it, that she had not actually ever seen Brenda's home in person. Brenda had dutifully come to Florida to see her parents at least twice a year, with the visit in the summer being a couple of weeks long, and her parents had occasionally flown north, but except for Brenda's visits south, Gloria had not seen her. Brenda and Marty had urged them to come up, to enjoy the beautiful fall weather or the summer breezes, or even for a peek at the snow, but somehow it just never worked out.

Gloria put her hands on her hips and surveyed the piles of clothing, and then glared at her small carry-on case. Yes, it was only a week, but still; it seemed she should take more. *Just in case. It isn't as if I can just borrow something from Brenda.* Brenda was not even up to Gloria's shoulder.

"Agonizing over the packing?" Bob inquired, leaning against the doorway. "It's just a quick week."

"Well, I don't know. You can't be too careful. It's good to have extra, just in case."

"In case what? You suddenly start spilling things on yourself? Don't Brenda and Marty have a washer and dryer?"

Gloria sighed, rolling her eyes. "You don't understand."

"I don't," Bob agreed mildly. "I'd bring enough for four days and figure a load of wash one night would take care of things."

Gloria sighed and pressed her lips together, hard. She started sorting things into different piles. Then she arranged them again. She unfolded a top and stared at it, and then glanced at the pants she'd selected. She wondered what to do about shoes.

An hour later she was sitting disconsolately on the edge of the bed, surrounded by stacks of laundry. She felt foolish. It seemed that packing for a few days for a friendly visit shouldn't be so hard. She wished Rachel were here. She sighed. Rachel had rolled a few changes of clothes tightly and wedged it all into a backpack. When Gloria had protested that Rachel was not sufficiently prepared, Rachel had said, "It's all very casual and if I need anything, I'll get it there. Everything goes with everything else, so it's fine. Mom, really. It's no big deal and this way I'm not worried about my suitcase ending up lost."

Gloria sighed, stood up, put four tops, three bottoms, a sweater, a nightgown, underwear, and some socks into the carry-on, tucked in a book and spare reading glasses, sighed, and shut the case. She wheeled it out to the foyer.

"All set?" Bob looked up from his book.

Gloria shook her head, frowning. "No, I'm sure I'm not. But I'm hopeful that if I put it here, I won't be tempted to do it all over again."

Bob glanced at the clock. "Honey. It's been two hours. You spent two hours putting what? A few clothes into a suitcase. It's Massachusetts, not the ends of the earth. Why don't you come sit down and read a bit? Relax before supper?"

"Relax? I don't have time for that. I have things to do," Gloria huffed, then bustled into the kitchen. She wiped off the clean counter and carefully aligned the canisters. She checked to see if the trash needed to be taken out; it did not. She wiped off the front of the refrigerator, removing the various magnets and carefully replacing them and all the reminders.

The day of departure, Gloria was up early, anxious, fretting about getting to the airport on time. Bob was not worried at all; Gloria wondered if he had ever even heard of rush hour. Bob finally acquiesced to leaving for the half-hour drive four hours before her flight. Gloria was sure she heard him say, "Whew," softly after she stepped out of the car at the curb, just before she slammed the car door.

It had been a few years since Gloria had flown anywhere. She went to the security area, fumbled for her boarding pass and driver's license. She noticed people showing their phones instead of paper and made a mental note to ask Brenda about this. She made an effort to not frown during the security checkpoint process. She waited anxiously for her carry-on to pop out of the X-ray machine and then her purse with the phone sitting next to it. Everything came through, and she clumsily gathered her possessions and made her way out of the security area. She then realized she had three hours until departure.

She filled the empty reusable water bottle Rachel had insisted she bring and, when she went to buy coffee, understood why the reusable water bottle was a good idea. Never mind concern about one more plastic bottle ruining the environment—airport prices were outrageous. Gloria's lips pressed tight and her eyebrows flared. She was, however, a prisoner and thus her options were limited. She bought a very expensive and, she had to admit, begrudgingly, very delicious large raspberry mocha coffee with whipped cream, and settled in to enjoy it and her book.

"How is it?"

Gloria sighed and lifted her face. The speaker was sitting next to her. Gloria noted with annoyance there were empty seats available and wondered why this person had chosen to sit, well, practically on top of her, when there were other options. It was a youngish woman, perhaps Rachel's age. She had strawberry-blonde hair, a spattering of freckles, amber eyes and, Gloria noticed, two bright-green streaks painted into one side of her hair.

"The book," the woman clarified. "I've heard the author interviewed and she sounded quite interesting. How's the book?"

"I've hardly started," Gloria said. She gave a benevolent smile. At least, if she were going to be crowded by strangers, it was a bookish one. Although there were those green streaks, she thought, but added, "It seems quite interesting. Draws you right in from the first page."

The woman leaned back with satisfaction. "Oh, good! It's on my list, so I'm glad that it will be a good one."

"I hope you enjoy it," Gloria said, nodding, and went back to the book. Reading, however, was not to be.

"Are you going up to Boston, too?" asked the woman.

"Yes," Gloria replied.

"I'm going up to visit my nana," the woman said, and paused. She turned to look at Gloria. "I'm Becky, by the way."

Begrudgingly, Gloria responded, "Gloria. Nice to meet you."

"Oh, that's a lovely name. Like Christmas Eve," Becky sighed. Gloria thought that was an unusual thing to say. "Angel songs. How nice to be named after angel songs."

It had not occurred to Gloria that she had been named after angel songs. She nodded thoughtfully. "Your nana?"

"Yes," Becky said. "She lives outside of Boston."

"Is she alone?"

"Oh, no," Becky said, firmly. "She lives in a retirement community, and she has her own place. She's got lots of friends and a gentleman friend she describes as her 'beau,' but I think it's just a friendly companionship thing. She's very busy."

"Well, it's good to be active," Gloria said approvingly. "I imagine she's rather ... elderly, after all."

"Oh, she's seventy-five," Becky said. "And you can't believe the kerfuffle about my not being married yet. I mean, I'm twenty-five and yeah, there's a guy ..."

Not so very elderly for such a grownup grandchild, Gloria thought to herself. "And the guy?"

"He's wrapping up medical school and then we're getting married," Becky said. "He won't know where he's settling down until then, and I'm an RN, I can get a job just about anywhere, so I'm staying close to family until we know where Frankie will be doing his residency."

"That sounds very smart," Gloria said approvingly. "You're quite an accomplished young woman and have a very clear plan."

"Oh, yes," Becky said happily. "We've agreed to a very small wedding—just the immediate families and a few friends, and we have the children's names picked out. We've talked about *everything*."

Everything, Gloria thought, barely containing an eye roll. *Only someone as young as twenty-five could imagine they'd talked of everything.*

"You probably think that's very naïve," Becky said, "and I suppose it does sound like it. But Frankie and I decided early to get married and we've really worked at having the good conversations. You know, about values and how we'll do charitable giving and volunteering and raising the kids, and whether or not to have them in religious school. You know, everything."

"That sounds remarkably prudent," Gloria admitted.

"But not good enough for Nana." Becky sighed and turned her coffee cup around in her hands a few times, staring down into the swirl of cream and coffee. She looked straight at Gloria. "I love my nana, but you know, unless it's her idea, it's a bad idea. She's just critical of almost everything. I love her so much, I just want her to approve of what I'm doing. Being a nurse, working in pediatrics, marrying a good man, having a plan, being conservative with our money so we can live simply without working too hard and have time to spare for what matters."

"I'm sure she must be very proud of you," Gloria said. She felt sorry for this young woman, clearly someone who loved her grandmother and was living what seemed to be an exemplary life.

"I hope so," Becky said. She shook her head. "She focuses on whatever she thinks is wrong. Like this." She ran the fingers of one hand through her hair, to show off the green streaks. "Yeah, I know. It looks dopey. But we had a kind of a pep rally, for the kids. In the ward." She paused. "I work with the kids with cancer. We had, you know, some clowns. One made balloon animals. Someone did a little facepainting. They had put makeup on their surgical masks so they could be clowns for the kids. I let one of them do this wash-out green dye thing to my hair, just to join in the fun. And they painted a tiger face on me. To cheer up the kids. Here—I'll show you." She poked at her phone, held it up: There she was, with white, orange, and black makeup and a tiger's snoot painted over the surgical mask.

"Very impressive facepainting," Gloria commented.

"But Nana." Becky paused, shaking her head. "She won't even give me a chance to explain. She'll just purse up her lips"—Becky made a face as if she had just sucked on a lemon—"and then say, 'Oh, I see you've been *experimenting*.' As if that was a terrible thing."

"That's so sad, dear," Gloria said sincerely. How dreadful, she thought, to have such good actions preemptively misunderstood and criticized. She shook her head in disapproval at this hectoring grandmother.

"Thanks for listening," Becky said sincerely. "I'm sorry to have dumped that on you. I guess I'm just a little nervous about the visit. You know, will we have any fun or will she just criticize and try to fix me all weekend?"

"Understandable." Gloria nodded. She closed her book and rested her hands on it. Perhaps this young person needed a friendly ear. She thought it would be prudent to appear open to hearing more. Becky did not need much encouragement.

"It's funny, but I think Nana's been like this all along," Becky said. "I mean, Dad laughs at me complaining. He says, you should have seen what she was like as a mother! I can't imagine what that would be like, she's been hard enough on me as a grandmother. And grandparents are supposed to be the fun ones! Enjoy them and hand them back, you know? That's what they say."

"How was she all along?" Gloria asked.

"You know. Everything orchestrated. Planned perfectly. Sometimes it was great," she emphasized. "I appreciate that talent! You should have seen her take over the First Communion party—everything perfect. And the time we went on a train ride through the Rockies—she had the whole thing planned. It was magical. But other times ..." Becky paused. "Other times, it's like, you can't do anything right. Not like that, dear. Becky, don't you think you ought to try doing it this way? Stand up straight. Stop playing with your hair. Haven't you considered—whatever. And she always thinks she knows what's best for everyone. *All the time.*" Becky heaved her biggest sigh thus far.

Gloria felt a little warm. She slipped out of her jacket. "All the time," she repeated.

Becky shook her head. "I love my nana. Like I said, she can be wonderful. But she never lets up! It's always a management project." She grinned mischievously. "And of course she's on the HOA! Ha, I bet they regret the day they invited the new lady to join the board."

Gloria pressed her lips together hard.

"Maybe," Becky said with a little sarcasm, "she's using up all her bossiness running the HOA and she'll give me a break."

"That would be nice," Gloria said. "It sounds as if you have your life very well together, especially for such a young person."

"Oh, not so young. I'm twenty-five," Becky restated. "I mean, Nana was married by twenty. So was Mom. Nana's afraid Frankie's going to dump me for a younger model as soon as he's an MD."

"Oh, leave you on the shelf, so to speak," Gloria said.

"Yes! Her words exactly," Becky said warmly. "I knew looking at you, you'd be an understanding person." She put a hand on Gloria's forearm. "I really appreciate you listening. Thank you!"

"You are very welcome," Gloria said, and wondered why her head was starting to ache. She was relieved when they boarded and it turned out that Becky was sitting several rows ahead of her. Gloria leaned her head on the cool of the window, closed her eyes, and pretended to be asleep. She didn't want to hear any more uncomfortable stories about disapproving grandmothers.

Chapter 29

"I'm so glad you were able to make the trip." Brenda had one hand on the wheel and the other lazily draped on the edge of the door. She had the windows and the top down on her little powder-blue convertible while they drove to her home from the airport. She glanced at Gloria, grinned, and said, "Don't worry, Gloria, I know how to drive."

"Of course." But Gloria did not approve of the casual hand at four o'clock on the wheel. She deliberately tried to relax her eyebrows.

"We're going to have such a great visit," Brenda asserted. "I can't believe you've never been up here before! I'll take you on a tour of the house and then later we can decide if we want a nice walk or to ride bicycles down on the path near the water." She switched driving hands to shift as they merged with traffic. "It's always a few degrees cooler there, and there are a lot of shade trees along the path."

"Nice."

"How lucky that Marty's away and Bob is all recovered and can spare you for a few days." Brenda changed her window hand to eight o'clock and rested her shifting hand lazily on her right leg. Gloria kept trying to look forward but Brenda's low-key attitude toward driving was distressing.

"Well, I'm not sure I'd call Bob all recovered," Gloria began.

"Oh, Gloria! He's fine. He's getting around. Before you know it, he'll be flying up to meet Joe—consider yourself blessed. He's a true miracle, walking around."

"Well, yes," Gloria admitted. "I'll grant you that."

Brenda glanced sideways at her; Gloria caught her glance behind the sunglasses. Brenda's eyes were crinkled up in a smile. "Okay—here's a deal. Let's have fun, okay? Not just talk family stuff. Whatever it is. Let's laugh and be Gloria and Brenda—best friends for always."

"That sounds lovely, dear," Gloria said, and turned her head to watch the New England scenery. "It's very pretty here in summer. I suppose I only ever see tourist-y autumn pictures, or snow photos."

"It's always beautiful in its own way," Brenda agreed. "You should see the spring! The lilacs and the fruit trees. The woods are full of white and pink and pale purple and the mistiest yellow-greens."

"Beautiful," Gloria said quietly. She wondered what it would be like, to live in a place that changed so much. Florida had its seasons, something the residents knew but visitors did not always perceive, but the … violence, she supposed, yes, the violence of these seasonal changes—as if it were a different place entirely, all the way to the drastic differences in the hours of light and darkness. *No wonder people went a bit batty*, she thought, *when you consider nature's always going crazy and chaotic in some new way.*

"I think you'd enjoy seeing it." Brenda smiled. "But I don't know if you'd like living here in it." She slowed as they exited the interstate into suburban traffic. "You know how you hate change."

"Oh, Brenda! I don't think that's fair."

Brenda shrugged. "Well, fair or not, it's true. Oh, Gloria! Remember how upset you'd get at the end of each school year, and then again when school started, because we had to change classrooms and teachers? You were always complaining that the kids should stay in the same room until eighth grade and the grownups should move because there was only one of them."

"You have to admit, as a suggestion, it does make sense."

"No argument on that. At least until everyone but me outgrew the desks. But it's an example of your resistance to change."

"Hmm."

"You know what I mean. Sort of the opposite of Vicky Stetson. Remember her?"

"Oh, goodness, Vicky! How could I forget?"

"Remember that time Vicky decided to be the first to iron her hair and she set the temperature too high and had to get a pixie haircut?"

Gloria chuckled, shaking her head. "Oh, yes! Who could forget all that beautiful, long, black hair turned into that little elfin style?"

"Or when she cut up her jeans to put in inserts to make them super-wide bell-bottoms and the seam split all the way up both legs before the dance was half over?"

"And she didn't care! She just kept dancing with her legs showing!"

"But only from the knee to the hip—the bell panels stayed in place." Brenda snorted with laughter. "And course, she had a perfect tan." She turned onto a side street. "All right! We're almost home." She pointed off to the right. "That property—the kind of wild looking one? That's a goat sanctuary."

"I see chickens."

"Oh, of course! Yes, the chickens. But mostly it's about goats who were injured somewhere or rescued from religious ceremonies, shall we say."

"You've got to be kidding."

"Wish I was." Brenda sighed. "Of course, some of them are pets that people couldn't handle. Everyone loves goats but they are smart, very mischievous, and a ton of work. So they send them here."

"Well, that's understandable."

"Yes." They slowed and Brenda turned into the driveway. "Here we are! Home sweet home!"

Gloria slowly got out of the car. Brenda put up the roof and rolled up the windows, and then hopped out to retrieve Gloria's bag from the trunk. Gloria gazed at the house; the original little Cape Cod was only discernible if you knew the history. The roofline had been altered, as Brenda had sketched so many years ago, to encompass all the changes. The wraparound porch was deep and inviting; boxes popping with warm-toned marigolds hung on the porch railing; hanging baskets were dripping with ivy; casually arranged seating was scattered into conversation groups. The grass was a bit overgrown, and shrubs framed the short steps to the porch and the dark-red door. The house was white; the shutters were also dark red. Thick, wild-looking forsythia and azaleas lined the fence along the property line, and a few pine trees stood in the front yard, towering over the house.

"It's good rabbitat," Brenda commented.

"Sorry?"

Brenda nodded toward the fence. "The bushes are a little crazy. And we let the grass get a little high, especially there. Helps the bunnies have places to hide from predators."

"Ah."

"How do you like the house?" Brenda asked.

"It's beautiful," Gloria said.

"Well, let's get inside and I'll show you the rest of it!"

The inside of the house was as inviting and comfortable as the outside. And like the outside, Gloria noticed, it was a little unkempt, perhaps. It occurred to her that in that regard Brenda was a bit like Alexa. They were the kind of women who actually thought toss pillows were supposed to be tossed at the sofa or chair, and who flung off a cozy shawl and let it droop over the back of the sofa. The refrigerator was a riot of magnets and pictures, with three separate list pads on the side.

Brenda, meanwhile, was heading down the hall. "The guest room is down this way," she said over her shoulder. "It's quiet and convenient to the bathroom, which is here." She nodded to the side. She pushed the door open and dragged the suitcase in. "Here you are!"

Gloria stepped in. The room was beautiful. It was in a corner of the back of the house, with a window overlooking the side porch and the backyard. The bed was made up with a light-weight quilt in greens and lilacs; the walls were the softest pale olive green. The furniture was light-colored and simple: a writing desk and chair, a chest of drawers, a nightstand on each side of the bed with a small lamp. There was another lamp on the desk. Photos of mountain scenery had been hung on the walls, and a cross sat over the head of the bed. "It's a lovely room, Brenda."

"Thanks," Brenda said. "I like it! So, do you need to rest a few? Change?"

"Maybe after the rest of the tour," Gloria said. "Then a little relaxation would be nice."

The rest of the house made for a short tour: Brenda and Marty's room on the other side of the living/dining room, two bedrooms and a bathroom upstairs. "Wait 'til you see what we've done upstairs!" Brenda chortled. "The kids were beside themselves but, hey, we have to use our house! And we find space for everyone when they visit."

She was taking the steps two at a time. Gloria puffed behind. Brenda stood at the left door. "So, this room was the boys' bedroom. And then Artie's after Aaron left for college." She pushed the door open. Any trace of a child's bedroom had disappeared; the room was painted a soft cream color and two walls were lined with bookshelves. Warm wood blinds let in sunlight filtered by pine trees. A worn tapestry carpet, two upholstered chairs in front of the bookshelves, each with a gooseneck floor lamp, and two desks with chairs completed the room. Except for the family photos that were tucked around and in front of books, it could have been any scholar's library.

"It's lovely, dear." Gloria pressed her lips together. "But the boys. Don't they feel hurt that—?"

"That Marty and I know they don't live here anymore?" Brenda laughed up at Gloria. "No, no, they're pretty well adjusted to us being onto the facts."

"Still," Gloria said.

"Well, wait until you see Alicia's old room!"

Gloria was not sure she wanted to see Alicia's old room, but Brenda bounced across the hall and flung open the door. The room was flooded with light; it had windows on three sides and the soft white walls added to the brightness. There was a small exercise bicycle and yoga mat along one side, with some weights and bands on the floor. On the other side were shelves and cabinets, corkboard on the walls covered with papers, and an easel. Gloria felt a bit lightheaded.

"Gloria? Are you okay?"

"Of course, dear. Just surprised." Gloria ranged her glance around the room again, slowly. "I suppose I wasn't expecting ... this." She flapped her arms helplessly.

Brenda shrugged. "Well, you know. You turn older and it's time to go for the gusto. I mean, if not now, when?"

"When." Gloria repeated. She shook her head slowly. *Another artist! No wonder the crazy big sunglasses, the apparently tossed toss pillows, the reading shawls thrown recklessly where they were used.* She started feeling a bit shaky inside, as if some sort of danger were present.

"I've always loved art! You know that. Oh, and wait until you see the garage! Marty's got a whole workshop in there. He's taken up woodworking. He made all the shelves in the library. That's why we don't use the garage as a garage, actually. In the winter we put up a little pop-up to shelter the cars a bit but otherwise, well, the house is for using!" Brenda went over to the easel. "So, what do you think?"

It was a painting early in the process; the drawing underneath was visible under a thin layer of pale brown. Gloria lowered her brows.

"It's got that sienna tint to give the next colors a bit of depth," Brenda explained. "It's going to be a late autumn scene and I want warmth."

"I see," Gloria said, but she knew she did not. "I'll look forward to seeing more, dear, but I'm terribly tired from the trip."

"I can imagine!" Brenda said sympathetically. "Let's get you back to your room. Can I make you tea? Coffee? A little snack?"

"I think," Gloria said, "I'd like to just unwind for a little while and perhaps have lunch in about, say, an hour or so? Would that be too late?"

"Too late? Of course not," Brenda tossed over her shoulder as they headed downstairs. "We're on vacation time! No hard and fast rules."

Gloria pressed her lips together hard, nodded, and said, "Thanks so much, dear! I'll be out soon."

It wasn't soon, actually; Gloria had lain down on the inviting bed and when she awoke the shadows had shifted quite a bit. She sat up drowsily and checked her watch; it was almost three o'clock! She started to get up quickly, sat down heavily, sighed, and stood up slowly.

She was smoothing her hair as she opened the door and headed out to apologize to Brenda.

She found Brenda on the porch swing, feet up, lemonade on the table next to her and a book propped up against the pillow in her lap. Brenda smiled and swung her feet down to the porch when Gloria stepped outside. "Gloria! Feeling better?"

"I'm so sorry," Gloria began.

"Sorry? For what? Clearly you needed a nap! Marty can always sleep on planes—time travel, he calls it—but I never can. I'm always exhausted when we land."

"But it's so late! You must be starving."

Brenda laughed and patted her belly as she stood up. "Oh, Gloria! As long as you've known me, you know that I've never been in imminent danger of starving! But you're probably famished and I could definitely eat. Let's go inside."

After a couple of glasses of iced tea, some crackers, cheese, and sliced apples, Gloria felt much more like herself. She nodded approvingly at the cheerful kitchen: the herb plants on the windowsill, the apron hung at the ready on a hook near the door. They chatted about the flight; Gloria told Brenda about the young nurse at the airport with green hair and a disapproving nana.

"What a sweet girl," Brenda mused. "How nice that you had someone like that sit next to you."

"I suppose," Gloria said slowly. She pursed her lips. "To tell the truth, I was quite relieved that she wasn't next to me on the plane."

"Oh?"

"I just didn't want to hear about her negative grandmother."

"I can see that."

"What's that supposed to mean?"

Brenda looked perplexed. "Why, just what it means. Who wants to hear someone gripe for three hours?"

"Oh," Gloria sighed and swirled her glass, watching the shrinking ice cubes tumble in the iced tea. "I guess I thought you were talking about me."

"About you?"

Gloria pressed her lips together. "My family, and even Alexa and Joe, and Miss Arlene next door—everyone's been on me lately! Since, well, a couple of months after Bob's accident. That I'm a concern. A problem."

Brenda sighed and put her hand on Gloria's. "Oh, honey! I'm sorry. I didn't know." She shook her head. "What's been going on?"

Gloria frowned. She gazed at Brenda's sweet, concerned face, her brows drawn together in concern. "I'd rather not talk about it now. I think now we should have a little fun. That's what I'm here for!"

"Of course. But at some point, Gloria, we should talk." Brenda paused and gave Gloria's hand a squeeze. "A real talk. Your life and mine. Like we haven't for a long, long, time."

"Agreed," Gloria said. "So how about a nice long walk? And maybe plan a morning bike ride?"

"Grab your sunglasses and walking shoes." Brenda smiled. "I can be ready in five minutes."

Chapter 30

The morning bicycle ride had been as beautiful as Brenda had promised: dappled sunlight through trees, the sun glistening on the water, the paved path wide and smooth. They'd come home, laughing and slightly sunburned despite the sunscreen, taken showers and lunched on Brenda's homemade leek-and-potato soup and some fresh fruit, and were now on the shady side of the house, feet up on the porch railing, with two glasses and a pitcher of iced tea. Gloria leaned her head back against the cushion and closed her eyes, sighing with satisfaction. She could tell, dimly, that her legs would be sore tomorrow, but a good morning walk would put things right, perhaps to that crazy goat sanctuary to pet some goats and buy some farm-fresh eggs.

"Gloria." Brenda's voice was quiet and soothing.

"Hmm?" Gloria asked lazily.

"Gloria. Let's talk."

Gloria scowled before opening her eyes and looking over at Brenda. "We've been talking. Since I got here."

Brenda had shifted to sitting cross-legged, half turned to face Gloria. She shook her head, smiling. "I mean really. Like, what's going on with you. With me." She paused. "You know. Like yesterday, you said everyone was … what, critical? Concerned?"

Gloria sighed. "Oh, it's worse than that. They orchestrated a little 'intervention,' I guess you'd call it. Over my getting upset over Bob's not taking his health seriously. I caught him eating ice cream. In the middle of the day. Out of the container."

"Was it the eating out of the container? Or the ice cream?"

Gloria shook her head. "The whole thing! He doesn't take this all seriously. I had a sort of, well, I had a bit of a tantrum."

"Oh, Gloria," Brenda said sadly. "No."

Gloria nodded guiltily, gazing past Brenda's shoulder to the tired-looking tomato plants in the back garden. "I sort of lost it, I suppose. Threw some things. Rachel came home and took pictures and called an intervention and they insisted I 'talk to someone.' So, I have. A couple of times, anyway."

Brenda looked perplexed and concerned. "Well, I'd be worried about you, too! Throwing things? At Bob?"

"Bob. The walls." Gloria felt her face growing hot. "It was a mess. I didn't realize how bad until later, when it was time to clean up."

"And? The talking to someone?"

Gloria told Brenda about the cranky Capuchin, Father Jack, and the parish counselor, poor widowed Andrea, who didn't have a family of her own. "She was a caregiver for her husband, though," Gloria remarked. Brenda nodded thoughtfully as Gloria summarized a few weeks into a few lines.

"And what's the deal?"

"What do you mean, deal?"

"Oh, Gloria. You know—what's the issue?"

Gloria shook her head. "Bob thinks I need to get the Jerzy part of me under control. Healed. Changed."

"Oh, that's harsh."

Gloria's shoulders sagged. "I don't know if it is, actually. When I think about it, yes, I do get upset when I don't get my way. However, unlike my father"—Gloria frowned—"my way tends to make a lot more sense. You can't imagine these people." She flapped her hand as if she were waving at her absent family. "It's chaos! Pure chaos! All the way down."

"Chaos?"

"Rachel's in Ireland! Chasing after some ... some Gaelic teacher!"

"The handsome man you're so fond of, whose uncle is a priest and who teaches history?"

"Well, yes."

"The one who invited her to visit his family and understand more about him as they're getting serious?"

"If you put it that way, well, yes."

"Is there another way to put it?" Brenda took a sip of tea and raised her eyebrows at Gloria. "You call it chasing but it seems like an invitation. A chance to meet his family and for them to meet this American girl he's apparently planning to marry."

"I suppose you could say so, yes." Gloria shook her head.

"And what else?"

"Bob! This fishing trip! He's an invalid."

"Is he?"

"Of course! He's diabetic," Gloria protested.

"And so am I! So are lots of people. But we do stuff." Brenda shook her head. "We live our lives."

"And he has heart problems."

"Admittedly. Is anything he's planning dangerous? To his heart? The cardiologist putting the kibosh on plans?"

"Oh, for goodness' sake! Dr. Arnold? That nut is trying to wangle an invitation to join them when they're in New England this fall!"

Brenda grinned. "That sounds like approval."

"Unfortunately, yes. One idiot encouraging another." Gloria frowned.

"And?"

"And I told you Veronica is pregnant again!"

"Yes; it's wonderful! This will be number three, right?"

Gloria stared at Brenda. Surely, she could see the trouble with this. "Veronica! The crazy photographer! The gentle parenting person!"

Brenda burst out laughing and said, "Oh, Gloria! It's a baby! Try to at least be happy about a baby!"

"Of course I'm happy." Gloria crossed her arms sullenly and realized, at Brenda's smile, that she was acting sulky. She uncrossed her arms and fussed with the hem of her sleeves. "But you know how lax she is with the children. Poor Kevin!"

"Kevin always seems happy enough when we see them," Brenda commented. "Does he seem unhappy to you?"

Gloria shook her head. "No. But you know how men are! There's something about creative women that makes them a little foolish." She clamped her lips shut as Brenda hooted with laughter.

"Well, you may be onto something there," Brenda gasped between laughs. "Marty still seems to like me well enough."

Gloria grimaced and said, "I'm sorry," but Brenda shook her head, laughing.

"No harm, no foul, Gloria." She took a shuddering breath and said, "Okay. Rachel's meeting Aidan's family. Bob's well enough to go fishing and his heart doc is all for it. Kevin and Veronica are still crazy about one another despite two kids and a third on the way."

Gloria nodded slowly. "I live in fear of another crisis. Not just for whatever the crisis is but because every crisis brings another baby. Kevin and Veronica," she said disapprovingly, "seem to have only one way to deal with stress." Brenda burst into another round of laughter, and finally Gloria could not help herself; she laughed, reluctantly, at her own description of her son's apparently happy marriage.

Brenda lifted one hand in surrender. "Gloria, seriously. I'm sorry … it's just—" More giggles burbled out. "It's just, you have a way of describing things sometimes that just tickles me."

Gloria gazed at Brenda with affection. Here was someone who would understand all of it. "I knew you'd understand," she said warmly. She hesitated. "There's more, of course. I probably mentioned on the phone that Cody's been spending a lot of time with Alexa's daughter, Sandy?"

"Right."

"Well, apparently, they're quite serious. And I have my concerns." She hesitated. "And I'm afraid I kind of blurted them out. To Alexa."

"Oh, gosh." Brenda grimaced. "How did that go?"

"About as badly as it could." Gloria frowned, shaking her head and closing her eyes, remembering the look on Alexa's face when Gloria had asked if she'd ever met her own daughter. "I'm afraid I insulted Sandy. Terribly." She sighed. "And of course Bob was on Alexa's side. And made me apologize."

"Wouldn't you have, otherwise?"

"I guess," Gloria said, and they both knew it was not entirely true. "I guess," she repeated, "I'd never thought about the whole thing from Alexa's side."

"Meaning?"

Gloria rubbed her temples. "I mean that Cody isn't exactly perfect on paper, as they say. He's a mess on paper—divorced. No annulment yet. A couple of kids. A wacky ex-wife who is in and out. I mean, well. Yes. On paper, he's definitely getting the better end of the bargain."

"That had to be hard to hear," Brenda said sympathetically. "I know you've always seen Rachel and Sandy as sort of the little immature girls in the family. While Cody—"

"Yes, Cody's wonderful. And I worry because Sandy is, well, Sandy. Flaky. A little centrifuge of enthusiasm."

"Sounds fun," Brenda said. "Is she kind? Happy?"

"Yes," Gloria replied reluctantly. "Both. Unflaggingly so."

"Then Cody should be very happy. Kindness and a happy disposition—that makes for a good life partner."

"Of course," Gloria said flatly. "Of course, you're right."

Brenda reached out to touch Gloria's arm. "Have you made things right? Really right? With Alexa?"

"We had breakfast and I apologized, and she's acted pretty typically since," Gloria said slowly. "I suppose things are okay."

"That's important," Brenda said firmly. "I'm glad." She gave Gloria's arm a gentle squeeze and leaned back, took a sip of iced tea and sighed. "So, that really is a lot to have going on."

Gloria sighed, nodded, and gave Brenda a tight smile. "I knew you'd understand," she said wearily. "There really has been a lot to handle. It feels very—" She paused. "Unsettling? I don't like it." She smoothed the rumpled khaki of her shorts. "Things should be neat. Orderly. Predictable." She lowered her brows.

Brenda chuckled. "When has life ever been orderly and predictable?"

Gloria looked at her sideways and felt herself relax just a little bit. Somehow, the same words just felt different coming from Brenda.

"You're right, dear. When I think about it, it seems that keeping things orderly is always an uphill battle."

"Which is why I do so little of it." Brenda stretched out her legs, flexing her feet and pointing her toes. "I like just a little chaos. Keeps things interesting."

"Interesting!"

"Sure." Brenda shrugged. "I can't control anything—at best I have some influence. So why make myself crazy?"

"Crazy," Gloria repeated quietly, nodding at the fence.

"Sure." Brenda clasped her hands behind her head. "Can you imagine? Trying to manage Marty's crazy work schedule and the mess in the garage? Keeping up with Alicia's latest 'thing' or trying to figure out *exactly* what Aaron does for a living or what Artie's next adventure will be?"

Gloria glanced at her, eyebrows raised in question.

"Artie's latest thing is using all his time off going on small-group adventure tours. Last year it was hiking up to Machu Picchu, hiking and camping in Utah, Scotland and, oh, what else? Oh, yes—the jungle tours in Belize."

Gloria frowned, lips pressed together. "That sounds risky."

Brenda nodded. "Yes. Some of it's downright dangerous." She shrugged. "But what can I do? He's an adult. He's enjoying his life and besides that, in the course of all this, I think he's met a woman who can keep up with him. Maybe out lap him, to tell the truth."

"Oh?"

Brenda smiled broadly. "We met her this past spring. She's a peds nurse in Montreal—taking advantage of her time off to get as far away from work as possible."

"Interesting," Gloria said. "That girl I met in the airport was a pediatric nurse."

"Yes, you mentioned that," Brenda said. "How funny! Do you suppose it takes that kind of open, friendly personality to handle pediatrics?"

"Perhaps." Gloria sighed. "So, you just don't worry?"

"Of course I worry! I worry about all of them! Alicia's decided she only eats grass-fed beef, butter, free-range chickens and their eggs. I worry she won't get enough nutrients. Although," she said reluctantly, "she looks very healthy. And Aaron's a nuclear engineer so it can't exactly be safe. And Artie's either griping about economics students or trying to fall off a cliff on some other continent. Or on this continent." Brenda wiggled her toes. "But I can't do a thing about any of it!"

"Don't you think you should try? You know, share the wisdom of age," Gloria said and added quickly, "Our age."

"I ask questions. That seems to work better." Brenda took a sip of iced tea. "They share more if I am respectfully curious. Once I start lecturing about danger or asking why, bam! Up go the walls and I get the polite minimum info."

"Bam," Gloria repeated.

"You know what I mean," Brenda said confidently. "And you know what else? This tea isn't iced anymore."

"I guess it is kind of warm out," Gloria said, "but it's so pleasant here on your porch."

"It never gets old," Brenda agreed. "Sitting out here! Savoring the weather. The birds. The breeze." She poured herself some more tea and asked, "More for you?" She filled Gloria's glass at her nod. "You and Bob have that nice backyard! I guess you have more time to enjoy it with the kids getting bigger—less eyes-on supervision, right?"

"Right," Gloria said, nodding. She wasn't sure she was enjoying it any more often. It seemed that most of her recent memories around the backyard had been arguments and annoyances. She tracked her activities the last few days and realized she had spent a lot of time roaming the house trying to keep things orderly.

"Gloria?"

"Hmm?"

"I was asking about the yard; what you and Bob had planted for this year."

"I'm sorry, dear. I was thinking."

"And?"

"And I don't think I have been enjoying the yard. Or the plants." She rubbed her temples. "Of course, Rachel has planted some beach sunflowers which, if they make it, will just spread into an absolute mess. She says it will be good for the pollinators, the bunnies and the birds."

"I'm sure it will be." Brenda sipped her tea. "So, what have you been doing?"

"Mostly just trying to keep things orderly."

"Ah. And how's that working?"

"It takes hours." Gloria frowned. "You can't imagine!"

"Why, yes, I can. Which is why I don't." Brenda grinned. "The Board of Health hasn't nailed my door shut, and I'd rather be painting. Or visiting the goats. Or riding my bike. When I'm not at work, that is."

"Aren't you afraid it's going to get out of control?"

"The secret," Brenda said serenely, "is never having the illusion that any of it was under control in the first place. Life," she added, "is more like a cat than anything else."

Gloria frowned and shook her head at the tomato plants. "I don't like cats."

"Maybe you should get to know one or two," Brenda suggested. "They have cats at the goat sanctuary, actually—they help with the mice and rats. Maybe we should lather on the sunscreen and grab sun hats and go visit some animals, buy some fresh eggs."

"Maybe we should," Gloria said. But she felt skeptical about it now, especially those unpredictable, uncontrollable cats.

Chapter 31

"I just can't stop thinking about the trip up to see Brenda. My best friend from childhood," Gloria clarified. She leaned back against the old couch in Andrea's office, shaking her head.

"It sounds as if you packed a lot into a short visit."

Gloria nodded. She tried to focus on Andrea's tilted, curious face and ignore the fact that she was sitting cross-legged on the oversized chair, more like Marta than an elderly therapist. "Yes, we did a lot and yet nothing in particular. You know, a lot of sitting around talking. Bike rides. Visiting the goat sanctuary down the street."

"Sounds like fun."

"It was. But there's more than that." Gloria pressed her lips together and shook her head firmly. "It's just that ... oh, spending time with Brenda. She's a lot like Alexa in some ways. I don't know why, but for some reason Brenda doesn't think she needs fixing. Yes, fixing. Yet I can think of a dozen things about her that seem to need fixing."

"Such as?"

"Well." Gloria sat up straight, pursing her lips. "The living room! You know, she seems to think you're supposed to take the term 'toss pillow' seriously. They're just willy-nilly! Stacked over there so she can put her feet up! A big one on the floor to sit on. One for lumbar support in Marty's favorite chair! And the throws! She *throws the throws.*" Gloria paused. "It drives me bonkers just seeing it. But I did not"—she nodded hard, once—"straighten them out."

Andrea laughed warmly and said, "So, did you practically herniate yourself resisting the urge? To straighten up your best friend's toss pillows?"

Gloria gaped at Andrea's little scrunched-smiling face and then felt the slightest burble of laughter in her chest. She shook her head in amazement and said, "Well, that was weird."

"Yes," Andrea said, "I get that a lot. Sorry—no offense intended."

"No," Gloria protested. "I mean." She rubbed her sternum. "I had the strangest feeling! As if I had a laugh stuck! Right here."

"Cool," Andrea said.

Gloria wondered what sort of therapist pronounced things "cool." She said, "Well, I don't know. It was quite odd!"

"When do you laugh, Gloria?"

Gloria shook her head. "Sometimes I have a little chuckle at the children's antics. But generally, not very often."

"That's terrible!" Andrea looked sincere. "I'm so sorry! Well, we have to do something about that. The key to misery is having no laughter, no humor, no joy."

"I have laughter. I did," Gloria admitted, "have a bit of a chuckle about the kittens. The ones at the goat sanctuary."

"Oh?"

"It's quite odd," Gloria mused. "You know, we'd been talking. About our adult children. And Brenda said something about life being like a cat. And the next thing you know, we're at the goat sanctuary and there was a litter of kittens. About eight weeks old, the worker said. Six of them, all mish-mash colors. From one litter! And, well, of course Brenda was on the ground with them, playing, and I knelt down and the next thing you know—well, chaos."

"Chaos?"

"One on my lap! One crawling up to my shoulder and purring in my ear. Another one trying to attack the tail of the one on my shoulder! And constantly switching which one's where." Gloria shook her head.

"It sounds adorable."

"It was." Gloria began to think that it actually had been adorable, and sort of fun. And funny. She smiled. "I was surprised."

"Well, kittens will do that. A good demonstration that Brenda was right."

"Hmm?"

"That life," Andrea said, "is like a cat."

Gloria shook her head. She didn't like that expression, that life is like a cat. Cats were unpredictable. Mischievous. Sneaky, even. Soft and cuddly and then suddenly full of claws and hissing and sharp little fangs.

"Which gives me an idea for homework," Andrea mused. "Perhaps you need to go spend time with kittens and cats. No allergies, right?"

"Right," Gloria said slowly. "Homework?"

"Yes. I think, hmm. Yes—I'm suggesting you contact a friend of mine. Lisa Stark. She's the volunteer coordinator over at Bethlehem Animal Shelter. You know, the non-kill shelter. They need a lot of volunteers. See when they have room in the schedule for someone to come in and just play with the kittens."

"Play with the kittens." Gloria rubbed her forehead. "How is that volunteer work?"

"The hope is for all these kittens to find homes, so they need regular socialization. That sets them up to be good companions."

Gloria pressed her lips together. *This referring to animals as companions is annoying.* "They're just pets, for goodness' sake."

"A lot of people adopt pets because they enjoy the companionship; cats can be such affectionate animals."

"Hmm." Gloria shook her head. "Okay, then. I'll take Lisa's number and give her a call."

Chapter 32

Gloria settled into the Adirondack chair, stretched out her legs, tilted her head back and closed her eyes. The breeze felt good; the late August morning was warm, but not uncomfortably so just yet. She flexed and curled her fingers, and then drummed them against the arms of the chair. She could hear Miss Arlene's sliding door open and her speaking softly to chattering blue jays. The across-the-street neighbor was already out trimming around his driveway. Life was about as peaceful as it could be. She scratched mindlessly at a long, dotted scratch down her left forearm and then at a set of shorter scratches on the right arm. *Kittens*, she thought with a sigh. *Those wild, unpredictable little cats.*

She pressed her lips together, shaking her head. She had called Lisa, at Andrea's suggestion, and arrangements were made for her to go in the following Wednesday morning. Rachel had been almost annoyingly enthusiastic, and Bob nearly as much, although he did wonder, more than once, if this meant they'd be getting any cats? No, no, Gloria had assured him. This was some sort of therapeutic intervention, she had said, sarcastically, and Rachel had smirked and asked if the kale in the salad was organic.

There was a special room for socializing the kittens. There were three rocking chairs, two of which were occupied by women. There were mats on the floor where two other volunteers were sitting. And there were kittens, seemingly everywhere: climbing on kitty condos, up and down on stepladders, in and out of boxes. The volunteers in the chairs were Sandra and Deena; on the floor were Leeann and Phil. Leeann and Phil were veterinary medicine students. Sandra and Deena were retirees. Gloria settled into the empty rocking chair, keeping an eye on the kittens. "Don't rock hard," Deena advised. "Their little paws and tails can get caught." Gloria tried hard not to rock at all.

A small, yellow tiger kitten with blue eyes started climbing up one of her legs. She felt the small, sharp points of claws through her slacks. She startled and Phil said, "Oh, they're all pointy at first; they don't retract their claws yet when they are this small."

"Oh. How ... convenient," Gloria murmured, and kept an eye on the yellow tiger. The little tiger made it to her lap and kept climbing up. It ended up on her shoulder and proceeded to rub its little face against her neck, purring loudly. She put up a tentative hand to pet it and it purred louder, nuzzling her neck. Gloria began to relax and then, without warning, the little kitten whirled sideways, grabbed one of her fingers between its paws and bit her, hard. She yelped and brushed the kitten down to her lap, where it romped in three tight circles and then headbutted her belly, curled up in a ball, and began to purr. Gloria held a hand near it, torn between petting it and being cautious. Sandra remarked on how mercurial these little ones were; so playful.

"Playful?"

"Oh, yes, it's all play. All getting ready to be cats who can survive in a very unkind world."

"Interesting." Gloria was not sure if it was interesting. She reflected on her kindergarten classes and how quickly chaos could ensue if she turned her back for a moment. Kittens were a lot like kindergartners, she remarked, and Leeann had commented that kindergartners were probably easier to control.

"Small animals are small animals," Gloria said with assurance. "I'm quite certain these kittens will learn to behave properly."

"Have you spent much time around cats?" Phil wondered.

"No, but I taught kindergarten for my entire career. I know a little about juveniles."

"Interesting," Phil remarked, and, on all fours, lowered his shoulders to let a couple of kittens climb up onto his back. Gloria watched the others. Sandra and Deena seemed to have a series of kittens, sometimes several at once, who were cuddling on them or climbing on and around them. Leeann and Phil played actively; both of them had more than a few scratches on their forearms. She watched with horror as Phil let his hand be a wrestling partner for what seemed like a totally possessed little black-and-white kitten with a smudged nose; it ended with the kitten letting go and leaping into the air with its fur sticking out and then running around in circles before curling up in a ball next to Leeann's thigh. Meanwhile, Leeann wielded a wand with a string and a feather on the end of it. Kittens chased the feather back and forth, leaping into the air, occasionally breaking into a wrestling match among themselves before reverting to chasing the elusive feather.

After an hour of socializing kittens, Gloria was exhausted.

"How did it go?" Bob asked when he came home at lunchtime.

"I don't quite have words for it," Gloria said hesitantly, "except absolute chaos."

Bob chewed his carrot stick thoughtfully, took a sip of water, and said, "Yes, that sounds about right."

The next week was worse than the first. Gloria's ankles were attacked three times. One kitten crawled halfway up her shin under her pants and resisted being removed with an impossible number of sharp, tiny claws. The small black kitten had crawled up her leg, belly, and chest, nuzzled her neck and draped herself over Gloria's shoulder, staying there most of the hour and having to be pulled off, unwillingly, when it was time for Gloria to leave. There were loopy snags of material all over Gloria's shirt. Meanwhile, Phil pretended to be a big animal on all fours, and kittens rode around on his back, with one perched on his head. Leeann held one at a time like a baby, and Sandra and Deena were tolerating all sorts of mischief inflicted upon them and their chairs.

She went home exhausted, complaining about the chaos, and again Rachel and Bob were enthusiastic. "You should go, if you think this is so jolly," Gloria grumbled.

The third Wednesday, Gloria started her morning listing all the good reasons not to go to the shelter. She was ticking them off on her fingers when Bob shuffled into the kitchen.

"No excuses." He smiled. Gloria lowered her eyebrows and frowned at him. He blew her a kiss and said, "Go, sweetheart. Just go."

"Of course I'm going," Gloria grumbled. "Heaven forbid! You all might call another little intervention."

"And I love you too," Bob said cheerfully. "So, what do you think? Scrambled eggs or oatmeal?"

"Oats. I'm making a quiche for dinner. Assuming," Gloria added darkly, "I still have all my fingers when I get home."

She drove to the shelter in time for her volunteer slot. She passed the Sunflower Beach shopping center and made a mental note to get Rachel to come clothes shopping. Even if she did insist on sitting on the floor with the smaller children, she could still manage to look more put together. Gloria pressed her lips together disapprovingly. She kept looking disapproving as she passed the college. Joe! Alexa! Their crazy so-called sabbaticals. She did not understand this drive to do foolish, reckless things.

She went into the shelter and signed in. Roberto, the volunteer at the desk, smiled at her. "Gloria! Good to see you. Here for the kittens?"

"Yes," Gloria sighed. "Good to see you," she added quickly. No use being rude; it wasn't Roberto's fault she was being prescribed this service.

"There's been a lot of turnover," Roberto commented, getting up to walk her into the back where the animals were.

"Turnover?"

"Adoptions," Roberto said. "A lot of our kittens got big enough to go to their forever homes. So, you'll meet new friends today."

Gloria frowned and wondered about the small, black cat who was so determinedly cuddly. "What about that little black kitty? The quiet one?"

"Oh, Darcy," Roberto said. "No, Darcy's still here. The black cats are the last to be adopted. And we never let them be taken in September and October, anyway."

"Why is that?"

"People are superstitious about black cats. And the black cats tend to be pretty smart, which seems to freak people out. Even cat people," Roberto added. "And then with wannabe pagan rituals, we just keep the black cats here in the fall. It's better that way."

Gloria felt a little sick to her stomach. She shook her head wordlessly.

"I know," Roberto said sympathetically. "It's terrible, the things we have to take into account. Well, here you go!" He swung the door to the kitten room open for her.

"Thank you," Gloria said warmly, and went in. She greeted Sandra, Deena, Leeann, and Phil—the regular Wednesday morning crew—and scanned the swirling kittens for Darcy. She found Darcy up on a box, in the corner, hunched down and watching the chaos. She smiled, went over, and, speaking softly, lifted up Darcy, put her to her chest, and took a seat in the rocking chair. Darcy made her way to Gloria's shoulder, nuzzled her neck, and proceeded to purr loudly.

"Well, don't you have a special friend!" Deena exclaimed. "That little one definitely likes you!"

"Well, I don't know about that," Gloria said, but she smiled and petted little Darcy, who purred even louder.

"It's always a compliment when a cat picks you out," Leeann asserted. "They pick us, not the other way around."

The conversation circled around this topic: how cats were the selectors, how they just "knew" who their person should be. Gloria found this quite odd. She wondered, briefly, if that miserable Jonah and his pathetic wife had picked, or been picked, by their pack of dogs. Gloria was assured by the whole crew that she was very lucky to have little Darcy pick her out, and she was beginning to feel more than a bit self-satisfied when Darcy suddenly roused and nipped her finger.

"Ow!" Gloria had exclaimed, and resisted pushing Darcy away. Darcy had shifted positions and seemingly went right back to sleep. "And what do you call that?" she asked indignantly. "Everything's fine and then, boom! And then everything's fine again. Except for the holes." She waggled her finger.

Sandra had smiled as she disengaged a small, pointy gray-and-white kitten from her calf and said, "Oh, that's cats for you! Cats and life.

You just have to learn how to roll with it and make the best of all the good moments."

Gloria kept thinking about Sandra's offhand "Roll with it." She poured herself some iced tea and made her way to the backyard. *Roll with it*, she thought, sinking into the chair with a sigh. Reflecting on the last three Wednesdays, Gloria shook her head against the back of the Adirondack chair. *Cats*, she thought. And then she thought about soft little Darcy, with her small, pointy face, the little mew and the eyes that had turned from pale blue to a pale jade green. She felt sad that Darcy would remain in the shelter all that extra time, and then felt a little relieved. It was nice to have someone to look forward to seeing. Then Gloria mused on thinking "someone" about a cat, of all things.

Chapter 33

As always, Veronica could not do anything without some sort of creative flare. Gloria rubbed her temples as she waited for the tea kettle to heat up. She glanced at the clock. It was 3:00 a.m., and finally the call had come through that mother and baby were fine—little Grace had arrived with a very loud cry at 2:26 a.m. Veronica had been working on some sort of photography project for the preschool website, editing photos or some such thing, and had kept insisting she didn't need to go to the hospital "yet." That was at 9:00 p.m. Then at 9:40 Kevin had called on his way to Gloria and Bob's with pajama-clad Bobby and Gina, and glowing, and occasionally moaning, very-much-in-labor Veronica. It had taken until midnight to get the children settled down, and then the long, restless waiting ensued.

"It's hardly worth trying to sleep, is it?" Bob shuffled into the kitchen. "Visiting hours start at what? Eight a.m.?"

Gloria nodded. "I believe so. So, baby Grace it is."

"Beautiful name," Rachel commented, joining them. "Are we having cocoa?"

"Herbal tea," Gloria replied.

"Maybe cocoa would be nice," Bob remarked and then, at Gloria's frown, sighed and said, "But perhaps herbal tea would be better."

"Suit yourselves," Rachel replied serenely. "I'm in a celebratory mood and chamomile won't quite do it." She rifled through the refrigerator. "Don't we have any whipped cream?"

"It's in a can. And not organic." Gloria couldn't resist, and then felt sorry she gotten that dig in when she saw Rachel's shoulders drop just a bit before she turned from the refrigerator with the spray whipped cream in hand.

"Well, it is a special occasion," Rachel said. "Wow, you guys have five grandchildren—one more and you'll need an extra hand to count them."

"True." Bob nodded.

Gloria poured two cups of chamomile tea and stirred them carefully. "Five."

"Well," Rachel said cheerfully, "I'm sure there will be more."

"For right now," Gloria said, "let's just be grateful Veronica and Grace are well." She lifted her phone; Kevin had sent a picture of a sweaty and slightly disheveled Veronica, eye makeup smudged, beaming, with tiny, pink baby Grace in her arms.

They were at the hospital the next morning with still-tired Bobby and Gina in tow. Gloria was glad the children were tired; it made them easier to handle. Kevin looked exhausted but he was smiling. There were hugs all around, and then they all went off to see Veronica and baby Grace. Veronica was holding the baby, sitting up in a rocking chair; Bobby and Gina rushed up and then froze, inches away.

"Bobby! Gina! Meet your baby sister Grace." Veronica's voice was quiet and peaceful. "You can touch her. Here—like this." She rested a hand gently on Grace's pink cheek. Gina reached out first, tentatively, stroked the baby, and then rested into her mother's one-armed hug. Bobby stepped forward then and touched the baby. Gloria held her breath, and let it out slowly as Bobby was very gentle, softly stroking the fine, dark hair on Grace's head.

Veronica smiled up at Gloria. "Grandma's next! Here you go." She handed Grace up. Gloria gently took Grace and cradled her, breathing the new-baby scent and softly tracing the surprisingly arched eyebrows, the little nose, the dimpled chin. She felt tremendous warmth rising up in her belly, felt her eyes moisten and gave in; she let a little sob come out and some tears escaped. Bob put an arm around her and put his hand tenderly on the side of Grace's head.

He looked at Veronica and Kevin. "Well! You two have done it again. One more perfect baby."

"Thanks." Kevin's voice was pleased. "We think so."

Rachel stepped up for her turn to hold Grace, and sat on the bed with her, with Bobby and Gina pressed in on each side. They continued marveling over Grace.

Kevin pulled over a chair for Gloria and then one for Bob; the room was set up for family visits.

"So, what happens next?" Gloria asked.

"Next?" Kevin wondered. "Well, we expect to get released later this morning. So, home we'll go. I'll have the staff reschedule my appointments for this week except for the ones Dad can fill in on."

"I can do a half day each day," Bob said. Gloria began to protest. He looked at her with a smile and a head shake, and she pressed her lips together firmly.

"So that should take care of a lot. I'll be home full-time for the week. Veronica's mom is coming in for two weeks, and then, Mom, we'll be leaning on you to help out a bit. If you don't mind."

"Of course not," Gloria said firmly. "I can manage a baby! And Bobby and Gina are no problem."

Veronica smiled and tried, unsuccessfully, to squash a yawn. "Thank you. I know we rely on you so much."

"And you must be exhausted," Bob said, standing up slowly. "Gloria? Rachel? Let's let Veronica get some rest before the doc comes and sends her home. Bobby, Gina, say goodbye for now to Grace. You'll see her later." He turned to Kevin. "Should we keep the kiddos another day or two? Or bring them home later?"

"I'd like everyone home together tonight." Veronica sighed. "I think it will be good. But we will take you up on the sleepover thing soon."

Gloria frowned. She didn't think a two-day-old baby should be subjected to life with Bobby just yet. On the other hand, she thought grimly, she didn't know if she felt up to life with Bobby just yet, either.

"Mom. It's going to be okay." Kevin hugged her. "I'll give you a call and be by later. Bobby, Gina—be good for Grandma and Grandpa. I'm going to pick you up later and we'll all be home together tonight."

Bobby and Gina promised to be good.

Chapter 34

Gloria took a careful sip of coffee, trying to focus closely on the conversation with Rachel and Sandy. They were having a snack at Gloria's kitchen table and updating her on Sandy's upcoming job. She was trying to make sense out of what they were saying.

Sandy was a little vague on the details, but was explaining that this job was a combination of research, which would build on her current research project, as well as developing and delivering education on Florida's plants, animals, and general environment.

"Research?" Gloria asked. "What research?"

Sandy flipped her long hair behind her shoulder and dipped a celery stick into the hummus. "The research I've been working on in my free time. For the dissertation. On the relationship between time in green space and improved cognitive function in seniors with mild cognitive decline."

Gloria pressed her lips together and tried not to make a cynical face at the green space perspective. "Really? That sounds ... unusual."

"Well, the Japanese have had a long tradition of forest baths—meaning really spending time in nature, immersing oneself in nature like you would in the tub. And there's research indicating even seeing pictures of nature reduces some dementia symptoms in the short term. So naturally we'd like to learn more and build education programs on that."

"So, education for senior citizens?" Gloria put her mug down and carefully set the handle parallel to the edge of the table.

"Not just seniors," Rachel said. "That's what's so cool. Sandy will be meeting with people in private schools, with homeschool co-ops, with public schools. Along with other scientists."

"I see," Gloria said. She imagined Sandy whirling around, flipping her hair and talking about how amazing sea turtles are.

Sandy smiled. "A lot of the plans are sort of like what you did for us in kindergarten, Aunt Gloria."

"Hmm?"

"You know! The nature walks! Between snack and naptime! When you would take us outdoors and challenge us. You remember! 'Okay, class, let's be very quiet and notice how many different bird songs we hear! Everyone, stand very still and look down at the grass. How many different colors do you see? Let's stop and look up at the sky. Who sees a cloud shaped like a chicken? Who can see the hippo?' That was great."

Gloria's eyebrows flared. "You remember all that?"

Rachel laughed. "Everyone remembers those walks, Mom. Ask anyone who was in your kindergarten class."

"So, imagine." Sandy leaned forward on her elbows, eyes shining. "Imagine a whole class of kids! Or an adult organization, out on a nature walk like that with an expert on local fauna, another on flora, and time to do a nice Q&A afterward."

"The Q&A," Gloria said. "I suppose that's to tell people how important it is to recycle and eat organic foods?" She shot a disapproving look at Rachel, who laughed and shook her head.

"No," Sandy said firmly. "The point isn't to tell people what to think or how to feel. The point is education. If people really know about the animals and plants that make up their environment, and learn how they are interconnected, the hope is they will naturally want to take better care of them."

"As opposed to a photo shoot," Rachel said, rolling her eyes.

Sandy snorted.

Gloria frowned, lips pressed hard. The girls were giving each other a sideways look and turning pink. "Now what?"

"Mom, nothing."

"Rachel, I'm not a fool."

"Fine." Rachel paused and glanced at Sandy. "So, last weekend Jenna and her video-boy were arrested for disturbing a sea turtle nest. They decided to do a little late-night video work—portable spotlight and all—which is of course totally illegal."

Gloria reached for her coffee, lifted it and put it down again without taking a sip. "No."

"It made the news," Sandy offered. "That's how Marta and Sean found out. One of their friends told them."

"Oh, no," Gloria sighed. "Those poor twins!"

"And Cody found out when about five patients in a row came in and asked if Jenna Quinn was any relation. That was a crappy day." Rachel shook her head. "The receptionist finally printed out a news report and wrote on it in big red letters: No relationship to Dr. Quinn! And hung it on the front counter."

Gloria raised one hand to rub her temple. *Maybe I should call Doreen at the practice, suggest she do the same.*

"So, obviously," Sandy said quietly, "there were people in the area who understood that bright lights at night will disorient hatchlings and potentially lead to them never making it out to the Gulf."

"Obviously," Gloria said firmly, and took a sip of coffee. Then she looked straight at Sandy and said, "Now, Sandy, dear. Tell me more about the kind of outreach you're hoping to do with this nonprofit job."

Sandy, was, of course, more than happy to oblige, piling on details and examples, including places they were already working out relationships to bring science to people from school age through the senior years, including botanical garden outings coordinated with various assisted living facilities. Gloria was impressed with the thoughtfulness of including even the frail elderly, and thought of Miss Arlene next door. "Miss Arlene would love that sort of thing," she commented.

"You're right," Sandy said. "You know, I might go talk to her. See if she's interested in participating. And if she has some artwork the program could use. You know, Florida artists, Florida scientists—all local talent."

The conversation continued, and later, as she rinsed out her coffee cup, Gloria looked out the kitchen window and thought what a surprise it was that little Sandy Bonhall had remembered those nature walks and turned them into a grownup project.

Chapter 35

"It sounds like a cross between kindergarten and the Christmas pageant. You should feel right at home." Alexa stirred her iced tea with a straw and wiggled her eyebrows.

Gloria frowned. "The kitten room is nothing like kindergarten! Not at all!"

Alexa shrugged. "Maybe I'm remembering wrong. From being 'class mother' for both Jonah's and Sandy's classes. Ha, remember little what's-his-name? The boxer?"

"Ryan Michaels," Gloria sighed. "And he wasn't any trouble."

"Not for you!" Alexa chuckled. "But some of the bigger boys! Bop! Pow! Ha, he was a little comic book character come to life."

"Still, not like a roomful of kittens," Gloria sniffed.

"Or what about the middle Bronson girl? The clingy one who kept having nosebleeds when she couldn't have her way?"

Gloria's eyebrows flared. *Yes, Ginny Bronson had been challenging. The nosebleeds were an original touch*, she thought. When Ginny started crying really hard, she would sneeze and splatter blood everywhere. "That was singular, and quite disruptive, yes."

"And the pageant! Joyce Senger and Todd Sampson practically got into a fist fight over the Star of David last year. And of course, the camel was stoned. Were stoned? Both ends, anyway. Again."

"And last year, of course, we had the costume swap between a Magi and a shepherd in the middle of the room," Gloria said pointedly.

Alexa grinned and shrugged. "Everything worked out fine in the end." She poked at her salad. "The avocado is perfect today."

Gloria nodded. "Yes, the salads here are always very nicely done." She paused. "I really appreciate getting to get together by ourselves. Before you leave for the mountains, especially."

"Of course!" Alexa said. "But I'm just going on a little sabbatical retreat—I'll be back the week before Thanksgiving."

"A lot can happen in that time," Gloria sighed.

"Agreed. I suspect so." Alexa looked straight at Gloria. "As we both know, we can expect an announcement from Cody and Sandy. Probably holding out until Christmastime when everyone's together."

Gloria pressed her lips together. "And Rachel and Aidan, no doubt." She shook her head.

"Well, that's all good news," Alexa offered. She leaned back against the worn cushion of the booth. "I'm expecting some not-so-good-news, too."

"Oh? What? Is someone ill? Your mom?"

"No, no. I think." Alexa hesitated. "I think there's real trouble with Jonah and Beth. Something's been not right for a while but lately, I don't know."

Gloria watched Alexa. *The poor thing, she looks worried about it.* "I'm sure Jonah will be all right," she said kindly, patting Alexa's hand.

Alexa smiled sadly. "It's not Jonah I'm worried about it." She pushed a floppy curl off her forehead. It fell right back into place. Gloria wondered when she would get a haircut. "Beth is sad all the time. Always."

Gloria nodded. *Here we go again*, she thought. *Who wouldn't be sad, married to that pompous little brat?* She pressed her lips together in an effort to keep the words inside.

"Well, naturally she's sad married to Jonah," Alexa said. "I mean, you know how he can be. But to see that girl struggling. Well, Sandy and I have been reaching out to her. And her best friend, Courtney, reached out to us. Asked if there was anything she should know. Or could do. And all I could do was ask the same thing. We pretty much just promised to keep one another in the loop."

"That does sound serious." Gloria frowned. "Any concerns about safety?"

"Oh, gosh, no. I mean, I hope not. No, I don't think so. But yeah, something to keep an eye out for and maybe even ask about. Outright, I mean."

"You're not worried about giving her any ideas?"

"Oh, no. No, that's not how suicide works, Gloria. People don't ask someone if they're suicidal and they suddenly think of it."

Gloria shook her head. She thought about how easy it seemed for Beth to just fix her problem: divorce Jonah and move on. Then she thought about how it felt to be trapped in Jerzy Grabowski's iron-clad control—always terrified of doing the wrong thing, drawing the wrong attention, and feeling like there was no way out. "The poor thing. She must feel absolutely trapped."

"Good word for it," Alexa said. "Trapped."

"I know what that's like," Gloria said slowly. She stared past Alexa's head, thinking of her mother climbing up to retrieve the hidden money, the checklist of tasks, the path to freedom her mother had so carefully orchestrated for each child but never taken for herself.

"Oh?" Alexa leaned forward. "Not now, right?"

"No, no," Gloria said hurriedly. She paused, took a sip of her iced tea, gazing over Alexa's head and then back to her face. "It was when I was eighteen, the summer after high school. My father wouldn't let me go to college." She winced at the memory of his words. *She's a monster. The girl stays here.* "But my mother, she made it happen. My God, she probably had hell to pay for it when she got home from dropping me off at school. But I needed that. I couldn't see a way out." She shook her head. "Couldn't see one."

Alexa reached out to hold Gloria's hand. "You never told me this story."

Gloria took a deep breath and told Alexa. She told her about Jerzy's cruel words and watched Alexa's eyes fill with tears. She told her about her mother waking her early, mysteriously, and the money hidden in books, and Alexa laughed aloud at the cleverness of hiding money in plain sight from someone who sneered at education. Gloria described the day of the haircut, makeup and new clothes, the early-morning ride out to the university, the appointment and dorm all arranged, and her mother's long trip home by bus.

"Wow," Alexa said. "Little Nora! Who would ever have guessed, looking at her? Brilliant. Bold."

Gloria pressed her lips together, feeling the wave of sorrow that sometimes came when she thought of her mother. She put her other hand on top of Alexa's and said, "Well, dear. I wonder if Beth needs a little of the Nora treatment. Something to get her unstuck."

"Ah. The Nora." Alexa grinned. "I like it. I like it a lot."

Gloria smiled with satisfaction. Alexa would figure a way to help that poor, putty-spined Beth, and her mother was now memorialized as an intervention—even a rescue mission, one might say. *Yes*, she thought with satisfaction, *the Nora was a fine intervention.*

"I think," Alexa said slowly, "if the opportunity—or something that seems close to one—avails itself, I'll invite Beth up for a little weekend away in the mountains."

"And violate your sabbatical retreat?"

Alexa grinned and lifted her glass in a toast. "Nora would do it."

Gloria smiled and lifted her glass. "Indeed, she would."

Chapter 36

Gloria waved to the kitchen crew as she passed them on the way to Andrea's office. She had given up feeling embarrassed and compelled to be secretive; apparently everyone had some sort of experience with Andrea and thus no one thought anything of it. In the process of coming and going from what she had imagined were surreptitious meetings with Andrea, a host of people she barely knew had felt free to walk up to her and share their Andrea stories. Nancy, the lady who handed out bulletins at the Saturday vigil Mass, had gone to see her after her granddaughter decided to take up synchronized skydiving. Richard, the head usher at the 9:00 a.m. Mass, had met with her before he felt ready to go to the grief support group after his wife of sixty years had passed away three years ago. The maintenance chief had worked on a snake phobia. The housekeeper at the rectory had talked about some old issues from young adulthood. A teenager who was helping make sandwiches and was homeschooled told Gloria about how Andrea had helped him with social anxiety before he started going to youth group. The assistant music director had gotten parenting advice, the preschool assistant had gotten some help with insomnia, and apparently the last two pastors had sent engaged couples to Andrea for at least one premarital session as a matter of course.

Gloria settled into the couch and tried to ignore the fact that Andrea was sitting cross-legged on the chair and that a long vest was draped all around her and past her knees toward the floor. "Andrea, you see all the engaged couples, don't you?"

"Yes, that's pretty much the way it works. Unless they're marrying outside of the parish." Andrea took a sip of tea. "Why do you ask?"

Gloria pressed her lips together. "Well, we're expecting a few announcements. Probably in the next few months or so, certainly by Christmas. That's the guess. My Cody and Sandy Bonhall. And my Rachel and Aidan. Aidan Mahoney."

"Oh, right. Monsignor's nephew. Over at St. Stephen's?"

"You know him," Gloria said flatly. *Of course, the woman knows everyone. Or everyone knows her, anyway.*

"Well, he's been around since he was a teenager so, yes, I've run into him. And his reputation precedes him. You do know"—Andrea leaned forward—"how many disappointed middle-aged ladies there are over at St. Stephen's? Who had their eye on Aidan for their daughters?" She leaned back, chuckling. "They're going to be just green with envy at you. Assuming your expectation for the announcement is correct."

"Well, I guess you'll be seeing both couples, then."

"Yes. And." Andrea straightened up, the signal, Gloria had learned, that whatever followed was very official. "And, of course, these conversations are never mentioned. And my conversations with them remain private except, of course, for the summary report for Father Anthony or Father Jack."

"Of course," Gloria said, nodding, and felt relieved.

"Now, tell me about the homework. You know, the kitten room."

"Well," Gloria pursed her lips, drawing her brows down. "To tell you the truth, it occurs to me that I'd forgotten it was homework. It's just something I do."

"Interesting. So, you like it?"

Gloria pressed her lips together. *Like it?* she thought. It had not occurred to her to use "like" about this. It was a commitment, certainly, but she couldn't recall just when it had become what she did, not something she had to do to keep her family from putting on another intervention. It just seemed normal, now. She put a hand up to her shoulder, instinctively, and smiled briefly, thinking of that little Darcy, and then frowned.

"Gloria? What was that?"

"What was what?"

"The smile. The frown."

"Oh." Gloria hesitated. "I was thinking about this one little cat. Darcy. She always climbs up my legs and then up to my shoulder and then cuddles with me for as long as I'm there."

"Nice."

"And then I thought ... well, she's on an adoption hold for now because she's black. And it's that time of year." Gloria waved a hand vaguely. "But that will pass. And a kitty that sweet will no doubt be snatched up in a minute."

"Huh." Andrea nodded. "Any other thoughts about that?"

"Well, of course I'll miss her," Gloria said regretfully. "She's quite the little sweetheart. Except she will suddenly get playful and then she has a lot of little sharp claws and teeth."

"They do."

Gloria moved her gaze from the landscape painting to Andrea's face and shook her head. "No, no."

"No what?"

"No, I can see it on your face. I've already heard it from Rachel. And the twins. And Matt and Tim." She paused and then added quickly, "I've heard it from everyone. And, no."

"No what, Gloria?"

"I can't possibly adopt a kitten."

"Has anyone suggested you adopt 'a' kitten?"

Gloria stared at her.

"I mean," Andrea asked, "have you considered adopting *Darcy*? Not 'a kitten,' but that *particular* one? The one who seems very fond of you?"

"Have you ever met a kitten?"

"Why, of course, lots of them. We had lots of cats over the years, all ages."

"Then you know what they're like," Gloria sniffed. "Chaos! All chaos!"

"And yet, you're sad that this little one will soon go off to a good home. Just not your home."

Gloria pressed her lips together. She sat up straight and reached unconsciously for her purse, caught herself, and put it back down. She thought about the months ahead: The twins would be bigger and spending more and more time at school, and with Sandy and Cody; she would be moved into a regular grandmother position rather than nanny/surrogate mother. Rachel would move out at last. The house would be so quiet, so peaceful, so ... "Empty," Gloria sighed. "The house will be empty soon. Except for Bob and me." She looked bleakly at Andrea.

"It must be hard," Andrea replied. "You worked so hard to help your children all grow up to be strong and independent, and then that means they leave—just like we hope. But how hard it must be."

"It is." Gloria shook her head. "I don't know if adopting a kitten—adopting Darcy—would be smart. Would I just be substituting the chaos of children with the chaos of a cat?"

"Maybe." Andrea shrugged. "Or maybe you'll find that after the kitten stage little Miss Darcy is a sedate lap cat who is happy to cuddle up most of the time and chase the occasional lizard that wanders indoors."

"So, the kitten stage is temporary?"

"Like kindergarten," Andrea replied, grinning. "You know a little about that."

Gloria nodded thoughtfully. A lap cat, she thought. A sweet little cat. She imagined herself coming home from errands and having little Darcy there, peeking out the front window and meeting her at the door. She pictured herself petting Darcy's head and giving her exactly the right amount of cat food and fresh water. She thought about having toys available and imagined Marta and Sean playing nicely. She grimaced at the thought of Bobby being a little rough and thought about those pointy claws; no doubt Darcy could take care of herself. *A cat.* She wondered what Bob would think about that. She looked straight at Andrea and said, "I would have to run that by Bob. Having a kitten, that is."

"No doubt," Andrea agreed.

Of course, Bob thought it was a great idea. Gloria shook her head in disapproval at the soapy dishwater and scrubbed a saucepan with unnecessary vigor. Now, she thought regretfully, there was no way around it. She'd have to ask about adopting Darcy, and soon. She glanced over at the calendar. It wasn't long before the no-black-cat policy would be lifted.

Rachel walked up and started drying the pots and lids. "So, Mom. A cat, huh?"

"You eavesdropped."

"I heard you and Dad. My door was open and you weren't exactly quiet," Rachel said. "You guys forget that your hearing is going, but mine isn't."

"Yet," Gloria said grouchily, and swatted a bit of dishwater at her. "Not yet. But if you keep blasting the music in your car like that—"

"I know, I know." Rachel laughed. "But the kitten sounds adorable! When is she coming home?"

"Not until they lift the ban. The black cat ban," Gloria added.

"Ah. That time of year." Rachel frowned. "That's so sad! That we have to worry about that, too!"

"They don't worry. They just don't let them go," Gloria said firmly. "Very prudent." She held up a pot lid, examined it, and wiped off a smudge before rinsing it carefully and handing it to Rachel.

"Maybe they won't make you wait. Since you're a volunteer and all," Rachel suggested.

"Maybe," Gloria said flatly.

"Aren't you excited?" Rachel asked. "I'd be excited! I *am* excited! We haven't had pets. You held out on us," she teased. "Oh, sure! Now that I'm practically gone, you're getting a cat and I'll miss all the fun."

"Well," Gloria said with a half-smile, "I'm sure you'll still be able to give me very clear instructions on the right organic food for Darcy."

"And the right kind of cat litter! And properly sourced toys," Rachel added. "Don't worry, Mom—I've got you covered."

"I'm sure you do," Gloria said, shaking her head. "I'm sure you do." She put another pot in the drainer. "And what do you mean, practically gone?"

Rachel shrugged, smiled, and said, "Oh, you know! I've been saving up for my own place." She rested her head on Gloria's shoulder. "Or maybe I'll just run away to Ireland with a dark-haired, handsome man."

Gloria patted Rachel's cheek and said, "Maybe you'll give your mother a heart attack."

Rachel straightened up, dried the last pot and, as she put it away, commented, "You know, Mom, you handled that way better than you would have a few months ago. That Andrea must be something."

Gloria pressed her lips together, and then replied, "Well, maybe you'll find out yourself one of these days."

Rachel hung up the dish towel and nodded thoughtfully. "No doubt," she answered. "I'm going to go for a walk. It's nice out. Want to come?"

"Yes. That would be lovely," Gloria agreed, a little surprised. "I'll just put my sneakers on and let your father know."

Chapter 37

"He's a monster, Gloria. My God in heaven, how did I raise an absolute monster?"

Gloria rubbed her forehead with her free hand. She wondered what to say. She agreed; he was a monster. She'd always known he was horrible but this—this was inexplicably evil, as far as Gloria could tell. Still, to tell her best friend, yes, your son is an evil monster ... Gloria sighed. "Are you sure, dear? Quite sure?"

"Oh, I'm sure." Alexa was barely comprehensible, she was sobbing so hard. "I had to call Joe! You can imagine how ... disappointed. Furious. Oh, God. What a nightmare."

"Oh, Alexa," Gloria said. She felt at a loss for words. There was a crash in the living room.

"Gloria? What was that? Is everything okay?"

"That wasn't me. It was Darcy."

"Darcy?" Alexa snuffled.

"The cat," Gloria explained as she lifted Darcy off the mantlepiece, put her down on the floor and picked up the two largest pieces of the vase.

"Cat?"

"Well, kitten. For now."

Alexa managed a weak laugh. "Okay, now I've heard everything. I thought"—her voice caught—"I thought I'd heard everything after we heard from Beth, but you may have even topped that."

"That seems a bit harsh, dear."

"No, no. I mean, we knew Jonah was a problem, I guess. But you adopting a cat—unless it's Rachel's?"

"No," said Gloria grimly, peeling Darcy off the drapes and putting her down on the floor with a gentle pat on the rump. "No, Darcy is apparently all mine."

"I'll look forward to meeting her," Alexa said.

"Well, you certainly will," Gloria replied. She sank into her chair, patted her lap, and, as Darcy eagerly bounded up her leg and then up her belly toward her shoulder, said, "Now, dear, let's talk a little. Are you quite okay? Should I come over? Send one of the boys?"

"No, no. But thanks. I think I need the thinking time."

"And you're quite certain that it's all … true? Not Beth being a bit dramatic?"

"No, no. Apparently, he's been lying to her about all sorts of things—and for the longest time, about whether he was likely to father any children. The poor thing took him at his word and has been throwing money away with all sorts of tests and specialists. Thinking there was something 'wrong' with her."

"Right, you said he lied about this," Gloria said soothingly. "And Beth didn't know anything?"

Alexa sighed and her voice wobbled. "She was, well, naïve. I think she saw Jonah as some sort of rescue project at first and was so eager to believe the best about him, she never verified. The medical report was right in their filing cabinet and she never checked it after he told her he was 'fine.'"

"Ah. Yes, naïve," Gloria said, drawing her eyebrows down.

"And yet I would do the same thing! I wouldn't look over Joe's shoulder at his bloodwork or something; if he told me things were fine, I'd believe him."

"Well, of course. That's Joe, dear. Not Jonah." Gloria carefully disentangled Darcy's left front paw from her dangling earring. *And this is the sort of thing that happens when you let people manage themselves.*

"It's her husband. Who lives like that? Peeking over their husband's shoulder? What kind of life would that be?"

Gloria nodded, thinking. "I guess ... you know Jonah. And so do I. And we always had distrust for him. But I guess Beth just sort of sailed in, an overly bright teenager, and took things at face value."

"Right. And she's been dragging him along." Alexa started sobbing again. "Oh, Gloria! What a nightmare!"

Gloria pressed her lips together. "Alexa, dear. It's going to be okay. You're okay. Joe's okay. Sandy is fine." She heard Alexa's breath begin to settle down. "Jonah's being Jonah. But you have Beth; she's turning to you, for heaven's sake. And you have all of us, and your mother, and your sister and her family up north. Everything will be okay, Alexa."

"Thanks, Gloria. I knew you'd understand."

Gloria stroked Darcy, who was purring and asleep, and shook her head wordlessly before continuing to try to calm Alexa. After they hung up, she put down the phone and sat for a long time, gazing out the window, pondering the problems they were all facing.

She was still sitting there when Bob came home at lunchtime. He came in, took in the pieces of the vase on the hearth, still not swept up, and the sleeping kitten on Gloria's shoulder. He smiled, kissed her on the cheek, and straightened up. "Looks like you and little Miss Darcy have had a time."

Gloria smiled up at him. "You can't imagine the half of it. It's been a ... singular morning."

Bob's eyebrows shot up. "Singular? That's not a word you use readily."

Gloria shook her head, lips pressed tightly. She sighed and stood slowly, one hand on Darcy, who shifted, sank a few pointy claws into her shoulder, and resumed purring. "Alexa called. What a nightmare."

Bob frowned. "Is everyone okay?"

Gloria headed toward the kitchen, Bob just behind her. "Well, about as okay as ever. It's Jonah. And Beth."

"Jonah and Beth?"

Darcy was awake; Gloria put her down and began putting lunch together while Bob started the coffee. "It seems that Jonah got fired and didn't tell Beth for weeks. Technically, he never did tell her; she found out by accident from a friend at work. In the meantime, he'd been heading out every day, dressed for work, spending money on God knows what, and settled into being even meaner to her than before."

"Losing a job must have been embarrassing," Bob offered. "I mean, to give him the benefit of the doubt."

Gloria shook her head and spread carrots and celery on a small plate next to the hummus. "No. No benefit. That's the tip of the iceberg."

"Not an affair?"

"Who knows? It's possible. A lot of money went out the window. No, what happened is probably worse. He knew he had almost zero chance of having children, and he let Beth think he was fine while she went on a wild goose chase from specialist to specialist."

Bob turned to stare at her.

Gloria continued. "Remember all those crazy exotic vacations and the dog sitting? No vacations. Just trips to specialists all over the country, looking for answers to her supposed deficit. He insisted on secrecy because he said Alexa was so Catholic she'd disapprove of seeking help with fertility. So, Beth's been thinking she's got some mysterious problem for years and pining after a family and meanwhile Jonah just lied."

Bob sank into a chair, mouth agape. He rubbed his forehead. "He's a monster."

Gloria sighed. For an instant, her mind flashed back to her parents' kitchen and her father's sneer. "She's a monster." She shook her head. No, she wasn't—but Jonah, well, maybe. Maybe. "Maybe," she said. "Poor Alexa! She was falling apart. Angry, hurt, blaming herself."

"No," Bob said firmly. "She can't own this one."

"Agreed," Gloria said. "But she's just a mess. At least Joe will be home soon."

Bob took a sip of coffee. He sighed, put the mug down, and put his hand on Gloria's. "Sweetheart, Beth's situation ... what an absolute nightmare."

"Chaos," Gloria sighed. "Truly wicked chaos."

"Right," Bob said. "That's what chaos looks like. Not having two happy adult children about to make good matches."

Gloria lowered her eyebrows. "Yes, I suppose. Chaos," she sighed, and stood up to retrieve Darcy from behind the sugar canister.

"Perhaps you should ask Andrea if there's a diagnosis for people who see chaos where none exists." Bob smiled, and Gloria tried to frown at him but instead just shook her head and kissed his cheek as she sat down with Darcy on one shoulder.

"There's a label for everything," Gloria said, carefully dipping a carrot stick into the hummus. "Including one for recalcitrant diabetes patients."

"And what's that supposed to mean?"

"It means"—Gloria reached across the table to brush his polo shirt—"that you didn't get all the powdered sugar off your shirt. Who brought donuts today?"

"Holes. Donut holes," Bob said. "That's the new policy! Donut holes only, and I have only one."

Gloria's eyebrows flared up. "One?"

Bob held up three fingers. "Scouts' honor," he said solemnly. "One! One delightfully airy powdered-sugar-coated donut hole."

"Hmph," Gloria said, and chomped on her carrot. Darcy roused, sniffed Gloria's breath, shook her head, and nuzzled back into her neck. Gloria patted her with her free hand and said, "Good girl."

"And is Darcy Irish for chaos?"

"No, that would be *Anord*." Gloria paused. "I did look it up, actually."

"I love you, Gloria Grabowski Quinn." Bob chuckled, shaking his head. "You looked it up. Of course."

"I was thinking of it as a kind of banner. For the whole year." Gloria sighed.

"I think miracle works better," Bob said. "It's been a year of miracles for us."

"Your recovery, yes."

Bob began ticking off miracles on his fingers. "My recovery! You finally going to visit Brenda! My getting to participate in Joe's sabbatical trip! Cody and Sandy! Rachel and Aidan! This." He pointed at Darcy.

"Veronica and Kevin having baby Grace! My semi-retirement! Good news after good news."

Gloria nodded, lips pressed together, and began to smile. "You're right."

"And even for poor Alex and Joe—and Beth—the rest of the year has been, well—the sabbaticals. Sandy and Cody—a match made in heaven. Alex coming out of her shell." He shook his head at Gloria's eye roll. "And, you know, in the long run, I think this Jonah debacle is going to turn out to be good. Because now Beth is dealing with reality, and she's going to be free to go after what she wants. I say, give it a year at most, and Beth will look back at this time and be grateful it happened."

"So soon?" Gloria mused.

Bob leaned back and took a sip of coffee, nodding. "Yes. A year at most."

"We'll see," Gloria replied, and peeled Darcy's left paw out of her earring.

Bob lifted his mug as for a toast. "A year! By Thanksgiving next year, everything will be different. Even for Beth."

Gloria gazed at the refrigerator. A magnet from Dublin, holding up a photo of a laughing Rachel between Aidan and his sister in front of Oscar Wilde's home; that beach cleanup picture with Rachel, Aidan, Marta, Sean, and Sandy all smiling for the camera and Cody gazing at Sandy. Her glance shifted to the pre-Christmas photo of Kevin, Veronica, Bobby, Gina, and Grace; the photo of Matt and Tim in front of their home from last Christmas season. She felt warmth in her chest, felt Darcy's comfortable purring, and smiled at Bob. "It's already different. And—" Gloria paused, surprised at the words herself. "It's already all good."

Bob reached across the table, putting his hand over hers, his eyes sparkling. "That's my beautiful Gloria," he said.

Chapter 38

Later, Gloria would laugh it off as "the perfect pincer movement," but now she was anxious, puttering in the kitchen putting supper together and glancing at the clock. Bob was setting the table and talking about fishing; she answered in half sentences and vague murmurs.

"Gloria."

She looked up. He was leaning on one side of the arch to the dining room, arms folded, head tilted.

"Gloria. We've discussed this. Neither one of us is surprised. Let's just listen. Enjoy the evening."

Gloria pressed her lips together firmly, nodded, and wiped at one eye. "I know. It's just—" She waved her hands vaguely.

"Just what, Mom?" Cody stepped in from the garage.

"Just a lot to get done," Gloria said firmly, "before we can all sit down for a nice meal. How was your day? Where are the twins?"

"The twins are making birdhouses with Matt and Tim this evening." Cody was unpacking the bag of groceries he'd brought in. "Cranberry juice. Whole grain bread. Leeks—three in the bunch."

"Thanks, dear," Gloria said. "So, it's just you and Rachel this evening?" She glanced at Bob, who nodded.

"That's right. She's not here yet?"

"She had to make a couple of stops on the way home," Bob said. "Should be here momentarily."

They discussed the upcoming holidays, the latest news from Alexa and Joe's family—the pending divorce between Jonah and Beth—and how the twins were doing in school. Rachel arrived and they all settled in for the family supper.

They had barely said grace when Cody put down his fork and said, "Well, Mom, Dad. It's not a surprise because I've discussed this with you both, and of course with Uncle Joe. I've asked Sandy to marry me and she's said yes."

"Congratulations, son," Bob said, putting his hand on Cody's shoulder. "We wish you every happiness."

"Yes," Gloria chimed in. "I'm very happy for you. Still surprised, I suppose—but very happy for you."

"I guess I'm surprised, too," Cody said. "I can't believe my luck."

"Luck," Gloria echoed, and took a sip of water.

"And," Rachel said, "as you know, Aidan was going to propose. And he did. I accepted. So, we're engaged!" She flashed her left hand, a simple claddagh ring.

"Did you have that on when you came in?" Gloria asked, taking Rachel's hand and admiring the ring.

"I hid it in my pocket until we sat down for dinner," she said. "I knew you wouldn't miss any details."

Good wishes were expressed all around, and then the conversation turned to plans. Cody, Sandy, Rachel, and Aidan had had multiple conversations about this, and the details were laid out. Sandy, they said, was having the same conversation tonight with her parents, so all the parents could talk later.

The official announcements would be Christmas Eve, after Mass. This was just a heads-up for the parents.

The weddings would be in early June; Cody's annulment should be wrapped up in time. They were having a double wedding in the chapel at church, with Aidan's uncle Seamus, the monsignor at St. Stephen's, coming to be celebrant. The rehearsal dinner for the three families would be here, assuming Bob and Gloria didn't mind; they did not. The dinner after the wedding would be at Joe and Alexa's. In July, both couples, with Marta and Sean, would go to Ireland, where Uncle Seamus would be visiting family, too, and would bless their marriages. He would also be baptizing two great-nephews.

Aidan's parents and at least one of his brothers would be here for the weddings, and staying with Aidan.

"In his apartment?" Gloria wondered. "Isn't it small?"

Rachel explained that they had already put in an offer on a house in Matt and Tim's neighborhood—just a few miles away. Assuming the sale went through, Aidan would live there alone until the wedding while Rachel stayed here at home. His parents and whatever siblings came might use the house or the apartment. Gloria assured herself that they couldn't be planning to run off to Ireland if they were buying a house in the current market.

She wondered about the wedding plans. "So simple. Don't either of you girls want something a little more?"

"No," Rachel said firmly. "We've had two big weddings—Kevin's and, well, Jenna's." She glanced at her brother. "Sorry, Cody."

"No offense taken," Cody said, shaking his head. "That was definitely Jenna's show."

The details kept coming. Sandy would continue working mostly remote, from home, in her new research position; any travel would be in-state. She would be spearheading local education outreach.

"It's interesting that a real job finally shows up just as she's getting married," Gloria remarked.

Cody grinned. "It probably looks that way. Truth be told, she's turned down a lot of offers for good jobs that she wasn't even looking for."

"Why would she turn down perfectly good jobs?"

"A lot of reasons." Cody shook his head. "None of them met her criteria."

"Criteria?"

"To support her research."

"Research. Right, she mentioned research." Gloria felt a bit thick-headed. She wondered where her vocabulary went.

Rachel leaned forward. "You know! Sandy's almost done with her doctorate and she wants to continue research."

"I didn't know that. Interesting, Joe didn't say a thing about it." Bob chomped noisily into a carrot stick.

"Probably because Sandy and Aunt Alex keep some things on the quiet side. Because of how Jonah gets," Cody explained. "It's some sort of girls' secrecy club."

"I'm in it," Rachel interjected. "The secret girls' club. So is Beth."

"And the new position combines research with developing, and presenting, educational materials for the public." Cody took a sip of water. "So that's one big reason. And it's why she was keeping the job thing kind of low-key. I think she underplayed the amount of work she's been doing even to Aunt Alex, to tell the truth."

"Interesting," Gloria managed to say. She was trying to make sense of a Sandy who was almost done with her doctoral research. She had imagined Sandy's new job something more like a docent at a nature center: something that required some knowledge but not necessarily credentials.

"And, she didn't want to go too far from home."

"For her parents," Gloria said approvingly. Finally, she thought, the conversation was making a little sense.

"Not exactly. Well, partly." Cody paused. "What she said, actually, was she was waiting around for me to grow up."

Bob laughed and said, "Isn't that always the way? How much older does a man have to be to be wiser than his wife?"

Gloria shook her head, smiling. "You can't catch up, dear."

"And don't I know it." Bob nodded. "Too bad about Jonah, huh?"

"Oh, I don't think so," Rachel asserted. "I think it's too bad it took Beth so long to figure it out. But I think everything will work out okay in the end."

"It always does," Bob agreed.

Rachel leaned forward on her elbows, grinning mischievously. "Maybe we can help Beth out. Cody, didn't Sandy mention the history department is hiring a new instructor? A young guy?"

"Stop," Gloria said, pressing her fingers on the table firmly. "Enough! Two weddings! All sorts of plans. Let's leave Beth and Jonah to get their divorce and figure things out a little." She rubbed her temples. "Well, originally I was quite surprised." She scanned the three faces around the table. "And I must say." She hesitated. "I must say, I'm delighted. It's a lot to take in, of course, but"—she drew herself up firmly with a crisp nod—"I'm quite pleased."

Rachel almost tipped over the table rushing around to hug her mother. Gloria felt Bob's hand on her shoulder, and saw Cody's teary eyes and bright smile as he reached over to touch her hand. She lifted the other hand to stroke Rachel's hair and then rest her hand on Bob's. Just for a moment, she felt as if maybe, now, everything really would be very, very right.

Chapter 39

Of course, it was absolutely necessary to get together with Alexa and Joe as soon as possible. Both couples agreed it was imperative. The very next evening, they were sitting on Alexa and Joe's deck, sipping hot cocoa. Alexa insisted it had been made with almond milk, so it was safe for Bob. Bob complained cheerfully about being starved to death, and Gloria rolled her eyes at him. Then they got down to the serious business of discussing the young people's plans.

Alexa had brought out a large manila envelope. She held it for a while as they discussed the general wedding plans and agreed that, simple as the plan was, it was perfect for their families and made it easy to have a similarly cozy, family-focused day in Ireland later that summer.

"I was thinking," Alexa said slowly, "about Sandy saying she'd known practically her whole life that Cody was the one for her." She shook her head. "That sounds so over the top. Romantic, idealizing: a lot of looking backward and re-interpreting history."

"Cody said the same thing," Bob said. "That he'd known forever but it was too weird. Well, kids with that much age difference, can you imagine? Being twelve and thinking you're in love with a kindergartner, just waiting for her to grow up?"

Joe shrugged. "And what boy hasn't had a major crush on a much younger girl and felt like a fool?"

Alexa shot him a look. "Jonah, probably, for one." Joe chuckled and shook his head. Alexa opened the envelope. "You know, I started looking at old photos last night, after Sandy went to bed. And then this morning." She fanned out a lot of old snapshots. "Remember the old days when we had all our photos printed?" She passed them to Gloria, who was on her other side. "Have a look."

The lights over the deck glimmered. The sky was streaked with sunset light. Gloria slowly shuffled through the snapshots.

A beach day for both families. Cody and Sandy were working on a sandcastle. He must have been fourteen and she would have been seven. Gloria recalled those beach days; she always told herself how nice it was that Cody was spending time with his sister. She studied the picture. Rachel had her back to both of them, diligently working on a moat. Cody and Sandy were clearly cooperating, but Sandy was studying the sand turret and Cody was looking at Sandy.

Sandy and Rachel at their first Holy Communion party, dressed in their white dresses, veils, and gloves. Rachel was grinning at the camera, hands properly together in prayer position but managing to look less than pious. Sandy and Cody were inexplicably side by side, smiling at each other and looking like a foreshadowing of a wedding couple.

Sandy waving out the window of the beat-up car that had survived her parents, and then Jonah, with Cody grimacing in the passenger seat and trying to get her to pay attention to her driving lesson.

The whole family gathered together around Cody and Jenna on their wedding day; all those happy faces and Sandy, off on the edge, looking a little sad and gazing past the camera. The tired look on Cody's face, the broad smile on Jenna's.

The pictures went on. There were a dozen; there could have been many more. Gloria blinked back a few tears, feeling a bit surprised at her emotionality, and handed the photos to Bob without a word. Alexa nodded, wiping a tear. "I know. It's so perfectly clear. I feel like a fool."

Bob shook his head. "It's hard not to envy them. Here it is—the answer, so easy." He winked at Gloria. "I had to deal with those office ladies just to get a little intel on my Gloria."

"Oh, you." Gloria waved a hand at him.

Bob snorted. "You have no idea! The torture. Pretending they thought I was interested in every other teacher!" He handed the photos to Joe, who began shuffling through them. "And just to get a little information."

"You know," Gloria said to Alexa and Joe, "Bob's never fessed up before this as to exactly how he managed to find out when I went to the library and the grocery store." She smiled at Bob. "So he could stalk me."

Bob just shook his head and made a zipping gesture across his lips.

Joe handed the photos back to Alexa, nodding. "Someone at school sold you out, Gloria." He paused. "And Aidan and Rachel? Are you happy with that?"

"I will be," Gloria said firmly, "once I'm sure they're not going to run off and live in Ireland full time."

"If the worst-case scenario is you have a place to go for months at a time every year while Matt and Tim keep an eye on your place, that's not so bad." Joe leaned back against clasped hands. "It sounds pretty nice. I hear," he said, grinning at Bob, "that the fishing in Ireland is quite something!"

"No. Stop it," Gloria said firmly, eyebrows lowering. She caught Alexa's glance and shook her head. "I think we wait until after the wedding and then," she said, turning to Bob, "then we'll know Aidan's family and we can wangle an invitation. I suspect Aidan's father knows about fishing."

Bob reached over to take Gloria's hand. "You never cease to surprise me, Gloria Grabowski."

Gloria squeezed his hand and smiled. "Bob, dear. Remember, we talked about visiting his family." She lifted her eyes to see the first stars, twinkling in the purple-blue sky. She thought, suddenly, of her mother. She wished Nora was here to see all this and then considered, that, of course, Nora knew. She'd probably known all along. She imagined she heard her mother's voice: *Gloria, darling, you remember. How it was even when they were children.*

"Yes, I remember," Gloria said quietly. She turned to Bob and smiled. "I was just thinking about my mother," she said. "About how happy she'd be."

Bob smiled and nodded. "Your mother probably saw this coming a long time ago. Nothing ever got past Nora."

"Funny," Alexa said. "My mother said she couldn't believe this took so long—Cody and Sandy—when we spoke this morning." She paused. "I think it's like a painting; you have to be the right distance away for it to all come together. Up close you get details but not the big picture." She sighed. "Maybe the moral of the story is to take more big steps back."

"Agreed," Gloria said with a nod. "A big step back."

The rest of the conversation turned back to the plans as the young people had laid them out, the surprising ease of the arrangements, and the demand that the parents keep things quiet until Christmas Eve.

"They do realize that no one in the family is going to be surprised, right?" Joe chuckled. "These have to be the two worst-kept secrets in the history of the world."

"It's what they want." Alexa shrugged. "They get to pick."

"I think," Gloria said firmly, "it will be lovely, and just the thing I'll need to be uplifted after the Christmas Eve pageant." She sighed. "We have the same teenagers for the camel this year."

"Ah, the camel," Alexa murmured. "Let's head in and wrap this up near the Christmas tree."

Gloria rose from her chair, still holding Bob's hand. They stood still, smiling at each other. Bob let go of her hand and wrapped his arm around her shoulder; she kissed his cheek and, smiling, they followed their friends into the warm light of the house.

Book Club Conversations

1. What were your impressions of Gloria as the book opened? In what ways did she confirm or challenge those impressions as the story unfolded?

2. Have you ever met anyone who reminds you of Gloria? Does getting to know Gloria impact the way you think about that person? If so, in what way?

3. What are your thoughts about Gloria's reactions around Bob's accident? Did any of those reactions make more, or less, sense to you later in the story?

4. What seems to drive Gloria? Do her motivations seem to change during the book? In what way(s)?

5. Gloria faces a lot of surprises; which surprises are most impactful in the short term? The long term?

6. Which character surprised you the most? Did any other characters share some of that person's characteristics? If so, which ones, and how did those traits impact the story?

7. Which character would you most want to play if this book were cast as a movie? What about this character resonates with you?

8. How would you cast some of the other characters, and why?

9. In what ways are Gloria's fears challenged? How have you chosen to challenge your own fears, and what changed for you?